"WHAT HAVE I DONE TO YOU, ANGEL?"

Trace stood for a moment, staring down at her—at the woman who had changed his life forever. This was the woman who had taken him to her bed, despite all her misgivings and without him ever having told her that he loved her. He had betrayed her, and she had responded with love.

Despite everything, this good, sweet woman loved him.

* * *

She knew he was telling her that he cared. But it was something neither of them were willing to put into words yet.

Rachel felt such disappointment—she actually ached from it. She should have felt hope and elation. This was the closest he'd ever come to saying that he loved her. But, instead, she felt empty and afraid. Her body ached for him—longed for him with a white hot passion she'd never experienced before. She wondered, though, if she would ever know his love again. . . .

CHEROKEE WIND

Clara Wimberly

Zebra Books
Kensington Publishing Corp.
http://www.zebrabooks.com

ZEBRA BOOKS are published by

Kensington Publishing Corp.
850 Third Avenue
New York, NY 10022

Zebra and the Z logo Reg. U.S. Pat. & TM Off.

First Printing: August, 1997
10 9 8 7 6 5 4 3 2 1

Printed in the United States of America

"O Spirit of the Cherokee wind, blow from the green mountains and fertile rivers of our homeland. Bring from the land of the rising sun, homeland of our Fathers, your cooling life's blood to the land of the setting sun. Blow O Cherokee wind, the spirit of our lost home to us in this harsh and barren land."

One

"Home," Sun Killer murmured. "I've come home to Rose-wood, Mother . . . just as I promised you I would."

Anyone hearing those words from the man astride the big, sand-colored horse might wonder at them. There was no joy on his face as he spoke, no excitement in his declaration.

Rather, he sat very still on the small rise overlooking the brick, white columned house, his black eyes narrowed and his jaw clenched. He hardly looked like a man seeing his home again after thirteen years.

Sun Killer climbed down from his horse and walked to a large crooked oak tree that hung over the edge of the hill. He had come to this very spot many times as a boy, sitting on the hill in autumn and watching the changing colors that surrounded the house.

Kneeling, he took a small pouch from his pocket and with a knife that he drew from his soft deerskin boots, dug a hole in the dry soil beneath the oak tree. He held the pouch toward the sky and closed his eyes. He spoke in a soft chant the Cherokee words he had heard his father use, words he'd learned well on the Oklahoma reservation. They were words of thanksgiving and accomplishment.

Opening his eyes, he pulled the string of the pouch and spilled its contents into his hand. It held two items. One was his mother's brooch which lay glittering In the sun. It was the only piece of jewelry she'd taken with her when she left Rose-wood. She had hidden it from the soldiers in her clothing. The other piece was a small beaten gold coin that matched the one on a leather cord around his neck. It symbolized his family's good name and his father's accomplishments as a spokesman and peacemaker for the Cherokee people.

And now Sun Killer had brought it home to be buried in a symbolic ceremony. It would remain on the land that once belonged to his father and mother, the land that should one day have belonged to him and his future children.

He slipped the brooch back into his leather pouch and stuck it inside his shirt quickly, with only a twinge of remorse. It was all he had left of his mother, and he wouldn't part with it unless it could be near his father's grave. If the soldiers had buried his father here, he would find him. Sun Killer had promised his mother as she lay dying that he would bring the brooch back here. She had told him it held her spirit and would somehow help her soul to travel from the dry, wind swept plains of Oklahoma back to the black, fertile soil of the Alabama and that she loved so dearly.

That promise, made as a young man, had stayed with him all these years. He thought it was the one guiding force that had brought him back here—the idea of reuniting his parents, if only in spirit. He had taken the brooch from his mother and had hidden it in his boot. Every night as he lay waiting for sleep, he remembered his mother's lone grave on the vast, barren plains and he swore that he'd honor that one last request, if it was the last thing he ever did.

He placed a flat rock atop the buried coin and stood up, his eyes turning once again toward the house his mother had named Rosewood. The house had changed since he was a boy. He thought it was more beautiful now than it had been then. Additions had been made over the years, and within the curve of the wide circular drive, there was a flower garden. He could only see the outline of it and the symmetrical lines of walkways crisscrossing through blurred dots of color. More space had been cleared for the lawn, which appeared quite green beneath the pale mid morning sun.

His mother would love it.

Sun Killer took a deep breath and reached up to his face, touching the thin white line of a scar that was hidden in his dark brows. It was hardly noticeable anymore, but touching the scar and being at Rosewood brought back the night the soldiers came in one bitter, humiliating rush.

His father had been a very important man among the Cherokee, even though he was half white. Because of his education and because he owned Rosewood, he was respected and listened to at Council meetings. Elijah Monroe was also a trusting man, more inclined to peaceful talk than to confrontation. He had worried about the latest treaty with the United States government, but Sun Killer could remember his father telling both him and his mother that nothing would come of it as far as they were concerned.

"We are titled landowners," he'd said. "I have registered this land under the white man's laws and they cannot take it away as they have other Cherokee land. It would be illegal."

"Illegal," Sun Killer murmured with disdain.

The soldiers had come. They killed his father and took the land and the house and forced a young boy and his mother, along with other Cherokees, to leave Alabama on a long, tortuous trip that would culminate in the dry lands of Oklahoma. They found a reservation so desolate, so miserable that many preferred death to living out the rest of their lives there.

His mother had never been the same. And neither had the boy the Cherokee called Sun Killer.

He'd sworn vengeance when his mother died and he had promised himself that he would regain this land and this house, in her memory. And that the white man who'd been granted the land as a favor from the government would die, if necessary, just as his father and mother had died. He hated the soldiers, and even though he was more white than Indian, even though one would never guess, because of his features and his sun streaked hair, that he even had Indian blood, he hated the whites, too. And because of that hatred, he knew that in the end, if he could not live here, if the soldiers came again . . . then he would die here.

Sun Killer's black eyes narrowed as he stared at the house below him.

Inside the house that Sun Killer called Rosewood, there was a flurry of activity. The carpets had been taken out, and the pine floors spotlessly cleaned and polished until they were a gleaming honey color. New candles had been placed in the hall sconces and the glistening crystal chandeliers. Crystal bowls, filled with rose potpourri, sat in the hallway and at various points throughout the house. Spring flowers spilled out of Austrian vases and added to the heavenly scent that filled the air. From one of the upstairs bedrooms, there was the sound of girlish laughter and chatter.

Rachel Townsend scurried across the room, dressed only in her corset cover under layers of muslin crinolines that were trimmed with ribbon and eyelet embroidery.

One of her friends pointed at her and giggled.

"Rachel, you aren't wearing pantalets."

Rachel brushed her auburn curls back away from her neck. "I cut the legs off," she said, smiling mischievously at the other girl. "It's too hot. We'll be outside all day, and it's going to be very warm, even for spring. Besides, who will notice?"

"Everyone," Amelia said. "If you race around the way you usually do, everyone will be able to see your bare legs. Mother says you're still a tomboy at heart."

"Your mother is probably right," Rachel said. "Mama Cleo says Father should have remarried after mother died, if for no other reason than to give me a more gentle upbringing. But you know what? I think I'm perfectly fine, just the way I am. But I promise, I will try and behave with gentility today. I will keep my crinolines down and my legs covered."

The other girl spoke up, a slender blonde who looked younger than Rachel and Amelia.

"Well, my brother certainly would agree that you're perfect just the way you are. Edmund says that you are the most beautiful, most spirited girl in the county. He says you are also the sweetest."

"Oooh," Amelia said, rolling her eyes toward Rachel.

Rachel laughed and went to sit beside the blond-haired girl. "Your brother is very sweet, Hallie. Edmund would be a good catch for any girl in the valley. He's handsome and kind and—"

"And wealthy!" Amelia said, standing suddenly and dancing around the room, her flounced skirts flying out from her body. She gasped when her dress hit a small table near the window, tipping it over and sending a glass figurine crashing to the floor.

Amelia stopped and all the girls stood horrified for a moment before they collapsed into laughter again.

"It's not funny," Amelia said, falling to her knees to pick up the pieces of glass. "I'm sure this is very expensive. Why, your father brought it back from Europe, did he not?'

They heard a tap at the door.

"Come in," Rachel said as she went to help Amelia.

"What you girls up to now?" The Negro woman who entered the room frowned sternly at the girls. Dressed in a black dress with a white gauze collar that crossed and tied over her ample bosom, she made quite a formidable sight. Standing there with hands resting on her broad hips, she frowned at the scattered glass on the floor.

"Lord, chile, your daddy is gonna have a fit. Here, let me do that. Why, you ain't even dressed yet! Get your dress there and get it on chile, before your guests arrive and begin to wonder where you at."

"Yes, Mama Cleo," Rachel said. She went to the woman and kissed her on the cheek.

The Negro woman drew back, pursing her lips and staring at the auburn haired girl through wide, twinkling eyes.

"Don't be wastin' them kisses on me—or that charm, nei-

ther. All them young men comin' here this afternoon gonna
be lookin' for a little o' that charm. Jes' better save it." She
turned to the two girls who were grinning at her and Rachel.
"Now, you two scat. Get on outta here or Miss Rachel ain't
never gonna get dressed. All this gigglin' and carryin' on."
She waved her hands as if they were a flock of chickens, shooing them from the room amidst more laughter.

Rachel watched the woman affectionately before turning to
the white dress that lay across her four poster bed. Mama Cleo
had practically raised her, and for all her bluster, she was nothing more than a lovable old mother hen.

"Can you help me with the buttons, Mama Cleo?" she
asked. She stepped into the dress and wiggled her hips, carefully pulling the soft white patterned muslin material up and
slipping her arms into the fluffy sleeves.

Cleo grunted as she got up from the floor and placed the
pieces of the broken figurine on a table. She went to Rachel
and pulled the dress together at the back and while Rachel
held her breath, she buttoned the long row of buttons.

"Looks nice," the woman said, standing back to admire the
girl and the dress. "Looks real nice. That's the prettiest dress
your daddy done ever bought you."

"Oh, Cleo, you say that about every dress I have."

"Well, it's the truth. Just turn around here and have a look
at yourself in that mirror."

Rachel turned, letting her hands move softly over the lace
edged flounces that fell in four layers from her waist to the
floor. The tiny dotted pattern of white on white made the material look light and airy, and she had to admit that the pink
rosette trimming with its green streamers was just the right
adornment for an outdoor party.

"I do love it," Rachel said.

"Don't forget your gloves. Your mama always said a lady
never goes out without her kid gloves. And your parasol. Don't
want to be frecklin' that pretty skin o' yours."

"Yes, Mama Cleo," Rachel said with a laugh.

She felt so good today that nothing could keep her from being happy—not even being forced to wear uncomfortably hot gloves and carry a parasol. This was her day and her party, the one her father had insisted she have.

Rachel Townsend frowned for the first time, thinking of the reason that he insisted she have a party. But then she took a deep breath and smiled at her image in the mirror.

Did it really matter that her father was practically announcing to the world that she was ready for marriage? It happened to every young woman sooner or later. And if there wasn't a man that she cared about in that way, did that matter, either?

Today, Rachel only wanted to have fun and visit with her friends, stroll in the garden and drink cool iced punch. She didn't have to marry until she was ready . . . until she found the man she'd always dreamed of finding, a man who would make her heart beat fast and whose touch would be a mystical confirmation that he was the one she would love forever.

Two

Sun Killer wanted to get a closer look at the house and at the people who lived there now. Then he would decide how he would go about regaining Rosewood.

He wasn't sure there was a way of getting the property back legally. Even a man with one sixteenth Indian blood had no rights, as far as owning land was concerned. Besides, there was no guarantee that he would be here long enough to accomplish his goal of owning and living in Rosewood. He was, after all, a runaway from the reservation in Oklahoma. He had purposely made friends with the white missionaries and teachers and had bided his time, gaining an education in the process, until the circumstances were exactly right for his escape. Indians left the reservation often, usually sneaking away at night. The authorities didn't bother hunting them down. But with Sun Killer, it would be different. He knew they would not take kindly to the way he had used them, the way he had seemed to befriend them. He knew that even now, someone could be looking for him.

As he held the reins tightly and guided his horse down the hill and through the trees that surrounded the house, he reached back with one hand to touch the long straight, shining hair that hung down his back. He thought no one in Holly Springs would recognize him now, but he'd have to change his name. And if he hoped to be accepted here as a respectable white lawyer, he'd have to change his appearance, too.

An Indian warrior's long hair was a symbol of his masculinity and his dominance. And Sun Killer had no intention of cutting his hair short, but as a necessary concession, he would have it trimmed and begin wearing it tied back. A bit old fashioned, perhaps, but still acceptable in the rural south.

As for his name, he would use his own English name and his mother's maiden name. He doubted anyone would associate him with the long-legged, skinny boy he'd been when he left here. Any of their Cherokee friends or relatives who managed to escape the march to Oklahoma were probably long gone from Alabama by now.

He exited the forest at the back of the house and rode slowly to a rambling white-washed building that he'd never seen before. A large green pasture behind it was enclosed by a white rail fence, and as he approached, he could see a worn path, obviously where horses were exercised. His horse whinnied at the scent of other horses in the area, and Sun Killer bent to pat its neck, murmuring softly to it as he grew nearer.

The stable buildings stood well away from the house and they were separated by a well kept back yard that contained rose covered trellises and neatly trimmed boxwoods. His father had planted those boxwoods. A wide brick walkway led through the yard to the stables.

As Trace drew his horse up at the front of the stables, two young Negro boys came around, smiling up at him.

"Yes suh, mister," one of them said. "What can we do fer ya?"

"I wondered if I could get some water for my horse."

"Sho," one of the boys said. He reached up for the reins and Sun Killer stepped down out of the saddle, watching as the boy led the horse to a water filled barrel.

"You want a drink, too?" the other one asked.

He couldn't help smiling at the two. They looked exactly alike, dressed rather formally for stable hands, wearing pale blue britches and white shirts, ruffled at the sleeves and neck.

He thought they were as sprightly and happy as any two young-sters he'd ever seen.

"Thank you," he said, taking the dipper of water that the young man offered.

For a moment, he closed his eyes, enjoying the cold water and trying to remember the last time he drank from a Rose-wood well.

"Good ain't it?" the boy asked, grinning. "Got the best water in Alabam'."

"I agree," Sun Killer said, handing the dipper back. "I do believe its the best I've ever tasted."

The boy fairly beamed up at him, and his black eyes wan-dered over the long hair and fringed buckskins.

"Where you headed mister? You ain't here fo' the party, dressed like that, that's fer sho."

"Party?"

"Miss Rachel's party," he said, pointing toward the rose col-ored brick house. "Senator Townsend's daughter. Mammy Cleo says it's a fishin' party . . ." he giggled as he said the words. ". . . fishin' for a marriage offer . . ." He laughed again at the phrase he'd undoubtedly heard adults use.

"Ah," Sun Killer said, smiling at the boy's bright eyes and big smile. "I won't be staying for that, no. I'm just passing through, on my way to Holly Springs."

The other boy came back, leading the big, sand-colored horse.

"Nice horse, mister. You is welcome to stay awhile, if you want. Senator Townsend don't turn nobody away from Wind-ridge."

"Windridge?" Sun Killer asked. He was frowning at the boy without realizing it. "Is that the name of this place now?"

"Yep," the boy said again, waving his hand toward the house. "Always was, far as I know."

Sun Killer hated the name. He found it harsher than the name Rosewood, but then he probably would hate any name that was not the one his mother had given it.

"I can't stay," he said. "But I would like to walk around a bit . . . stretch my legs. Do you think the owner would mind?"

"No suh. He won't mind atall. We keep yo horse til you gets ready to go."

"Thank you."

Sun Killer walked through the yard, letting his eyes scan the boxwoods that his father had planted. Several Negro women moved back and forth, carrying dishes of food from the spacious outside summer kitchen into the back of the house. They smiled at him when he walked past.

One side of the house was shaded by large wisteria vines that hung from iron trellises. Sun Killer could remember playing there in the summer. It was always cool and dark, the perfect place for hide and seek or for just being alone to think. A walkway had been added, along with white iron benches at the edge of the trellis.

From the front of the house, Sun Killer could hear laughter and the low murmur of conversation. He looked around the edge of the house, being careful that no one saw him. The fishin' party that the Negro boys spoke of, seemed to be in full swing. Couples strolled through the garden in front of the house and along the tree lined driveway. Young women, dressed in beautiful pastel colored dresses, sat in white rocking chairs on the wide front porch. There was even a group of musicians seated beneath the trees, playing quiet melodies for the guests.

Sun Killer stepped back around the corner of the house and let his back rest against the cool brick wall. He knew he should leave before someone saw him, but he couldn't resist letting his eyes wander over the drooping blooms of purple wisteria, letting the sound of laughter and music take him back to those days when their lives here had been so happy.

God, how he wished his mother were alive to see it in all its beauty.

Suddenly, out of the corner of his eye, he saw a movement as two people walked from the front yard out toward the wisteria arbor. Sun Killer quickly walked the length of the house until he was standing at the back corner, hidden from the approaching couple by the wisteria vines.

They stopped very close to where Sun Killer stood and sat on one of the benches with their backs toward him. He held his breath, his black eyes narrowing as he saw the girl.

She was the most beautiful thing he'd ever seen. Her hair tumbled in a shining auburn mass over her shoulders, entangled with the same green colored ribbons that adorned her white flounced dress. Her skin was soft and creamy, the color of magnolia blossoms.

For a moment he actually had to close his eyes as he imagined how that skin would feel beneath a man's hands . . . how she would smell and taste.

"You know I'm going to ask your father for your hand," the young man was saying.

"Oh, Edmund, I'm flattered, but—" Her voice was soft, tinged with the quiet, sweet lilt of the south.

"Don't," Edmund said, taking her hand and bringing it to his lips. "You don't have to say anything. I know how you feel. I realize that you don't love me, at least not the way I love you. But you will, darling . . . you will. After we're married—"

"But Edmund, I'm not sure I'm ready for marriage. You're very sweet and you're . . ."

Her words trailed away as Edmund stood up, looking with a frown toward the front of the house. "Oh, drat—they're calling me for the next hand of cards, sweetheart. You're coming, aren't you . . . to watch me win?"

"You go," she said. "I just want to sit here in the shade awhile, where it's cool . . . and quiet."

"All right," he said, laughing down at the girl. "We'll talk about this later. Don't be long."

Sun Killer's eyes darkened as he watched the slender young man walk away. He thought that the slightly built man she called Edmund was much too ordinary for this exquisite, auburn-haired creature. But, then, it wasn't any of his business.

He stood for awhile, deliberately watching her, letting his eyes have their fill of her sweet, curvaceous body, her creamy skin and shimmering hair. He found himself wanting to see her face more than anything, and for a moment, he considered walking up to her and introducing himself.

"Fool," he muttered softly.

She stood up suddenly and turned toward him. He had waited too long and now he was captured. He thought as he looked at her beautiful face that the word "capture" was probably more telling than any he could have used.

Rachel gasped as she saw the stranger standing in the shadows at the corner of the house. His manner of dress and his long hair gave her a start for a moment. But then she saw his eyes, partially hidden because of the dim light. He was staring at her and there was such a look of curiosity in his eyes that, for a moment, she stood perfectly still, staring back at him.

"The man's a fool," he drawled. "To leave a woman like you for a hand of cards."

"I . . . I . . . thank you," Rachel whispered, hardly knowing what to say, or what to make of the stranger's softly spoken compliment.

"May I help you? Are you looking for my father?"

"No," Sun Killer said. His voice was husky and soft, and he didn't bother stepping away from the house where she could hear him better. "I just stopped for water and I was . . . curious." He glanced toward the front of the house, where the sounds of the party could still be heard.

Rachel could feel her heart pounding, and for a moment, she could do little else but stare at the handsome stranger. Was it only fear that made her heart beat so wildly?

"Do you live here? Are you Rachel?" he asked, his eyes narrowing. He didn't want her to be Senator Townsend's daughter, didn't want her to be the daughter of the man he'd come to unseat from this house.

"Why . . . yes. But how—?"

"The two stable boys," he said. "They told me all about Miss Rachel's party."

"Oh, yes," she said. "Jim and Jared . . . they're our twins."

She smiled at him and a small dimple appeared at the corner of her mouth. The unexpected tingle that raced through Sun Killer surprised him. She had a smile so sweet, so enchanting, that it fairly lit the dark enclosure beneath the wisteria.

He shook his head to clear his mind. He thought it would be wise to get away from here quickly, and away from this girl whose loveliness reached out and grabbed a man's very soul. He didn't need this complication. He didn't have time for it.

"Well, if you'll excuse me," he said, turning. "I should be on my way."

"Wait," she said. Rachel moved toward him, reaching her hand out as if she would touch him. "You're welcome to stay, if you like. Rest awhile and have something to eat . . . join the party."

"Thank you, but no. I have to be going."

His dark lashes came down, closing away his potent gaze and making it hard for her to see what he was thinking. And as he walked away, her eyes took in every inch of him, from the long hair that flowed over his broad shoulders to the buck-skin covered hips and the fringe that swayed at the sides of his muscular legs. She thought he was the most devastatingly handsome, the most masculine man she'd ever seen.

She wanted to beg him not to go until she found out who he was and where he was going. She couldn't bear the thought of never seeing him again. And she had the strangest, most breathless feeling in her heart.

She knew it immediately. This was the man she would marry. With a woman's instinct, she knew it as surely as she'd ever known anything. This man was the one she'd dreamed about and waited for, whose gaze had unexpectedly caused her heart to accelerate.

This stranger was the one whose touch would make her forget every other man in the world except him.

Three

Sun Killer, using the name Trace Hambleton, spent the next few days in Holly Springs, where he found a simple, but respectable room and a tailor who made him several suits of clothes for a reasonable price. He intended to set up practice as a lawyer, and in order to do that, not only would he have to look the part, but he would also have to procure an office.

In the meantime, he became acquainted with the people of the small town, passing the word around that he was a lawyer and would be starting his practice in a few days. And for the first time, an idea began to formulate in his mind, about just how he would regain his family's land and Rosewood.

He was going to marry Rachel Townsend.

When the idea first came to him, Trace quickly dismissed it from his mind because it involved the girl. There was something about Rachel Townsend, some intangible feeling that she triggered in him, some deep lost longing that made him feel things he never wanted to feel—not for someone like her and never for a white woman.

But, as the days passed, the idea became more and more intriguing to him. He would court her as gallantly as any of her other ardent southern beaus. He'd seen the interest in her eyes when she looked at him. She hadn't tried to hide it, and more than that, he had felt an undeniable spark pass between them. When his office opened, he would be an established, upstanding citizen of Holly Springs, and her father would have ample reason to accept him as a potential son-in-law.

It was the deception that bothered him more than he thought it would, something he couldn't understand fully. He hated the white people for what they had done to him and his family. Senator William Allen Townsend had no doubt coveted Rosewood and its land long before the order came to drive the Cherokee out of the area. It was this rampant greed for land possession that caused them to lose their homes, that caused men like Senator Townsend to do anything in order to get it. America was land hungry, and having a president who agreed with that premise had made that obsession impossible to fight.

Trace told himself finally that his guilt was unfounded, that his reluctance to involve the beautiful auburn haired girl was foolish. He would do whatever he had to do to regain his home and his land and that included deceiving Rachel Townsend, if need be. As it turned out, it was an easier task than he had dreamed.

One morning, Trace was working at the office he had rented. His sign had arrived, and he had gone outside to hang it above the door. He was practically bowled over by a young woman hurrying along the wooden sidewalk with her arms piled high with packages. It was Rachel Townsend.

"Oh," she said, as the packages scattered along the walkway and into the dusty street.

"Here, I'm sorry . . . let me . . ."

Rachel stooped to pick up the packages just as Trace knelt on one knee. He was very close to her and when her lashes lifted and she actually focused on him, her eyes grew wide with surprise and disbelief.

"You . . ." she whispered. Her incredulous gaze took in his dark suit and crisp white shirt, the shining hair that was held neatly with a leather thong behind his head.

It was him. There was no doubt about that handsome face and those incredible eyes. She knew she would recognize this man a hundred years from now, even though she had only seen him once. He smiled and Rachel thought the smile fairly transformed his face.

"It's nice seeing you again," he said. His eyes skimmed quickly over her smooth, ivory skin, noting the black fitted riding dress she wore. He liked the bell shaped sleeves that allowed her soft white blouse to peek out beneath and he thought the hat she wore with its dark veil blowing against her face was sensuous and completely enchanting.

"Yes . . . you, too." She glanced at the piece of lettered wood in his hand and felt a quivering in her chest when she realized that he was putting out his sign. He was going to stay here in Holly Springs. This incredible man that she was afraid she might never see again, actually had set up shop in her hometown.

Trace thought she was a vision, as beautiful and desirable as any woman he'd ever seen. And he had a feeling from the look in her eyes, that she was ready and willing to accept his attention. Perhaps this conquest was going to be more enjoyable than he ever thought possible.

"So," she said. "You're a lawyer. How interesting. You should find a lot of people in this town who need your services."

"I hope so," he said. "If not, I might find myself conducting business from the town's livery stables."

Rachel thought that his smile made him look young and boyishly handsome. She liked the way he looked. In fact, she was beginning to think that she liked everything about him.

"I . . . I don't even know your name," she said rather breathlessly.

"Trace," he said taking her hand. "Trace Hambleton." He didn't release her hand, but stood looking down at her. For a moment he wondered what she would do if he simply pulled her into his office and kissed her.

He was surprised at the sensation that the whimsical thought sent rushing through his body. And by the touch of her small hand in his. Rather like an arrow, he thought—swift and straight and to the mark.

But he was going to have to proceed slowly. This was no

barmaid, no roughshod young woman that one could pull into the shadows and kiss until she was breathless and begging for more. Rachel Townsend was a young woman of quality and breeding, and no matter how anxious he was to reclaim his home and see her father ousted, he knew he had to win her in a right and proper manner.

She was still looking at him, studying his face with eyes that twinkled. Trace couldn't help smiling back at her.

"And you already know my name. I'm Rachel Townsend."

"Yes, I do. I've always liked that name . . . Rachel." His voice was deliberately low and intimate as he said her name.

When she bit her lip, Trace smiled. He found himself almost reaching forward to brush his fingers along that sweet sensuous mouth. Instead he took a step backward and bowed slightly.

"I should get back to work," he said. "Perhaps next time you're in town . . ."

"Mr. Hambleton," she said, leaning her head to one side. "I'm sure my father could help bring you some business. He knows everyone in town and in the region, too, for that matter. He might be very helpful to you."

"I wouldn't want to impose," he said.

"Oh, but you wouldn't be. I'll tell you what—why don't you come out to the house for supper one night. Father is home from Washington right now, and I'm sure he'd be delighted to meet you."

Trace felt only the slightest twinge of guilt at what he was doing. He'd known instinctively that she was going to ask to see him again and he had deliberately let her be the one to take the first step. He'd found that women were always more interested in a man when he was just slightly out of their reach.

"That sounds very nice," he said, careful not to appear too eager.

"Tomorrow night?" she asked, biting her lip again.

Trace was finding that little habit quite charming. There was almost a shyness in her, an uncertainty that, despite her beauty, told him she was not arrogant or conceited. He liked that.

"Tomorrow night would be fine."

"Seven o'clock then," she whispered. "I'll look forward to it."

"Seven o'clock."

He helped with her packages and stood watching as she walked down the sidewalk, skirt swaying, her auburn hair glimmering beneath the black veil of her hat. He took a long, slow breath of air and let it out.

He was certain that she hadn't a clue about who he was or that he was part Indian. Neither had the people he'd met in town. For one moment yesterday when he'd seen Mrs. Findley, his old schoolteacher, at the General Store, he'd held his breath, waiting for her to recognize him. But she had only smiled and nodded and walked on past.

As Rachel disappeared into one of the stores, Trace found that he was looking forward to tomorrow night. He had to admit it wasn't entirely because he was on his way to getting Rosewood back.

A few weeks later, Rachel lay in bed, thinking of all that had happened to her.

She was in love. Oh, but she'd never met a man like Trace, never found anyone who excited and challenged her the way he did. He might be a businessman, not unlike her father, but there was something about him that was untamed and daring, something deep inside those passionate black eyes that he seemed to hold in reserve—a secret perhaps. And she found herself determined more and more every day to discover that secret. She wanted to know everything about him, to delve into his very soul, if possible.

That first night when Trace had come to Windridge, her father had been as charmed as she. He and Trace had talked for hours, it seemed, and she had had to be content with listening. Not that she had minded. It had given her a chance to watch this tall, handsome stranger, to listen to his carefully chosen words and his opinions about everything.

Sometimes, while he listened to her father, he would turn, suddenly catching Rachel's gaze on him. And he would smile, that odd knowing smile that made her heart turn over.

But no matter how charming he was, or how certain Rachel was that he was as attracted to her as she was to him, he still remained distant and aloof. And it had driven her crazy. She wanted him to touch her, to kiss her and yet every time she thought it might happen, he would draw away and look regretfully down at her, with just a hint of amusement in his eyes.

Until last night when Trace had kissed her. Even now, thinking of it, she had to close her eyes against the breathtaking emotions she'd felt. He had come to the house for supper again, and since there were several other people present to engage her father in conversation, she had actually managed to get Trace outside alone.

They were walking in the gardens and the sun was just setting behind the line of trees in the west.

"You have a beautiful home here," he said. "I like the rose garden addition."

"Addition?" Rachel asked.

Trace closed his eyes and took a deep breath. Why had he said that? He was going to have to be more careful in the future if he didn't want Rachel to guess that he knew more about this place than he pretended.

"It looks new is what I meant."

"Oh . . . well, actually my mother had the rose garden built. But for me, it's always been here. This is the only home I've ever known," she said, letting her fingers trail along the newly opened rose petals.

"You said your mother died when you were young?"

"Yes, I hardly remember her. I was three when she died.

There was another child . . . a sister. My mother died giving birth to her."

"What happened to her . . . your sister?"

"She died, too, just a few days later."

"I'm sorry." Trace stopped, turning to look down at Rachel. Her head was bent and when she looked up at him, her eyes glittered with unshed tears.

"Don't," he murmured. He had been so careful these past few weeks to restrain himself where she was concerned, to repress the desire she brought out in him. But tonight, seeing her tears, he didn't think. He only reacted.

He pulled her into his arms, telling himself he meant only to comfort her.

"Don't cry," he whispered. For the first time, he allowed himself the luxury of touching her hair, of breathing in the sweet scent of roses and, for a moment, he had to actually close his eyes against the rush of desire that washed through him. "I didn't mean to make you cry." She snuggled against him and he wondered if she had any idea what the feel of her soft breasts against him did to his reasoning.

"It's not your fault," she said. She laughed softly and shook her head. "I don't know what's wrong with me. It was so long ago that I hardly remember it, and I don't usually let myself get so sentimental."

"It's not sentimental," he murmured. He let his fingers trail down the side of her face, then downward to lift her chin. "It's sweet . . . very sweet." As she looked up at him, her eyes so trusting, her lips parted expectantly, he knew he was lost.

He had meant to be gentle and patient. But Trace had not known much gentleness in the last few years. And when her arms slid around his waist, when she moved so restlessly against him, he couldn't help himself. As his lips took hers, he felt an actual physical ache in his chest, a wrenching blend of disbelief and triumph at her sweet, urgent surrender. He found that he couldn't withhold the hunger he felt for her any longer and he was amazed that she seemed to feel the same way.

"Oh, Trace," she whispered as he lifted his head and stood in the darkening twilight, staring down at her.

"Rachel . . . little one, I'd better get you back to the house."

"Why?" she whispered. "I don't want to go back to the house. And I don't think you want to, either."

"I don't, but if I stay here any longer . . . holding you, kissing you, then—"

"I don't care." Her voice was breathy as she moved back into his arms, as she lifted her lips for his kiss. "I've never met anyone like you, Trace," she whispered. "Never."

"Rachel," he groaned. "Sweetheart, you're making this very . . . difficult . . ." He felt her soft kisses against his jaw, trailing to the corner of his mouth and he couldn't resist any longer. He tightened his arms about her, almost lifting her off the ground as his mouth searched and explored, as he gave in to all the curiosity and emotions he'd felt about her for the past few weeks. He could hardly believe it. She was falling so easily into the trap he had set.

"Am I?" she whispered against his mouth. She took his hand, pulling him away from the garden and across the drive toward the dark shadowy area near the wisteria arbor.

"Wait . . . Rachel." He withdrew his hand from hers and stood away from her. "You're a young woman of breeding, from a respectable family. I can't just drag you away into the bushes like a—"

"Why?" she asked, smiling up at him, her eyes teasing. "Why can't you?"

"Dammit, you know why," he said, shaking his head. "A man like myself . . . a girl like you. It isn't done. We should be married before—"

"Married?" she whispered.

Her hands went to her mouth and her eyes grew wide with delight as she saw him grin.

Trace hesitated. This was his chance. *Take it,* a voice whispered.

"Yes, married," he said, laughing. "That is, if your father would approve and if . . . you would say yes."

She threw herself into his arms, her small body actually rocking him and bringing a small laughing grunt as he caught her and enclosed her in his embrace.

"He will," she said. "And I would. Yes, oh yes, Trace. I want to marry you more than anything. I thought you would never ask."

He kissed her and looked down into her sparkling eyes.

"But didn't I hear you telling a young man not so long ago, beneath this same bower, that you weren't ready for marriage?" he teased.

"That was before I met you," she whispered.

Trace tilted his head back and laughed aloud then. She was such an odd sweet blend of teasing femininity and guilelessness. And, for one brief moment, he didn't want to think about why he was doing this. He simply wanted to enjoy the feel of her in his arms, the softness of her body against his. He wanted to pretend, if only for awhile, that tonight was truly real.

Rachel lay back on her bed remembering his kisses and staring dreamily out her windows at the twinkle of stars in the dark heavens.

She was in love. And she was going to marry Trace Hambleton.

Four

Trace couldn't sleep. It had all happened so quickly and so easily. Everything was going the way he'd planned, and in only a matter of weeks, instead of months. He couldn't believe how suddenly things had fallen into place. Or how easily Rachel had accepted him . . . how effortlessly she'd fallen in love with him.

Rachel.

It seemed he could still smell her rose-scented skin, still taste the honeyed sweetness of her mouth against his. Still see the sparkle of desire in those innocent, yet teasing eyes.

Trace thumped his hand against the bed and pushed himself to a sitting position.

"Are you going to do it *Ahs-gay-yah?*" His voice was fierce, as if he meant to hold onto the anger and bitterness he'd felt inside for all these years. "Are you going to avenge your family's disgrace? And make sure that the land where you buried the spirit coin is yours forever?"

Trace sighed and leaned his head back against the bed.

"Are you going to take this woman to bed? Take her virginity as if it is your right as a loving husband?" His words grew softer, more thoughtful.

Restlessly, Trace swung his long legs over the edge of the bed and got up. He pushed his long hair back from his face as he walked the floor of the small room. There was an odd little ache in his chest—not physical, exactly, but something he couldn't quite explain. Almost the same feeling of grief he'd had when his father was murdered and then after his mother died.

"Dammit," he muttered. His fists were clenched, his face fierce with determination as he walked to the second story window that looked down over the street. Pushing open the window he could hear laughter from the saloon down the street. And below him came the quiet murmur of men talking, and the scent of tobacco smoke.

"Damned injuns."

The phrase made Trace recoil for a moment. It had been spoken fiercely, angrily, by someone below him. He felt his heart accelerate, and instinctively, he stepped away from the window, and into the shadows of the room, flattening himself against the wall as he listened to more of the conversation.

"Seen one on the edge of town today. Had a squaw and two kids with him. Filthy heathen. Don't matter how poor or dirty they are, seems like they're still able to breed."

The men's laughter rose upward, the sound of it causing Trace's stomach to recoil in disgust. At that moment, he wanted nothing more than to go downstairs and confront the ignorant men who were speaking.

It was instinct, he supposed, that need to defend himself and people like him. Those first few years at the reservation, even the sight of an Indian was enough to send one of the guards into an abusive rage, either physically or mentally. Trace had wanted to fight. He'd wanted to kill them all, and it had garnered him more than his share of beatings. He thought sometimes that he had lived through them out of sheer fury and determination.

Thinking about killing the soldiers was all that had gotten him through the nights. He'd lie on his blanket, his mind alert, his heart beating rapidly as he envisioned a million agonizing ways to kill the white men who had shattered his life forever.

And now in one quick flash, he was back in that rundown building at the reservation, the dust of the earth strong and harsh in his nostrils, the ground hard beneath him.

"What'd ya do, Ned?" one of the men below asked. "Chase the injun out of town?"

"Nah," the man replied. "Weren't worth my time. The young-uns was squawlin . . . from hunger, most likely. And the squaw was so scrawny, she wouldn't even be worth the bother." The men laughed.

Trace gritted his teeth and leaned out the window.

"Hey," he shouted. "How about holding it down." It pleased him that his voice didn't reflect the fury he felt inside. If nothing else he had learned to disguise the rage that boiled inside him.

"A man can't get a decent night's sleep in this town."

"Oh, hey, Mr. Hambleton," one of the men said, gazing up at the open window. In the dim light from a doorway below, Trace saw the sheepish look on the man's face. "Didn't mean to disturb you none." The man turned to the others as he started walking down the street. "Let's move on down to the saloon, boys," he said. "Let the man sleep." Glancing over his shoulder and back up at Trace he said, "Sorry, Mr. Hambleton."

As a lawyer, Trace supposed he was given more respect than some. But, at the moment, he didn't really give a damn. He'd have welcomed the man's anger and his refusal to quieten down. He would have enjoyed going downstairs and beating the daylights out of the ignorant fool. He was almost disappointed that the man had been so obliging. He wondered what they'd think if they knew that he was one of those "filthy heathens" they seemed to hold in such contempt.

It was hours before he slept. By then, the words of the men below were firmly planted in his mind. They overrode any of his earlier doubts about marrying Rachel Townsend and his reluctance to involve an innocent like her in such a dirty, sordid charade as the one he intended.

Over the weeks, he'd seen for himself that not only was Rachel sweet and innocent and loving, she was good. Down to the soles of her small, well formed little feet. Only yesterday she had driven into town with a basket of food for a woman whose husband was sick and couldn't work. She'd asked Trace to come with her, and as he stood back and watched, he'd been amazed . . . touched even by the way she pretended that her actions were nothing. By the way she tried to salvage the man's pride when she insisted that the money she gave them was only a loan that she was sure he would repay when he was able.

Trace had walked away from that house with an odd feeling in the pit of his stomach. Rachel had done nothing to deserve what he was about to do to her. She was only a sweet, innocent young woman who happened to be the daughter of a man who owned Trace's home and had taken a land grant from the president of the United States. But Trace was willing to bet that Senator Townsend knew it belonged to Cherokees. Like the rest of the settlers, he simply hadn't cared.

It was the white man's right, wasn't it? They saw it as their destiny to possess every blade of grass, every tree . . . every living thing that they saw and coveted. In their greed for land, the Anglos hadn't cared who died, or whose lives were shattered in the process. After all, the Cherokee hadn't really mattered. Indians, like slaves, were considered to be less than human. Trace's father had made the mistake of thinking that just because he owned property and a fine home . . . just because he lived like a white man, that he would be treated like one.

Trace knew in his heart that Rachel was not like those men who had come for them that night. She wasn't responsible for anything that happened to him and his family. He supposed that was one of the reasons he was having doubts. He hadn't been sure if he could really involve Rachel after all. But involve her he would—if he wanted Rosewood back, that was exactly what he had to do.

Rachel turned around gingerly on the small stool on which she stood. The white satin skirt of her wedding dress belled out around her. It was so voluminous that it almost obliterated the tiny seamstress who was on her knees pinning up the hem.

Just then, Cleo came into the room and stood watching, her eyes round with excitement and pleasure. Rachel laughed when she saw her.

"Oh, Mama Cleo, have you ever seen anything so beautiful in all your life? It just arrived from Boston and Mrs. Tavindy says there are only a few alterations to be made. Look at this lace. Isn't it gorgeous?"

"It's called blond lace," Mrs. Tavindy said. "And, believe me, it costs a pretty penny."

"Looks pretty with the girl's hair, don't it?" Cleo said. Her large round eyes held amazement as she stared at the rich lace and shimmering satin material.

Mrs. Tavindy looked at Cleo and grinned, even though she held several pins between her lips. Finally when they'd all been pinned into the gleaming white material, she stood up and glanced at the Negro woman.

"Well, Cleo . . . what do you think?"

"Law me," Cleo said, her eyes sparkling now with just a hint of moisture. "It's about the purtiest thing I done ever seen. So shiny and all. And that lace jes sets it off, don't it? Yessir, fair to middlin' sets it off. Bet that dress cost the Senator a purty penny."

"I don't even want to know," Rachel said, smiling. The one tiny dimple appeared at the corner of her mouth. "Knowing how much it cost would only spoil the pleasure."

"Well, at this point, I'm not sure anything could do that, my dear," Mrs. Tavindy said. She winked at Cleo, then bent to pull the dress's train out behind Rachel, letting it fall to the floor in a soft, swishing cloud. "Have you ever seen anyone more in love?" she asked Cleo. "Not that I can blame her."

The woman pushed back her graying hair and lifted her chin a bit. There was a hint of envy and a faraway look in the slender woman's eyes as she spoke.

"That Trace Hambleton is just about the handsomest man

I've seen in an age. That long hair . . . those brooding dark eyes." She sighed. "My . . . some say he has an air of mystery about him, too, and you know how intriguin' that makes a man."

Rachel frowned and the dimple at her mouth disappeared. Trace *was* mysterious. There were so many things about him she didn't know. And no matter how hard she tried, or how many times she asked about his family and his past, she couldn't get anything out of him.

"He's just a very private man, that's all," Rachel said, her voice pensive.

"I'm sure you're right. And, to my mind, that's just one more reason to like him. Folks in town say he's a good lawyer, too. Going to make you a prosperous living some day. Might even follow in your daddy's footsteps—become a senator, if Mr. Townsend ever decides to retire."

"I wouldn't mind that," Rachel said dreamily. "Papa would never let me stay in Washington with him. He says the city is too harsh for a young woman. But if Trace ever decides it's what he wants, then I'll finally get to see Washington."

"That you will," Mrs. Tavindy said. She gathered up her sewing box and her gloves and placed them on a table near the door. "Now, let me help you take off the dress, dear. I'll have to stay up all night getting it done before tomorrow, as it is. If you ask me, your young man is in a mighty great hurry to get you married. Don't know what we'd have done if the dress hadn't arrived in time. 'Tis bad luck they say to postpone a wedding."

Mrs. Tavindy lifted her brows with only a slight disapproving look as she stepped to unbutton the dress.

"I wouldn't have postponed this wedding, no matter what happened," Rachel said. She sighed and her eyes twinkled as she seemed lost in her own thoughts. "I have many beautiful dresses. I'm sure any of them would have suited just fine for a wedding dress."

Mrs. Tavindy met Cleo's eyes and they both smiled. Mrs.

Tavindy then shook her head and carefully pulled the dress away from Rachel's shoulders and helped her step out of it and off the small stool.

Later, when Rachel entered the dining room and saw her father sitting at the long mahogany table, she smiled and hurried to him. "Good morning Papa, isn't it a beautiful day?"

William Townsend looked up as his daughter entered the room. Seeing the look on her face, he smiled knowingly and stood up to greet her. He pushed his glasses up on his nose and brushed his hand over his thinning brown hair.

"Well," he said. "Some women have last minute doubts before their wedding, they say. Looking at you, I don't see even a hint of that on your beautiful face, daughter."

"None whatsoever," she replied.

Rachel stepped forward and hugged her father before sitting down at the table across from him. She hardly noticed the crested silver teapot that held her hot chocolate, or the arrangements of fresh flowers that always sat in the middle of the mahogany table. She couldn't seem to think of anything this morning except Trace and the fact that tomorrow she would be his wife.

Before William Townsend took his seat again, he stepped to the mahogany sideboard behind him and took an envelope which he handed across the table to his daughter.

"A wedding present," he murmured. He sat down and placed his napkin in his lap again. But he didn't continue his meal. Instead, he sat looking at his daughter's beautiful face, which seemed so much like her mother's. He couldn't help feeling a small hint of loss. Rachel had been his alone most of her life and now he would have to give her over to the young man she had chosen to marry. That thought gave him a feeling of immense pride and sadness at the same time.

Rachel glanced curiously at her father as she opened the envelope and pulled out a piece of paper. She studied the paper a moment before frowning at him.

"It's the deed to Windridge," she whispered.

"Yes. The house is yours now . . . and your new husband's. After the wedding, you'll want to go down to the land office and have the registrar add Trace's name. Of course, it would have come to you when I'm gone anyway, but . . ."

"You know I don't even like to think about that," Rachel said.

"Well, now you won't have to," he said with an indulgent smile. "This is your home. More than it ever was mine even. Since your mother died I'm afraid I've never felt the same about the place. I bought it for her, you know."

"I know," Rachel said. "I'm not sure this is where Trace will want to stay. We haven't actually talked much about the future," she said, her voice turning wistful and shy.

"It doesn't matter. It's yours now. You're an Alabaman born and bred," he said, his dark eyes turning thoughtful. "Like your mother. It's only right that this land where she is buried should be yours to do with as you please."

Rachel's blue eyes sparkled with unshed tears as she watched her father and heard the catch in his voice. He had loved her mother very much, and she thought he had never stopped grieving for her, even after all these years. No woman ever seemed to hold his interest for long, and he seemed to have no desire to remarry.

That was the kind of love Rachel wanted. It was what she would have with Trace.

"Thank you Papa," she said. Quickly, she stood up and catching up her lavender colored skirts, she ran around the table and hugged and kissed him. "Thank you so much."

She stood for a moment, holding the deed in her hand.

"Papa, you like Trace, don't you?"

"Of course, I like him, my dear. Why, is there some—"

"No . . . no, there's nothing wrong. I don't have any doubts, if that's what you're wondering. I love him so much, daddy," she said softly. "I never realized a woman could love a man the way I love Trace Hambleton. But . . ."

"What is it then?" he frowned now as he saw the troubled look on his daughter's face.

"Mama Cleo thinks it's all happened too soon. And she thinks I should know more about Trace and his family before—"

"Oh," her Father scoffed. "Mama Cleo. Why darling, of course she's going to think that. You're her baby. She isn't quite ready to let you go yet. But she'll come around. She always does where you're concerned, doesn't she?"

"Yes, I suppose," Rachel said, smiling. She sat down and glanced into her father's eyes. "But I have to admit, I don't know much about Trace . . . his background, where he's from . . . what his family was like." Trace has never even told me he loves me, she wanted to add. But somehow she couldn't. That was hardly something to be discussed with her father.

The senator laughed and picked up his coffee cup. His dark eyes sparkled across at her.

"You love him. He's a handsome, hard working young man who will make you a fine husband. That's all that matters now. You'll have a lifetime to learn all about him."

"Yes," Rachel sighed. "You're right . . . a lifetime."

Finally she smiled, putting the troubling thoughts out of her head as she reached for her cup of chocolate.

Five

The morning of the wedding was perfect: a balmy day with just the hint of a breeze wafting through the open front door and ushering in the scent of spring flowers.

Rachel couldn't sit still. She had rushed through the house yesterday, overseeing the cleaning and now, this morning, only a few hours before the guests would arrive, she did the same thing with the placing of flowers. When she went outside to the kitchen, Mama Cleo met her at the door.

"Whoa it right here, gal," Cleo said. Her hands were at her broad hips and the look on her face was rather stern—as stern as Cleo could make it where Rachel was concerned, anyway.

"I just want to make sure the hams are just right. You know, with the brown sugar and island spices that—"

"The hams is perfect," Cleo said, still refusing to move. "Since when you know so much about cookin' anyway?"

"And what about the pastries?" Rachel continued. "Did Lula make the strawberry tarts that I wanted?" Rachel looked around Cleo toward Lula, an enormous black woman who turned and smiled sweetly at Rachel.

" 'Course she did," Cleo huffed. "What's wrong with you, anyway? Ain't you got nothin' else to do but pester old Lula?"

"Mornin', Miss Rachel," Lula said. "Would you like a sample of the ham? Cleo said you didn't eat enuff breakfast this mornin' to keep a bird alive."

Cleo's defenses seemed to weaken a little and she took one

step aside so that Rachel could speak with Lula without having to look around.

"Oh, no . . . thank you Lula. I couldn't." Rachel's hand was on her flat stomach. She was so nervous that even now, smelling the aroma of food that drifted from the summer kitchen, she felt a bit nauseated.

"She ain't been eatin' nothin' lately," Cleo said, giving Rachel a stern look. "Jes look at her. Got a waist like a wasp. Don't see how food gets down through somethin' skinny as that." Cleo fairly grunted with worry.

"I'm just a little anxious, that's all," Rachel said. "I'm sure by tomorrow I'll be back to normal."

"She's right," Lula said, nodding at Cleo. "It's her weddin' day and she's nervous. Ain't nothin' wrong with that. Nothin' wrong with having a waist like that, neither." Lula's big belly shook when she laughed loudly. "Can't recall as I ever had one."

Rachel leaned back against the frame of the door and sighed contentedly. This was what she'd needed—this bantering, Cleo's fussing over her and the aroma of Lula's cooking and her infectious laughter. This was Rachel's family. She'd never known any other. And if that seemed odd to others, she couldn't help it. She didn't think she'd want it to be any other way now.

Rachel crossed her arms over her breasts as she said, "I can't just sit upstairs in my room doing nothing. I'm going crazy. And don't tell me just because I'm getting married I have to start acting like the lady of the manor. I'm not and you know it. When I want to come to the kitchen, I want to come to the kitchen!"

Cleo's lips were clamped together and she shook her head, but her eyes had begun to twinkle and finally she smiled. "Well, it's yore kitchen chile," Cleo said. "Along with everything else I reckon. So I can't keep you out. I just think you ought to be restin' a mite. It's goin' to be a long day."

"And a longer night," Lula added with a grin.

The dimple appeared beside Rachel's mouth and she blushed.

Cleo leaned a little closer to Rachel.

"Is they anything you need to know, shug?" she said, her voice quiet. "Any questions you want to ask ole Lula and me?"

"No . . . I don't think so." Rachel wasn't embarrassed by Cleo's remarks. They'd talked about such things before. Her reluctance had more to do with the way she felt about Trace than anything. It was not something to be shared—not even with someone as dear to her as Cleo and Lula. Whatever she needed to know, she wanted Trace to teach her.

"Well, then . . . why don't you go on out to the stables . . . have Jim and Jared pull you around the grounds in that little buggy your daddy bought you last year?"

Rachel nodded. Perhaps it would do her good to get away for a while. See the blooming shrubbery, feel the warm breeze against her skin. And think about the wedding . . . and what would happen tonight.

The twins were delighted to take Rachel for a ride. She had little time for thinking because they chattered the entire way. Finally, she laughed and leaned forward to the front seat where they sat together.

"Do you boys never stop talking?"

"Nope . . . reckon not," Jared said. He would turn around in the seat and grin at her from time to time as he talked. He was the more outgoing of the two. Rachel also found it amusing that he did most of the talking for his brother. "Brother Justus says we was talkin' when we was borned. I said hello, I'm Jared, and this here is my twin brother Jim."

Jared pushed his shoulder against his brother's and they both laughed. Rachel thought they were the happiest children on the plantation. She rarely saw one without the other and she never saw them with a frown on their faces. It made her happy just to look at them sometimes, including this morning.

She sighed and leaned back in the shade of the buggy. Her

nervousness was waning a bit. This was her world. Despite having been raised without a mother, Rachel couldn't say she had ever wanted for anything. Not love or attention and not the contentment that she was feeling at this moment.

It was this place . . . this house that gave her security and peace. And whatever happened, she would always have that.

"Jared, honey, drive me over by the cemetery."

"Yes'm Miss Rachel." Jared pulled the reins and turned the horse toward the circular drive in front of the house. From there they pulled onto the main road a few yards before turning onto the short road leading to a stand of very large live oaks. The cemetery stood just at the edge of the house's wide lawn. It was close enough that Rachel and her father often walked here in the late afternoons. Because of the trees, however, the cemetery was hidden from the house.

When the buggy stopped she climbed down while the boys stayed in their seats.

"I'll be right back," she said.

She lifted her skirts and walked along the large stonelined pathway toward the area fenced by spiked black iron posts. The iron gate creaked on its hinges when she opened it and went inside. Yellow daffodils and white narcissus lined the inside of the rectangular fence. The scent of them drifting in the early morning air was sweet and poignant.

Rachel bent and picked a few of the buttery blossoms and walked to her mother's grave. She bent, her dress billowing out around her as she placed part of the flowers on her mother's grave and the rest on the smaller grave beside it.

"I'm getting married today, Mother," she whispered. "To a man that I love so much." She reached out and placed her hand on the grass that covered the rounded earth. "But I'm a little scared, Mommy. I'm afraid something will happen to end the way I'm feeling now. Like with you and Papa. I can't bear to think that I would be separated from Trace the way you were separated from Papa." Rachel took a deep shuddering breath and squared her shoulders. "Please be my guardian angel, Mother. I want this to last forever."

She stayed there for a while longer and when she rose, she looked at the only other grave in the cemetery at the edge of the fence. This simple grave had been here as long as she could remember. No one knew who it belonged to. But, even before her unexpected death, Rachel's mother had ordered that the grave and surrounding area be enclosed and made into a family cemetery. The stranger's grave had been the only one here for a long time. Rachel went to pick a few more blossoms and came back to place them on the grave that was marked only by a simple uninscribed stone.

Back in the buggy, she was very quiet going back to the house. Her restlessness had left, and she had become eager to go back to her room and dress for her wedding. She was anxious to get on with her wonderful new life.

At exactly twelve noon, Rachel met her father in the hall outside her bedroom. He kissed her and held her away from him for a moment so that his eyes could take in the entire vision of her. Cleo and Mrs. Tavindy stood in the doorway watching with brimming eyes.

Cleo wore a new silk dress with a white lace bertha and she fidgeted with the collar nervously as she watched the girl that she had raised so lovingly.

"How beautiful you are darling," her father said. "You look so much like your mother that it takes my breath away."

"Thank you, Papa," Rachel whispered.

Cleo and the dressmaker stepped forward and straightened Rachel's train behind her. They fluffed out the wisps of hair that curled around Rachel's cheeks and adjusted the flowered wreath that held her long, lace bridal veil.

"Are you ready, my dear?" Mrs. Tavindy asked. "Hallie and Amelia are already downstairs in place. Everyone must be wondering where the bride is by now."

Rachel could hear the music from the parlor, and part of her wanted to hurry. She thought she could hardly wait to see

Trace in his wedding suit. Even now, the girls were probably watching him, whispering behind their fans, as they admired those broad shoulders and striking good looks.

Still, a part of her wanted to slow the pace, to look at her father this one last time as an unmarried daughter. He planned to depart for Washington soon after the wedding—to discreetly leave her and Trace alone at Windridge, she suspected. Also, he wanted to go partly because he never seemed satisfied here for long. The exciting city on the Potomac called to him too strongly. Rachel needed him to know that he was leaving her with a husband she loved dearly and that she was happy.

"This is all I want, Papa," she said. "Trace and Windridge are more than enough to make any young woman happy."

"I know that, daughter. Trace Hambleton is a fine and honorable man. I haven't a qualm in my soul about what you are about to do."

"Then . . . I'm ready," she said.

Her father offered his arm and she took it as they walked down the hallway toward the stairs. The formal parlor, though very spacious, was overflowing with people. There were several couples standing in the hallway and even more out on the front porch.

Rachel smiled, although her heart was pounding so loudly she was sure they all could hear it. And her father, true to his political nature, waved to their friends and nodded to others as he escorted his daughter into the parlor. They hesitated at the doorway only a moment, until the musicians saw them and began to play. But it was long enough for Rachel's eyes to seek and find Trace.

He stood waiting at the front of the room, looking tall and handsome in his dark cutaway coat and white ruffled shirt. A black satin stock was tied just beneath his square jaw and he wore a stylish brocaded waistcoat fastened with gilt buttons.

Rachel thought she'd never seen a man so completely handsome, or so thoroughly masculine. Just looking at him made her knees tremble. He stood proudly, almost like some ancient royalty, she thought. His head was lifted, yet there was that slightly cool, aloof look on his face that puzzled Rachel sometimes.

But, when the music began, and he turned and saw her in the doorway, the look disappeared. For a moment, as they looked at each other, it was as if the world stood still. The music seemed to vanish and there were only the two of them, looking into each other's eyes.

There was an odd look of surprise and disbelief on Trace's handsome face. Then he smiled, a slight, sweet smile that just curved the corners of his sensuous mouth. And as Rachel and her father began to walk toward the front of the room, Trace turned toward her and waited, his eyes never leaving her face.

When her father placed her hand in Trace's, Rachel couldn't stop her fingers from trembling. The pale pink roses she held in her left hand quivered from her nervousness. Trace squeezed her fingers, his hand warm and reassuring.

Rachel was aware of Cleo as she slipped into a seat at the front of the room, just as Rachel had insisted. She saw her bridesmaids, Amelia and Hallie, dressed in their beautiful rose colored satin dresses. Both of them smiled brightly at their lifelong friend. But then, everyone and everything faded away. There was only this moment and Trace. The rest of the ceremony seemed to go on without her. It seemed over before it began.

"I now pronounce you . . . husband and wife."

Trace took her in his arms—gently and carefully, aware of propriety—as he kissed her lightly on the lips. She looked up into his eyes and smiled and she could feel the world coming back into focus.

Finally her heart could beat, and she could breathe again. As she and her new husband turned and walked toward the door, the music soared with the majesty and joy of the occasion. The entire room then erupted into soft laughter and quiet murmurs of approval.

For Rachel, it was the happiest moment of her life.

Six

In the hallway, Trace stood holding Rachel's hand tightly.

"Your hands were freezing," he said. "I was afraid you'd faint on me."

"Never," she whispered, gazing into his eyes. "Nothing could stop me from becoming Mrs. Trace Hambleton."

He bent slowly and kissed her. If Rachel had always regretted his aloofness and his propriety with her, this time she couldn't say that was true. His mouth was warm and soft and there was an urgency in his kiss that she had never noticed before. The new look of possessiveness in his eyes warmed and delighted her.

She practically sighed aloud with joy and contentment.

Before she could say a word, they were being hurried out to the front porch. Garlands of flowers and streaming ribbons encircled the large white columns. Linen table cloths, covering tables that lined the porch against the house, fluttered in the afternoon breeze.

Jim and Jared and several other Negro children, dressed in their house clothes, stood at the tables waving huge fans over the elaborate array of food. Rachel went from one child to the other, bending and placing a kiss on their cheek.

"Thank you all for helping today." She pinched Jared's arm gently and whispered, "Have you sampled Lula's famous ham?"

Jared nodded, his eyes wide with glee.

"And the pastries, too?" she asked, feigning horror.

"Yep."

Jared and the other children giggled. One of the girls dropped her fan. Finally Cleo came forward, muttering reprimands and urging the children to return to their duties.

Trace watched his new bride with the children. Her patience and sweetness never ceased to amaze him. Even if she were aware of some of the looks of disapproval she received, he doubted she would let it affect her behavior. She seemed to genuinely love these children, slave or not. But then, he warned himself, it was easy to love when one had been afforded every luxury one could ever desire.

The guests lined up at the tables and then wandered out onto the lawn or back into the house to eat. Many more seemed to want to stay with the bride and groom, including Amelia and Hallie.

Once when Trace was engaged in conversation with Senator Townsend, Rachel turned to Hallie.

"I'm so sorry Edmund didn't come."

Hallie's beautiful eyes darkened and she brushed her hair back self-consciously.

"Edmund is very hurt. You know he always expected that the two of you would marry. He said you told him you weren't ready for marriage." She looked up and her eyes met Rachel's. "I understand Rachel, really I do. You didn't plan on meeting someone like Trace and falling in love so suddenly."

"I know," Rachel said. "I know he's hurt. I'm sorry for that, but—"

"Sorry?" Trace had moved closer without Rachel noticing and now he pulled a chair out and sat next to his bride. "Why would my beautiful bride be feeling sorry about anything on her wedding day?"

Rachel turned her head slightly. There was a tone in his voice that she'd never heard before. Sarcasm perhaps. Or a bit of bitterness. His gaze was steady, challenging almost. But then he smiled and the moment was gone.

Rachel shook her head slightly and returned his smile.

"I was just feeling sorry that Hallie's brother wasn't able to come to the wedding," she replied.

"Ah," Trace said.

He knew Rachel had no idea how much he had overheard of her conversation with Edmund that first day he came here. Rachel's relationship with the man was not even something he had thought about again. But now, seeing the look of sadness on her beautiful face, he felt a tiny spark of resentment.

"Edmund, you mean," he said. Slowly he sipped from a crystal goblet as he watched the expression on Rachel's face. He glanced at Hallie and saw her eyes dart from Rachel to Amelia and he wanted to laugh.

Did they think he was a fool? A man like Edmund? One of those epicene young men whose passions were cards and horses. Who dressed garishly and waved their lace trimmed handkerchiefs in front of their nose if they ever caught a whiff of anything odorous . . . or real. Trace suspected some of them even disguised their masculinity in the presence of ladies and pretended to be whatever the women wanted them to be.

There had been no such men at the reservation. The men Trace grew up with had been independent and rugged and brutally honest. They offered no apologies for being a man. Perhaps he would enjoy teaching his new bride the difference.

"Yes . . . Edmund," Rachel spoke before Hallie could— mostly because she saw the spark of jealousy in Trace's eyes and she didn't want him to think she was trying to hide anything. "Edmund and I were . . ."

"Sweethearts . . ." Trace drawled.

"No, not exactly sweethearts," Rachel demurred.

Trace thought Rachel seemed frustrated and not sure what to make of his words, or his attitude. He smiled and leaned toward her, pulling her forward for a kiss that surprised her.

"It doesn't matter," he whispered against her mouth. "You belong to me now . . . and no one else."

The day passed quickly, in a whirl of laughter and good natured teasing from the guests. Rachel enjoyed it tremendously, but she was also a little nervous . . . and a bit anxious about the night.

Late in the afternoon when the guests finally began to leave, Rachel could feel the tension returning. Every time Trace looked at her, she thought she could see impatience in those unusual midnight eyes . . . and a passion she'd never encountered before.

Every time he was near, he made a point of touching her, sometimes the gesture so intimate that it made her catch her breath. Then, as if he were completely aware of what he did to her senses, he would smile that enigmatic smile, and walk away to speak to one of the guests.

He puzzled Rachel and delighted her at the same time. She found herself anxious even for her father to leave. If Trace's actions were deliberate . . . if he had a purpose to his provocative actions, she had to admit it was working. Her legs were positively weak and shaky when Trace was near.

All the guests had gone and it was almost dusk when she and Trace walked with her father out to his waiting carriage. Cleo and Lula and the other house servants busily walked on the porch, removing the dishes and linens from the tables.

A cool breeze wafted through the trees where the night birds twittered and nested. Crickets joined a loud chorus from the lawn and, from the distance, came the sound of a lone whippoorwill. It was one of those spring evenings that always brought a pang of longing to Rachel. It was almost too beautiful for words.

Her father turned to Trace first.

"Trace . . . welcome to the family. I couldn't be prouder of anyone that my daughter had chosen." He reached his hand forward.

Trace shook the senator's hand and nodded.

"Thank you sir," he said.

"Papa, it's going to be dark soon. Why don't you stay until morning, at least."

"No, my dear. I've already made up my mind, and besides,

we'll be at Steele's Inn before you know it. I'm actually looking forward to the trip and to getting back to Washington. It's the first time I won't have to worry about leaving you here alone, or feel guilty that you have only Cleo and Lula to look after you instead of a father."

"I never felt alone," Rachel protested.

She felt Trace's arm tighten around her waist and she leaned back into his embrace, enjoying the strong feel of his body against hers. And the intimate touch of his thigh against her hips.

"You know what I mean," the Senator said. He leaned forward and kissed Rachel. "I'm sorry I was not more of a father to you child, after your mother's death." His voice cracked just a bit and then he cleared his throat. "But . . ." he said, focusing a broad smile on the two of them. "You're in capable hands now, I'm sure. And you hardly need me here interfering as you begin your new life together. So . . . I'll be on my way."

"Goodbye, Father," Rachel said. "Don't forget to write." She kissed him and then stepped away from the carriage as her father climbed in. She didn't feel sad. She had seen him leave so many times that it seemed perfectly normal to her. Besides, he was right . . . she had Trace now and it was time for them to begin their new life together.

They watched the carriage drive out of the circle and disappear into the gathering darkness. Then Rachel turned in Trace's arms. For only a moment, Trace let himself feel the triumph that had been building all day. He stood there in front of the magnificent house, resplendent with its wedding day decorations, teeming with activity as the servants put everything back in order. The lights from the house spilled out over them.

All this was his now. The house his father had built and his mother had decorated with such love and pride. The house and land. All of it . . . his.

And Rachel Townsend besides.

He pulled the flowered wreath from her hair. The long veil trailed along the grass as Trace carelessly tossed it aside and pulled her tightly against him.

Oddly, there was a part of him that wanted to hurt her. He thought of seeking his vengeance here and now with the only person available. To see the fear in her eyes that he'd seen in his mother's. But despite his bitterness and triumph, despite his right to revenge, he knew he couldn't possibly hurt a woman. Especially not this woman.

Still, when his fingers tangled in her hair and loosened the pins, he was not gentle. He pulled her head back. Her beautiful face, eyes puzzled, lips parted, was so very appealing. Quickly, Trace bent to take her parted lips. His hard mouth covered hers without holding back any of the lust and victory he felt. Trace was distantly aware of her quiet murmur of surprise, even a slight flinching away, he thought.

Only Trace knew that his kiss was more about possession and control than love. Rachel was much too innocent to know the difference.

And too much in love.

She stepped closer, her arms sliding around his waist as she pressed herself against the length of his body.

"Oh Trace," she whispered when he pulled away. She gazed up at him with complete adoration.

He stared down at her, a slight frown on his face as he pulled her toward the house.

"Let's go in," he said, his voice harsher than he intended. He bent to kiss her mouth again, this time only brushing his lips against hers. He felt her shiver and pulled her closer against his side. "Are you afraid?" he whispered as they moved up the steps and onto the porch.

"With you? Never. I trust you, Trace. I love you."

Trace frowned again and shook his head. *Don't trust me,* he wanted to say.

Her sweetness . . . her goodness made him feel and want things he could never have. It even made some part of him think this was all real. He had to remind himself that it wasn't. It was a sham, and he couldn't afford to let himself believe everything he felt when he was with her. He had to keep his pain closer . . . steel himself against her appeal, if he were to accomplish his goals. He had to remind himself every day that she was his enemy, every bit as much as her father was.

But that didn't mean he couldn't enjoy the rewards of what he had accomplished this day. That included making love to her any way and every way that he wanted.

On the front porch, Trace scooped her up in his arms. Rachel laughed softly and pulled the train of her dress up into her arms so that he would not trip. She was hardly aware of Cleo or Lula watching from the far end of the porch, nor of the servants who had grown silent as they watched the newlyweds. Some of the girls giggled softly and others murmured quietly to one another.

As Rachel clung to him and nuzzled her face against his neck, he carried her into the hall and up stairs, taking the steps two at a time.

Seven

The door to Rachel's bedroom stood open. The room was lit by fluttering candles and upon the bed's counterpane lay sweet herbs and mock orange, their scent filling the room.

"Oh Trace, look," she whispered. "Amelia and Hallie must have done this." Her arms were around his neck and she turned to look into his eyes.

He stepped into the room and kicked the door closed behind him. Then he set her gently on her feet.

Rachel felt a little dizzy and, for a moment, she was afraid that her shaking legs would not hold her. She clung to him, her gaze meeting his. All afternoon, she had been so keenly aware of him. Of his lean, muscular body, graceful and sure. Swaying toward her, touching her. She realized now that it all had been a prelude for this . . . almost like a beautiful male pagan dance.

Even now she could feel her heart beating wildly, with a rhythm that was as old as time. Her entire body felt hot, desperate for his touch . . . his kiss.

"Oh Trace . . . you make me feel so . . . so . . ."

"What?" he asked, his voice husky. His arms moved around her and he pulled her against him. "Tell me how I make you feel, love."

Trace found her shyness irresistible. There was no need for further propriety, no need for him to hide his desires any longer. Her sweet confusion and vulnerability moved him and made him want her as nothing else could.

The moment was here. The moment he would make Rachel his for good . . . and Rosewood with her.

His hands slid from her tiny waist down to the swell of her hips and he pulled her closer. He moved against her, letting her become aware of what he was doing, letting her feel his need for her.

When Rachel gasped and closed her eyes, Trace couldn't resist kissing her parted lips. He wanted to laugh when she responded just as he hoped she would. She clung to him, her small body trembling with a desire she didn't understand.

"I . . . I feel so hot . . . so . . . so strange," she murmured. She was kissing him wildly, and when he placed small kisses across her jaw and down to her neck, she thought she might go crazy. "I don't . . ."

She pulled his head down to hers, wanting to taste him, wanting to feel the erotic, forbidden thrust of his tongue. Trace laughed softly at her passion, so unexpected . . . so completely irresistible.

"Then I suppose we'll have to get you out of all these clothes," he said, whispering against her lips.

He turned her around, letting his hands linger on her slender shoulders as he trailed kisses down her neck. He felt her shiver, felt the heat of her skin beneath his mouth and he smiled. She was breathing heavily, but he had to admit, no more than he.

He unfastened the long row of buttons, cursing beneath his breath at their minuscule size beneath his large hands. He was finding himself more anxious than he thought to see her, to touch her naked skin and hold her slender body against his. Finally when the dress was free, he slipped it from her shoulders, steadying her as she stepped out of the billowing mass of satin to stand before him.

Trace's eyes glittered in the light of the candles. He took a step backward and let himself take in all of her, let his eyes have their fill of the beautiful woman standing before him. He loved the sight of her in the lacy corset that cinched in her already tiny waist. But he preferred seeing her without it even more. Her breasts above the lace trim, rose and fell rapidly. Trace was pleasantly surprised to see that Rachel wore no pantalets and once she stepped out of the layers of crinolines her creamy bare legs appeared long and slender. He could hardly believe she was his for the taking or that her eyes had grown dark with desire for him.

"You are so . . . beautiful," he whispered.

He stepped to her, holding her hands when she reached for him, making her wait as he reached out to pull the pins from her hair. When her hair fell he combed his fingers through it and smoothed it back from her shoulders.

He took strands of the auburn locks and rubbed them between his fingers, then pulled them forward to his nose and mouth. He closed his eyes, breathing in their rose scent. It was the first time he'd seen her this way with her long hair spilling over her shoulders and down her back. And he found it more enticing than he'd ever dreamed possible.

Every instinct in his body was telling him to take her now. To pick her up in his arms and carry to the flower strewn bed. But he intended to wait . . . to make her want him even more desperately than she did now. It would make it easier for both of them.

He let the strand of hair fall from his hand, then traced its length with his fingers where it fell from her shoulder down over one of her breasts.

Rachel shuddered and closed her eyes. She swayed toward him, reaching out at the last moment to steady herself against his chest.

"Trace . . ." she gasped. "If you don't . . . if you don't kiss me, I think I'm going to go crazy."

Trace stepped to her and put one arm around her waist. With the other he cupped her breast, still hidden beneath her camisole. Rachel trembled violently and lifted her face for his kiss.

He was a bit surprised when he felt her small fingers tugging at his shirt and tied stock. He helped her and followed her hands as she unbuttoned the gilt buttons of his waistcoat, then the shirt beneath.

It was Trace's turn to gasp as her hands moved inside the shirt from his naked stomach, up to his chest, lingering on his nipples before moving up to his neck. When she bent her head and placed hot little kisses over his bare skin, he held his breath, closing his eyes against the primitive, urgent need that rose in him.

"God . . . Rachel," he whispered.

Rachel thought she would explode when she heard the passion in his voice. When she felt his hard body against hers and felt his hands, unsteady now, cup both her breasts, when he kissed her, a wild urgency in him emerged. His mouth was hot . . . searching, as if he could not get enough of her. Suddenly his fingers jerked at the ribbons that held her corset together.

"I want to see you," he murmured. Trace cursed his clumsiness and felt Rachel's hands helping him.

When he saw her standing before him completely unclothed, her eyes wide, her look still a bit shy, he lost all patience for waiting. His eyes were hot, ravishing, as he let his gaze move slowly over her, from her perfectly formed breasts, her skin the color of magnolias, down to her tiny waist and gracefully flaring hips.

His mouth grew dry, his breathing unsteady as he looked at her.

Trace had never taken a white girl to bed. And never any woman as innocent as Rachel.

He stepped forward and swept her up in his arms. Going to the bed, he raked the flowers away and lowered her. Hastily, he stripped away the rest of his clothes and joined her on top of the flower scented counterpane.

In the dim candlelight, Rachel stared at Trace, mesmerized by his bare body. She reached her hand out to touch him and felt him flinch slightly as she brushed her fingers against his flat stomach. She felt his hand on hers, felt him push her hand downward to explore and discover for herself what a man was like.

She held his gaze, trusting him, amazed by the heat and hardness of him and amazed, too, that she did not feel as shy as she had thought she might. Anticipation consumed her. Every time he touched her, she wondered if the moment had come. He pulled her into his arms and his hands touched her everywhere, tracing seductive patterns over her breasts, and down her stomach until she was gasping with pleasure.

Her breasts felt hot and swollen and when he bent and kissed her, she arched against him instinctively. When he took her nipple into his mouth, she began to tremble violently. She couldn't breathe; couldn't speak of the pleasure, the heat that his actions caused to race over her in one fiery burst.

When his hands caressed her hips and legs, then moved between her thighs, she tensed and went dead still.

"It's all right," he whispered against her hair. "It's all right. Relax . . . I won't hurt you. I'll never hurt you."

She hadn't expected this. Hadn't expected him to touch her this way, to make her feel this exquisite torture. She moved against him, stunned at what he was doing and how he was making her feel.

"Trace," she whispered. She was breathing rapidly, clinging to him, wanting . . . what?

His movement became quicker, more urgent, and the incredible heat building in her seemed to envelop her in its wild fury. Finally, not understanding what was happening, she tensed her arms out beside her as the heat built and grew.

"Trace!" she cried as her body seemed to explode with pleasure, and Trace captured her scream with his mouth, holding her as she writhed in his arms. Rachel returned his kiss with a fire she'd never known.

Trace moved on top of her. His blood rushed through his veins now in one white hot river. He murmured to her, holding her still as he finally entered her.

Rachel was still warmed by the throes of their passion, but

the sudden pain she felt made her cry out for a moment and made her slender body shudder.

"It's all right," Trace said. His own body was trembling as he tried to hold back.

When she opened her eyes to look up at him, he began to move again, making love to her with slow, hard pleasure. He watched her face, saw the pain leave it, to be replaced by a look of wonder. She began to move with him, learning the rhythm quickly and wanting to give him the same pleasure as he had given her. She sensed a change in him—an intensity and urgency that thrilled and delighted her even though she didn't truly understand what was happening.

She heard and felt his groan as he clasped her tightly and shuddered hard against her.

"Trace," she whispered. "I love you . . . oh, I love you so much." She ran her hands down his powerful back, to the tapered area at his waist and on down to his hips. Her boldness surprised even herself. But it seemed natural and wonderful that she should share such intimacy with the man she loved.

Trace shifted his weight so that his body was not entirely on her. He looked down at her and gently pushed her damp hair away from her face. The heat of their bodies had released the scent of mock orange and sweet herbs into the air and he thought it was an erotic smell that would remind him of this night for the rest of his life.

He lay beside Rachel and held her in his arms as he frowned into the darkened room.

He hadn't expected this. He had prepared himself to feel triumph, and anger, and even a certain amount of guilt.

But nothing could have prepared him for the surprise of the sweet, intoxicating pleasure he'd found in her arms.

Eight

Rachel gazed up at Trace. His handsome face, caught in the flickering candlelight, looked hard and for a moment, savage and untamed. And, in that brief moment, she felt a jab of fear in her heart. She hardly knew this man who had just taken her to bed and made love to her with such soaring passion.

Trace felt Rachel tremble and he looked down into her eyes. He tightened his arms around her.

Rachel felt the moment's fear dissipate. She didn't know what was wrong with her to have such odd fancies.

There were so many things she wanted to ask, so many things she wanted to say to him. But she was relaxed and warm, and so exhausted from the past week's frantic activities and all the events leading to this night. She only meant to close her eyes for a moment to rest.

Trace knew that Rachel was falling asleep and he didn't try to rouse her. Actually, he breathed a sigh of relief, for he had no idea what kind of small talk he could engage her in. Their lovemaking had surprised him . . . had shaken him so completely that he needed a moment to remind himself of the reasons for his deceit.

But he couldn't seem to stop himself from gazing down at the sleeping beauty in his arms. The dark lashes closed against her cheeks. The luscious mouth, soft and pink. Hair that lay in tangles about her face and shoulders and only seemed to enhance her beauty.

Again, he felt that odd ache in his chest, as some unwanted

emotion moved within him. For all her sensuality moments ago, for all her passion, hidden so exquisitely from the rest of the world, she was still an innocent. She trusted him . . . loved him, even. And he had taken advantage of that.

Trace pulled part of the coverlet up over her naked body, but even so, he could still see the outline of her curves beneath it. He found himself wanting to trace the outline of her hips, fondle her warm breasts and kiss the lips parted so softly in sleep.

"God . . ." he muttered. "What the hell have I gotten myself into here?" He closed his eyes against the image of her and laid his head back against the pillow.

He had expected Senator Townsend's daughter to be willful and petulant. The first time he saw her there beneath the wisteria bower, he had noticed her classic beauty and the confident air that the aristocracy sometimes carried. He had even imagined how he would bend her to his will, make her suffer for what her father and his rich white friends had done to his family.

But Rachel's haughtiness had vanished when she came to him and sweetly invited him to join her party. Beneath her cordiality had been a teasing quality, innocently sensual.

Looking at her again, he decided she was too damned sensual for her own good.

And for his.

For the first time, Trace was unsure about how he would continue.

Rachel wasn't the one he'd wanted to hurt. She shouldn't even be embroiled in this revenge he was seeking. He should have concentrated on her father instead.

But it was too late.

He grumbled beneath his breath and shifted his weight.

Rachel stirred in his arms, opening her eyes for a moment and gazing up at him.

"Trace?" she murmured, her voice husky with sleep.

"Shh. Everything's all right," he said. "Go back to sleep."

As he lay there holding her, his mind wandered back. And, as always, he remembered his mother.

She had been the kindest, most loving and generous person he'd ever known. She could soften his father's sometimes stern behavior and turn his frowns into laughter. The entire household loved her.

And Trace had loved her most.

This had been his parents' room. His mother's. It looked different now. The furniture was more opulent and expensive, the floor covered by a patterned rug. His mother's tastes had been simpler . . . more austere.

Trace's mouth was set in a grim line as he thought of the irony. He had come back to claim Rosewood, accomplishing that task on a bed in his own mother's room. He should have felt a much keener sense of justice than he did.

He let his eyes move slowly about the room. Despite his reluctance to think it, he knew his mother would approve of the changes.

She would approve of Rachel, too.

"Dammit," he muttered.

Rachel stirred again and he slowly pulled his arm from beneath her and got out of bed. He moved silently across the room, not bothering to clothe himself, and stood before the front window that overlooked the curving drive and wide lawn. As he stared at the scene below him, the shadowy trees, the soft streams of light from the house, he felt himself transported back to that horrible night so long ago.

Trace had been wakened along with the rest of the house by a pounding on the front door. The soldiers had not even had the decency to come during the day, but had descended on this house in the darkness, like a swarming horde of locusts. In their blue uniforms, with their sabers gleaming in the moonlight, they had been an awesome sight.

Trace had run to the top of the stairs and watched as his father opened the door to them. They argued for a moment, then one of the men hit his father, knocking him to the floor.

Trace closed his eyes. He could still see the dark line of blood coming from his father's nose and spilling onto the pale pine flooring. The men in the shadows, swords glittering like those of avenging angels. Faceless entities hidden beneath the shadow of dark, broad brimmed hats.

The entire household had erupted into chaos. His mother screamed and ran to her husband, falling to her knees beside him. The servants rushed forward and were stopped by the eerie sound of a dozen hammers cocking against metal.

"Nooo," Trace screamed, racing down the stairs toward his father.

It might have been all right if his father had stayed down, if he had not resisted. Elijah Monroe had chosen the worst time possible to put aside his peaceful ways. And Trace always wondered if, at that moment, his father had purposely chosen death.

Trace threw himself against the men at the door as they struggled with his father.

He had been proud of his father, this meek, studious man, as he dragged himself up from the floor and turned into a savage warrior. He'd fought with all the instincts of his ancestors but he was outnumbered. He was dragged out into the yard and beaten into submission.

The servants had held Trace back, but it was his mother's quiet, tearful voice that made him grow still.

"Please, son," she said. "I can't lose you, too. Please . . ." Then she had walked slowly to the yard where her dying husband lay. With dignity, she had knelt beside him, ignoring his bludgeoned face as she bent to kiss him.

The soldiers had stepped back from her, forming a wide circle through which Trace walked. He could remember the tears falling down his face in hot rivulets as he stared into their eyes. One after the other. He'd made them face him and he'd made them turn their eyes away from what they had done to his father.

In the end, his defiance hadn't mattered. They had taken them from the house almost immediately, allowing them time only to gather one change of clothes. That was when his mother had hidden her brooch, a wedding gift from her husband.

They had not even let them stay to see to his father's burial. Trace had yet to discover the grave and it ate at him to think they'd left him like an animal for the vultures. It was the worst torture for a Cherokee—not knowing where the body lay or its spirit wandered.

It would give him a great sense of peace and accomplishment if he could at least bury his mother's brooch with his father, but he had no idea where his father was or even where to look. Trace took a deep shuddering breath and stepped away from the window, turning back toward the bed and the woman who lay sleeping there.

She *was* innocent in all this. And she didn't deserve to pay for the white man's sins.

But pay, she would. It was fate.

When Rachel awoke the next morning, she blinked, then stretched out in bed like a lazy cat. When she realized Trace was not there, she sat up, quickly looking around the room.

He was standing at the window, dressed in riding pants and boots and a white shirt. When he turned toward her, she saw that he held a steaming cup of coffee in his hand.

"Well," he said, moving toward the bed. "I thought you might sleep all day."

Rachel could feel a flush moving over her face, and when he looked at her naked body in the quiet morning light, she felt herself blushing from head to toe.

He put his coffee on a table and sat on the bed beside her. Rachel leaned her head against his chest.

"What time is it?" she asked sleepily.

"Almost noon," he said. There was a hint of humor in his deep voice.

She wondered how long he'd been up—long enough to bathe

and dress. His hair was still wet and this morning, instead of being tied back, it was loose down his back.

She had never known a man with hair like Trace's. It had caused some comment among her friends. Maybe it was different and unfashionable, but she loved it.

She inhaled deeply, letting her senses have their fill of his clean, masculine scent. She lifted her face and snuggled against his neck, feeling as content and as safe as she'd ever felt in her life.

"I love you," she whispered.

Just then there was a light tap on the door and Trace pulled away with a hidden sigh of relief.

Rachel shrieked and pulled the coverlet over her naked body. "Wait," she said. "You can't . . . I'm not . . ." Not only was she still in bed at noon, leaving everyone to guess that she was completely exhausted by her wedding night, but they hadn't even bothered to turn down the counterpane and she had slept atop it, with only her husband's strong body to keep her warm.

Trace grinned as he handed her a dressing gown.

"It's all right," he said. "It's only Cleo. I asked her to bring you your morning cup of chocolate. You and I have things to do, you know."

"What things?" she asked.

Rachel pushed her arms into the sleeves of the ivory-colored silk dressing gown, then quickly turned down the rumpled, stained counterpane and slid beneath it before nodding for him to open the door.

Cleo's eyes were bright with curiosity as she entered the room. She didn't look at Trace, but went directly to the bed and placed a tray across Rachel's lap.

The older woman bit her lip self-consciously as she glanced at Rachel. Her features softened a bit when she saw the look of shy pleasure and happiness on Rachel's face.

"Good morning, Mama Cleo," Rachel said softly.

"I won't bother you'uns none," Cleo said. "Mr. Trace says you goin' to show him the plantation today."

"Oh," Rachel said, glancing up at her husband. "Am I?"

She was a little surprised. She had not expected the day after her wedding to be spent touring the estate—not that she minded.

Perhaps she was being naive to think that she and her new husband could be completely alone for the next few days. After all, the work at Windridge couldn't stop just because she was married. And even if their fieldhands could run things on their own very well, Rachel still preferred spending a great deal of her time supervising. Besides, she enjoyed it.

She told herself she should be pleased that Trace wanted to be a part of that now. But she had to admit, if only to herself, that she was disappointed they had to leave this room.

After Cleo left, Rachel turned to Trace.

"I had thought we might have a quiet day together . . . just the two of us," she said.

Trace could see the disappointment in her blue eyes. Even if she didn't say it, he knew she was puzzled about his wish to see the acreage of Rosewood so soon after the wedding. *Windridge.* He'd have to be very careful not to use the wrong name—not just yet, anyway.

"It will be just the two of us." Trace came and sat down on the bed beside Rachel. He took her hot cup of chocolate and placed it on the table. And when he pulled her into his arms, he wasn't pretending.

Her mouth tasted of chocolate and the scent of mock orange still clung to her skin and hair. For a moment, he considered locking the door and making love to her again. It was what she wanted . . . what her eyes were trying to tell him. And if he would allow himself to admit it, it was what he wanted, as well.

"I've asked Lula to prepare a picnic for us," he said. "We'll take a buggy, perhaps a quilt in case we need to rest . . ." He wiggled his brows and grinned at her.

She pushed his dark hair back from his shoulders, letting her fingers continue to caress its texture. When he smiled at her that way, she couldn't resist. Besides, the idea was beginning to sound better and better all the time.

"Well," she said. "You seem to have taken care of everything."

"You don't mind, I hope," he asked, frowning slightly.

"No," she whispered. "Of course, I don't mind." She leaned over to kiss him one more time before pushing the covers back and swinging her legs over the bed. "I think perhaps I might even learn to like having someone take care of me." She looked under the bed for her slippers, then turned to him as she placed them on her feet. "My father was rarely ever here, you know. I suppose I've grown used to being on my own . . . to doing as I please."

She walked to him and stood between his legs as he sat on the bed. She put her arms around his neck and smiled at him.

"I want to share everything with you now, Trace. This plantation . . . the house, my friends and neighbors." She placed a warm, seductive kiss against his mouth. "My life . . . this bed . . ."

Trace found himself reacting against his will to her kiss, and to her generosity. He groaned slightly and stood up. Then he gave her a light, playful push toward the door and swatted her on the bottom.

"Go," he said. "Or else we'll still be here in bed when the sun goes down."

"That doesn't sound so bad," she said, turning from the door. "Does it?"

She was a vision, Trace thought. Standing there with her burnished hair tumbled down her back, her creamy skin blushed and rosy, her eyes warm and tempting with desire as she challenged him.

He had to shake himself back to reality and to his purpose.

"Not so bad at all," he murmured. "But there will be time for that . . . I promise. There will be time."

Nine

It was a beautiful spring day and Rachel thought she had never noticed it more, or appreciated it as much as she did that morning with Trace.

Rachel was acutely aware of the housegirls' stares and whispered giggles as she and Trace walked through the house toward the back. They heard Cleo reprimanding some of the girls, and Rachel smiled at Trace.

The touch of his hand at her back sent tingles up her spine. Yet, if he noticed, or felt the same way, she could not tell. The expression on his face was pleasant . . . she couldn't say anything was wrong specifically. But he seemed so cool, so different this morning from the man she shared such intimacies with last night.

And that was exactly the opposite of the way she felt. She would never have believed that anyone could feel the way she did. His kisses and touch . . . his lovemaking had opened her eyes and her heart to all the wonders that could exist between a man and a woman. And she wanted to know that he felt it, too.

Was something wrong with her? To feel this strongly, this passionately about her husband? She had no idea. None of her friends were yet married and this wasn't really something she wanted to discuss with Lula and Cleo. Just then, Trace smiled at her and she brushed away all her doubts and all her foolish, unfounded fears.

Outside at the summer kitchen, Trace stepped inside to get

the picnic basket Lula had prepared. Rachel stood at the door, feeling a bit shy until Lula turned from where she was kneading bread and smiled brightly.

"How do, Miz Hambleton," she said with a grin. "You be lookin' mighty pretty this mornin' in that new blue dress. Don't she, Mr. Hambleton?"

"Very pretty," Trace agreed. For a moment, he gazed at Rachel, seeing the flush on her cheeks and the sparkle in her beautifully expressive eyes.

Then he took her arm and pulled her toward the stables.

"Bye, Lula," she called over her shoulder.

Trace had not spent any time the past ten years in a beautiful, well kept house. And what he remembered from his youth was not the same as he observed here at Windridge.

"You seem very close to your slaves," he said, as they approached the stables.

Rachel stopped. She seemed a little disturbed by his words and she frowned at him before moving once again to walk beside him.

"I'm sorry," she said. "Just hearing you refer to Lula as a slave took me aback for a moment. I know she is a slave, but she's much more than that to me. So is Cleo."

"Yes, so I noticed," he said quietly.

"Do you disapprove of the relationship I have with them?" she asked.

"No . . . not at all." Trace stepped into the stables just as Jim and Jared came around the building leading the horse and carriage.

"Mornin' Mr. Trace," Jared said. "Miss Rachel. Brung you a nice horse. Nice and gentle for a nice ride. Want Jim and me to come, too? We's good drivers and we be quiet as two mice in a hen house."

Rachel laughed and bent to place a kiss on first Jared's cheek, then Jim's.

"No, darlings, I don't think so. Not today."

"Why not?" Jared asked. He looked curiously from Trace to Rachel.

"Because . . ." Trace began. His glance toward Rachel was teasing, more lighthearted than it had been earlier. "Miss Rachel and I would like to be alone. You'll understand about being alone with beautiful young women when you're a little older."

Jared frowned and stepped back, but Rachel could see the disappointment in his eyes. It was probably the first time she'd ever denied them the opportunity to come with her. But she was too happy that Trace wanted to be alone with her to change her mind.

"Next time, boys . . . all right?"

Trace helped her into the buggy and they pulled away, going around the stables, past the smoke house and the row of martin gourds. She didn't have to tell Trace which way to go; he seemed to know. So she sat back and enjoyed the scent of peach blossoms and the warmth of the sun against her shoulders.

"How many acres?" Trace asked, his eyes scanning the land.

"Over two thousand," Rachel replied. She watched him, noting the hungry way his eyes took in everything. For a moment, she thought she even saw a hint of longing in those deeply expressive eyes.

She reached across the seat and touched his shining hair, tied back now at his neck. When he turned and looked at her, his eyes were dark.

"I suppose I'm not a very attentive bridegroom," he said, his voice quiet. "I should have told you how beautiful you look today and I should have asked how you're feeling."

He found her blush charming and he reminded himself that despite her passion and her delightful responses to him last night, she had been a virgin.

"I feel wonderful," she replied, her gaze not leaving his. "Is that normal?"

Trace laughed and pulled the horse to a stop. Then he

reached across and drew her closer to him, placing a kiss on her mouth that made her sigh.

"How would I know?" he teased.

"Haven't you . . . I mean, I know I couldn't possibly be the first woman you've . . ."

He laughed again, even as the images of the squalid reservation came back to mind. The girls he'd lain with had been like him—poor and needy, shamed by their environment and the treatment of their white teachers and keepers.

Their nights of passion had been furtive, filled with urgency and guilt. Sometimes it was on their blanket, set against the dusty, dirt floor. Sometimes in a darkened shed, with the musty smell of animals nearby. There had been no sweet herbs and mock orange, no servants respectfully carrying up hot chocolate or water for baths.

"That's not a question a wife should ask," he said. He tried to keep his voice light, to continue the teasing attitude that had permeated their conversation earlier. He wasn't sure he succeeded.

Trace gritted his teeth and moved away from Rachel, flicking the reins against the horse's back as they moved on.

"Are these the slave quarters?" he asked, turning left toward a long row of houses that were split by a wide sandy road.

"Yes." Rachel pushed away the doubts and questions that continued to plague her. Like any man, she told herself, Trace was interested in the land. She should let him enjoy it.

Behind the rows of houses, there were large garden areas. Negroes overran the newly plowed patches, some with hoes and some with seed sacks hung over their shoulder. They looked up as the carriage moved slowly down the lane. Some of them waved and some of them merely went back to work, seemingly uninterested in the mistress and the new master.

Trace noted there were many more slave houses than his father had and that they seemed well kept and in good repair. Several had been newly bricked and stood out in stark contrast from the gray wood sided ones.

"You have a brick kiln?" he asked.

"Yes, father added one just last year. Eventually, we hope to brick all the cabins—it makes them warmer in winter and cooler in summer. But it's such a slow process, and we don't have enough people to work full time at the kiln."

"How many slaves?"

"Two hundred."

Every time Trace said the word "slave," Rachel had an odd feeling. There was a hint of something in his voice . . . not disapproval, exactly. Something she couldn't quite put her finger on.

"Did your family not own slaves?" she asked, thinking finally that was the reason for his odd behavior.

"At one time, yes." he said. His eyes continued to roam over the houses. "But not so many."

His father had tried too hard to fit into the white man's society, even owning slaves as they did. It was a mistake to think he would be accepted, his people told him.

And they'd been right.

Trace didn't intend to repeat his father's mistakes.

Where had the Rosewood slaves gone? Could some of them still be here? And if so, would they recognize him? It was something he'd have to be careful about.

"Turn right here past the last house," Rachel said. "We'll drive over to the gin house and you can see where all the skilled work for the plantation is done."

Trace did as she asked, but he couldn't resist one last look back over his shoulders. As a child he had thought little of owning slaves—it was merely a way of life here in the south. But now the quarters reminded him too much of the reservation, and he wondered if the Negroes working in the gardens felt the same way he had in Oklahoma. Did they desperately long for freedom and hate the white people who enslaved them? It was something he was going to have to deal with, sooner or later.

"Trace . . ." Rachel said, breaking into his thoughts.

"Where did you say your family was from? You don't have an accent like anyone around here."

"No?" He relaxed his shoulders and forced a smile to his lips. "That's odd—I wouldn't have thought there was that much difference between a Tennessee accent and an Alabama one."

"Tennessee? Which part?"

"Hey, look there . . . isn't that the gin you were talking about?"

"Yes," Rachel said. "There are work shops here, too, and a spring. Papa calls the shop area Townsend Springs because it's gotten so big it actually looks like a small town."

Trace bit his lip. The nearby springs had been sacred once. This had been a gathering place for the Cherokees—his father and mother's families. The meadows surrounding the tree-lined springs were often crowded in summer by tents and wagons as the clan gathered to sing and dance and celebrate the planting and gathering of crops.

And now the Senator had turned that beautiful, sacred land into a work village to enhance his wealth and position.

He felt Rachel's hands on his, felt her tugging the reins from his fingers, and when he turned he found her staring at him, her blue eyes troubled.

"Trace . . . what's wrong? You're so different this morning. Everything I say seems to bother you . . . anger you, even. Have I done something? Is it the plantation? Do you disapprove of something? Or—"

"No," he said quickly. "No, Rachel . . . you haven't done anything." He reached for her, taking her shoulders and pulling her toward him. Without rationalizing what he was feeling, he took her mouth with a hard urgency, grinding his lips against hers, tasting with his tongue, punishing her with bruising kisses that made her gasp, then submit. When he pulled away, he shook her gently, gazing into her wide, surprised eyes.

"You please me very much Rachel," he whispered.

That much wasn't a lie, at least. He might have to keep

reminding himself that none of this was her fault. In his heart, he knew she was sweet and guileless, that she had nothing to do with her father's greed for ownership, or the changes he'd made here on Rosewood land. But it was very difficult to hide his reactions from her, seeing his home again after all these years. He had to be careful that when the final confrontation came, Rachel understood why he had to do this.

She loved him. As unbelievable as that seemed, he knew she loved him. He could see it in her eyes, hear it in the sweet tremor of her voice.

No genteel southern woman would have given herself so completely . . . so passionately, if she weren't in love.

That was his trump card—her love.

If he wanted the relationship to grow . . . if he wanted her support when the end of Windridge came, then he had to make sure her feelings for him didn't change. And he had to guard against arousing her suspicions by his behavior.

Ten

As they drove past the large cotton gin, Trace could see the changes that had taken place here, too. The meadows were no longer wide and filled with wildflowers. Instead, buildings stood where grass once had grown and a wide dirt road ran between the dozen or so buildings. Another road led to the stand of willow and sycamore trees where the spring lay in its mossy hideaway.

Trace remembered the taste of the water. Cold and sweet. Like nothing he had tasted since.

"There's a wonderful spring there among those trees," Rachel said, seeing Trace's look.

He nodded and flicked the reins against the horse. One day he would come back to explore the springs alone—to remember the ceremonies and the spirit of what once had been. But now he was curious to see the shops, or the village, as Senator Townsend had dubbed it.

The carpentry shop was first.

"Stop here," Rachel urged. "I want you to see something."

He tied the horse to a wooden rail in front of the building and went around to help Rachel down from the buggy. Her hands lingered on his arms, and he felt her sway against him briefly. Trace closed his eyes and touched his lips against her hair.

There was activity between the various buildings. Negroes peered toward them, one going into a building and coming back with another Negro man behind him. Rachel motioned

Trace into the carpentry shop. The scent of freshly cut wood filled the air inside the small shop . . . the aroma of cedar was strong.

"Good morning," Rachel said to the two men working there.

Trace was surprised that one of the men was a white man who turned to them now with a smile. The flat brimmed leather hat he wore looked soft and worn with age. He set aside the long carpenter's plane he had been using and smiled, white teeth visible behind his dark beard.

"Well," the man said, dusting his hands against his rough apron. "This must be Mr. Hambleton."

"Yes," Rachel said, beaming at her tall, handsome husband. "Trace, this is Mr. Copeland, a master joiner. Father hired him to teach our hands the skill of carpentry and cabinetmaking. This shop hasn't been in use very long."

Trace stepped forward and clasped the older man's hard, calloused hand.

The man helping Mr. Copeland was a Negro. He didn't step forward, but had stopped his work and removed his hat. Now he stood waiting, his eyes shifting from the two men to Rachel.

"And this is Marshall. He's lived at Windridge as long as I can remember and he makes the most beautiful furniture to be found anywhere in Alabama. I defy anyone to tell his work from a genuine Chippendale."

Trace had been watching the man named Marshall. And something in his brown eyes made Trace step forward and offer his hand, even though he knew it was not considered proper to shake hands with a Negro.

"Marshall . . ." he said.

Marshall hesitated a moment. He glanced from Rachel to Mr. Copeland. Then with a slight lift of his chin, he stepped forward and took Trace's hand.

"You look like somebody I know," Marshall said, studying Trace.

Trace held his breath. His father had once owned a young slave named Marshall. He and Trace had played together.

Mr. Copeland cleared his throat.

"Well," he said. "We're honored that you visited our humble shop on this first day after your wedding."

"I'm very proud of the work," Rachel said, determined not to blush at the reference to how she was spending the day after her wedding night. "And I wanted Trace to see what you and Marshall are working on. Look, darling," she said.

Rachel's face was aglow as she glanced back at Trace. She couldn't contain her excitement as she reached for his hand and pulled him with her to the back of the room where a cotton cloth covered and hid a large piece of furniture.

She pulled away the material and glanced again at Trace for his approval. The armoire, though large, had a grace and fragility that was missing from many pieces made by plantation craftsmen.

"It's cherry wood," Rachel said. "Cut from Windridge property."

"Well . . ." Trace couldn't resist touching the wood. It held such a rich color and the grain stood out as if illuminated from within. "I'm impressed."

"Do you like it?" Rachel seemed especially anxious for his approval.

"Yes, very much," Trace said, smiling at her enthusiasm. "It's beautiful. I don't think I've ever seen anything quite like it."

"Miss Rachel designed it," Marshall offered. "Drew a picture and a plan for it." His voice held a hint of pride for his mistress.

"I didn't really design it," Rachel said, shaking her head modestly. "I once saw a piece in New Orleans much like it. All I did was draw what I remembered."

Trace turned to Rachel, a glint of surprise in his eyes. He found her humility sweet and appealing.

"It's for you," she said rather shyly. "I had them start it when we became engaged."

Trace's lips parted and his eyes narrowed as he gazed at

Rachel. He was taken completely off-guard by her thoughtfulness and her generosity. No one had given him anything, probably since his mother's death.

"I . . . I don't know what to say," he said.

"You don't have to say anything," she said. Despite the two men watching him, she leaned forward and took his arm, hugging it against her as she smiled up at him. "I wanted to do it for you. Besides, you'll need somewhere to put your clothes."

They told the two men goodbye and left.

"Thank you for the gift," Trace told Rachel as they stood on the wooden sidewalk in front of the buggy. "It's beautiful."

Rachel stood on tiptoes and kissed him. Her eyes were warm and filled with such love that Trace had to look away.

"You don't have to thank me. I told you before . . . everything I have is yours. Come on . . . we'll leave the buggy here and walk to the other buildings."

Trace had to admit he was impressed by the variety of work being done on the plantation. Besides the blacksmith and farrier, there was also a cooper whose shop was filled with various sizes of wooden barrels, kegs, buckets and tubs. There were barrels for storing dry goods and others for liquid items. All of the shops were operated by Negro men.

Stepping into another building, Trace whistled, as his gaze took in the amazing variety of pots and pans hung from the rafters and around the walls.

"We even have a whitesmith, or tinsmith, really," Rachel said proudly. "They use thin sheet iron, plated with tin to keep the pots and pans from rusting. We can even make our own lanterns and candlesticks."

It was mid-afternoon when they walked back toward the buggy.

"I'm surprised that you know so much about each shop and the work being done here," Trace said.

"Oh," Rachel said with a shake of her head. "I love it. If I were a man, I probably would like being a carpenter, or even a tinsmith. Despite Cleo's disapproval, I've been coming here since I was old enough to sneak away on my own. I'd stay here, asking questions and being a general nuisance until someone would shout that Cleo was marching down the street looking for me." She laughed and the sound echoed merrily along the street.

Trace shook his head. He was watching her expression with wry amusement. He could just imagine the sight: Rachel, perhaps in pigtails, her beautiful expensive clothes smudged with dirt, defying everyone in order to come here and see something that interested her. Work that should not have interested a young, well bred girl. This was a Rachel he had never seen before—a lovely young woman filled with joyous enthusiasm, with more than a hint of little girl playfulness.

"Well," he said, helping her into the buggy. "Are you hungry? Shall we have our picnic now?"

"Oh, yes, I'm starving," she said. "How about the springs? It's so beautiful there. You'll love it, Trace."

Trace had not wanted to share the springs with anyone, not even Rachel. But he could hardly refuse to go there. And he found he didn't really want to see that beautiful smile leave her face by suggesting somewhere else.

As he drove toward the grove of trees, Trace could feel himself growing tense. He could almost hear the chanting and see the silhouetted figures as they danced around a fire in the middle of the meadow. He felt a fierce pride, an appreciation for his heritage that had been beaten down almost to nonexistence in Oklahoma. There he was merely a red savage, one of thousands that needed to be contained and controlled through scorn and ridicule. And pure physical power, if need be.

Here, he was a man, a part of a land and history that no one could take away from him ever again.

"Trace?"

In his subconscious, Trace recognized the question and concern in Rachel's voice. He hadn't realized until then that the buggy was still. He was too deep in thoughts, too lost in the very smell and feel of this sacred place.

"Sorry," he said, shaking off the visions. "Forgive my distraction. It's just that this place is so . . . beautiful."

Rachel smiled, instantly forgiving his seeming disinterest.

"It's one of my favorite places," she said.

Trace wasn't sure if it was the wistful quality in her voice, or the look in her eyes when she said it. But it made him realize that she loved this land, too. And that was something that took him a little by surprise. He had concentrated so long on getting here, on accomplishing his long-held desire of possession and revenge. He had never even considered that the people who lived at Rosewood now could care about it as much as he did.

"I knew you'd love it," she said.

She took the quilt from the back and Trace carried the basket, heavy with food and drink. He stood for a moment, gazing at the clear blue waters of the springs.

Here nothing had changed. No house or covering had been built over it as he feared. Even the road stopped outside the stand of trees so that nothing was disturbed by man's intrusion.

It was as if he stepped into another time, the time of his youth, when he was happy and life was good here. Trace could almost feel the strength and vitality of this place, with its hundreds of years of ancient rituals, moving over him and into his very soul. It empowered him and made him want to shout to the heavens with a joyous abandon that he knew Rachel would not understand.

Instead, he turned to her and took the quilt from her arms. He placed the basket on the ground and pulled her toward a large willow on the other side of the water. There, he knew all too well, the area beneath the tree was dark and hidden, secure from the eyes of anyone who might venture here.

He wanted her. And he wanted to take her here and now, where the voices of his ancient fathers cried out to him, where the primitive chanting filled his head with a rhythm as erotic and sensuous as this beautiful woman before him.

Rachel knew his intentions. She could see it in his eyes, in the way they darkened and intensified. She felt a thrill move over her with a delicious shudder.

Something had changed in Trace's eyes. Perhaps it was the possession of land, the well-kept shops that he knew now belonged to him. Perhaps it was this place, filled with such beauty that it touched an ancient place of longing in his soul as it always did hers. But whatever it was, he was different. A man she hardly knew. But one she wanted with a desperation she never thought possible.

Perhaps, Rachel thought, her tall, beautiful husband was beginning to love her and want her and need her as much as she already loved him.

Eleven

In the shadows of the huge willow, Rachel stopped and turned to her husband. The long trailing limbs of the tree, like fragile green curtains, enclosed them.

Trace stepped close to her, his expressive eyes sending an unmistakable message of how much he wanted her. He untied the ribbon that held her hat in place and gently slipped the delicate blue material from her head. Tossing the hat aside, he brought his hands to span her midriff, letting his fingers splay upward to cup her breasts.

Rachel's eyes sparkled and she swayed toward him, wanting his kiss, wanting him to take her in his arms. But he continued to caress her body, letting his warm fingers slide down her shoulders and bare arms, to encase her wrists, then her hands. She moved with him, letting him touch her, caress her, while leaning toward him in a silent offer of surrender.

Even when she began to tremble with desire, he continued to touch her and to move his hands sensuously over her arms, her neck, then ever so briefly her breasts, until she was gasping with pleasure. His eyes seemed to burn right through the material of her dress and she wondered why he didn't undress her. Yet she hesitated to do it herself.

The thin material of her dress clearly outlined her hardened nipples. His touch and his intense gaze made her feel weak and breathless . . . helpless beneath the spell he always seemed to cast over her.

Everything she experienced with Trace was so new to her.

She wasn't sure what was happening to her. When he touched her, she felt as if he held some powerful control over her . . . something that left her pliable and willing. So willing.

Suddenly, he took her hard against him, running his hands down over her crinoline covered hips and pulling her even closer. His hands cupped her rounded hips, caressing and kneading until Rachel gasped and arched her head back.

"Trace . . ." she whispered.

"You belong to me, Rachel," he murmured fiercely. He bent his mouth to her neck, tasting, exploring, letting his teeth nip at her sweetly scented skin. His voice was gruff, his arms like steel bands around her.

"Yes," she gasped.

His mouth, hard and hungry, covered her soft lips. She opened her lips to him. The invasion of his tongue made her wild with the same longing she'd felt last night. The kiss was hard and deep . . . hot.

Trace pushed her down and back onto the grass, forgetting the quilt, forgetting everything except the taste and touch and scent of her. Quickly, he pushed their clothes out of the way and moved over her, taking her with a hot urgency that again surprised himself.

Rachel gasped for air, thrilling at the feel of him, at the total maleness of him. His heated skin smelled clean and good. She pushed her face against him and inhaled, letting her every sense experience his lovemaking. As she felt the ecstasy building, she cried out, her fingers digging into his shoulders.

Moments later when Trace lay still against her, breathing heavily, Rachel opened her eyes. She smiled with wonder as she looked up at the willow and let her gaze take in the long trailing limbs.

She could hear the birds now and the rustle of leaves where a squirrel played. She even became aware of the ringing of an anvil in the distance.

She should feel ashamed . . . making love in the woods like

an untamed animal. But she didn't. She felt wonderful and more happy than she'd ever been in her life.

Softly, she laughed, and Trace moved away from her to lie on his side, watching her.

"What's so funny?" he asked, his eyes warm and teasing.

"A year ago I could never have imagined myself doing something like this," Rachel said.

"Well, I hope not," he said, bending to place a kiss against her forehead. "Because you didn't know *me* at the time."

Her face grew more serious, and she put her arms around his neck.

"You're joking, but it's true, you know. I could never feel the way I feel today with anyone else in the world except you."

Trace grew very quiet until Rachel frowned and reached up to touch the tiny scar at the edge of his brow.

"Trace? You seem so far away sometimes . . ."

"Do I?" He pulled her hand away from his face and kissed her fingers one by one. "I'm sorry—I'm just finding all this a little hard to accept, I guess."

"What?" she asked, her eyes growing dark with concern. "That I love you?"

"That anyone could love me," he said quietly. "And, especially, someone like you."

"Trace . . ." she said, her voice so soft he could barely hear her. There was such sympathy in her eyes . . . such love.

Trace didn't know what made him tell her such a thing. He certainly hadn't intended it. Perhaps it was the moment . . . the feelings she so sweetly evoked in him. And because he found himself growing softer . . . weaker when he was with her, he knew he had to be more on guard. He was beginning to think that one of the biggest dangers of his charade was this woman—this sweet, beautiful woman who was now his wife.

And who would hate him when it all ended.

"We should go back to the spring," he said. He stood up and straightened his clothes and wiped the leaves and grass from his trousers. "Before someone comes here and finds us. What would they think?" he asked, his voice light and teasing. "Finding the mistress of Windridge frolicking beneath this tree with her new husband." He reached down and took her hand, pulling her up and helping her brush her skirt. He turned her around and gently plucked the grass and leaves from her tangled hair.

"They'd think we're in love," she said quietly.

She didn't turn around to face him when she said it. She wasn't sure she wanted to see his eyes when he heard her words. When she felt him stiffen, then move away from her, she closed her eyes. Her lips trembled and she shook her head, blinking away her tears and biting her lips until she felt her control coming back. Then she turned with a brilliant smile.

"Well, I'm starving, aren't you?" she said brightly. She picked up the quilt and walked past Trace, pushing aside the trailing willow and moving back toward the other side of the spring.

Trace stared after her for a moment. He knew what she'd wanted him to say . . . that he loved her. But he couldn't. The words of love she needed to hear were foreign to him, something he probably would never be able to say to anyone.

Brushing her disappointment aside, Rachel spread Lula's lunch on the quilt. Nothing ever smelled as delicious as the mingled aroma of Lula's fried chicken and moist Sally Lunn bread.

Trace came and sat across from her. He watched her for a moment, noting her brilliant smile and sparkling eyes.

She couldn't fool him; he knew how much he'd hurt her. He hadn't intended it. He didn't want her to be hurt. Perhaps he should lie and tell her what she wanted to hear. What difference would one more lie make in the end? But somehow, looking into her trusting eyes, Trace couldn't make himself do it.

It was growing late when they left the spring and the grove of trees. But Rachel had not forgotten that one awkward moment when she stood waiting for him to tell her that he loved her. She thought about it as they drove silently back through the village, past the corn shed and animal pens, then through the beautiful orchard that was in sight of the house.

Rachel thought something must have happened in Trace's childhood to hurt him very deeply. He had told her that his parents were dead, yet he hadn't seemed unduly grieved when he said it. She knew they died when he was young and he'd been on his own for a long time. How long, she didn't know. She could never seem to get a direct answer from him about that.

Perhaps he was distant and brooding sometimes because he had been raised without parents. Rachel knew all too well what it was like to lose a beloved mother. It was confusing and painful for a child—even when one had the delightful, warm life she'd had with her father and Cleo and the others here at Windridge.

Whatever was in Trace's past, she wanted to know because she adored him and wanted to comfort him. And she was determined that, because of that love, he would one day feel the same way about her. She would see to it by making a safe, warm home here—a place where he felt loved and secure.

Impulsively, Rachel slid across the seat, looping her arm beneath Trace's elbow and laughing when he gave her a look of surprise.

"Where to next?" he asked, his look warm and inviting. "Are you ready to go home?"

"One last stop," she said. Rachel grew very quiet as her eyes scanned the distance. "I want to introduce you to someone."

They drove on past the house. Rachel guided Trace past the cotton fields until they were on the main road leading to Holly Springs. Then she pointed to the right, leading him to the same road where she had gone just yesterday with the twins.

Somehow that seemed so long ago. She was a different person now—a woman. She glanced at the man beside her. Her husband . . . the man who would share this beautiful land and home. The one who would father her children and share her old age. And for her, she thought that would not be near enough time.

The sweetness and the sadness of it made her shiver.

They turned toward the cemetery and Trace glanced at her curiously again.

"This way?"

"Just there," she said. "Where the old live oaks are."

Trace pulled up to the iron fence surrounding the cemetery. He glanced briefly at the graves and walked around to lift Rachel down from the buggy.

Silently, they walked inside the enclosure. She held his hand and pulled him to the foot of her mother's grave. The flowers she had placed here yesterday looked as fresh as if they'd just been picked.

Trace read the words etched on the large marble monument.

"Mary Ann Townsend, beloved wife and mother." Then he turned to Rachel. "Your mother."

"Yes . . . my mother. And my baby sister there beside her."

"Do you remember them?" Trace could see that Rachel was still touched by the sight before them. His voice was low and quiet, out of sympathy and understanding.

"A little," Rachel said, smiling wistfully. "I was very young when it happened. I think I remember my mother's essence, more than I actually remember her. You know?"

"Yes," he said. "I know." He put his arm around her small waist and held her against his side for a moment. Then he motioned toward the other grave that lay unmarked near the fence.

"Whose grave is this?"

Rachel shrugged her shoulders and took a deep breath, then she walked toward the grave.

"We've never known. Papa says it was here when he received the property. Perhaps someone traveling through here . . . a slave . . . maybe even a Cherokee," she mused.

"There used to be a great number of them here you know . . . before their removal to the Oklahoma territory."

Trace gritted his teeth and frowned. He wasn't thinking now of the march. That last vision of his father came to him in one swift, heart wrenching flash. Lying bloodied and so still with the soldiers all around him. All of Trace's attention, all his being, was focused on the lone, unmarked grave.

Was it possible? Could this be his father's grave?

"Papa said Mother felt very sad about the grave . . . it being unmarked and all. She decided to enclose the area and make this our family plot."

Trace shook himself. He didn't want Rachel to see how deeply the grave affected him.

"Didn't it bother her that it might have been a Negro . . . even a Cherokee, as you said?"

Rachel looked up at him and frowned.

"No, of course not. My mother wasn't like that."

Apparently not. Surely Mrs. Townsend had considered those possibilities when she had the cemetery fenced and included this grave.

"The grave could be very old," Trace said.

"Well . . . not too long before Papa acquired Windridge, at least. That would be . . . mmm, ten . . . twelve years perhaps."

Trace felt a tingle race down his spine. The same tingle he'd felt when he first saw the grave and stepped to it. This was no stranger's grave, no wayfarer passing through the land. It was his father's grave, he was certain of it. It wasn't just the time period as Rachel had told it. It was a feeling . . . an age-old instinct that had never left Trace, not even when the white soldiers had tried to beat it out of him.

This was something that spoke to the heart. And if he could be here alone, he knew he would hear it even stronger. He might even hear the voice of his father, speaking to him from the cold ground and surrounding trees.

He wanted to lean back his head and shout of his great unexpected discovery. To chant with the ancient words of his ancestors. Instead, he clenched his teeth and stepped to the grave, kneeling on the grass and reaching out to caress the flowers that lay there like bright butterflies.

"The flowers are still fresh," he said, almost to himself. "Who would—?"

"I did," Rachel said.

She was touched by Trace's actions, although she didn't fully understand them. She knelt there in the grass beside him and leaned her head against his shoulder.

"You?" Trace asked.

"I came here yesterday morning before our wedding. You'll probably think I'm crazy, but I came to speak to my mother. And to tell her about you. When I leave flowers for her, I always place flowers on this grave, too. This was someone's mother or father . . . someone's sister . . . brother." She shrugged her slender shoulders and continued gazing at the grave. "He or she is alone here except for us, with no family to respect the grave, no one to place flowers here on special occasions. So I do it."

Unexpectedly, Trace felt tears welling in his eyes. He clenched his teeth hard against the ache in his throat and the terrible pain gathering in his chest.

Dear God, what was he to do with her? This sweet, enchanting woman who even now, here at the foot of his father's grave, managed to make him want her. She threatened to wind her way into his heart and soul, despite all his self warnings and the hatred of her people that ate at him daily.

Quickly, he stood up, reaching down to grasp her upper arm and pull her up with him.

"It's going to be dark soon," he said, his voice gruff as he tried to hide the unexpected emotion that flooded over him. "Are you ready to go?"

"Yes, my darling," she said, sliding her arm around his waist. "Let's go home."

Twelve

Rachel was typically an early riser, but the next morning, when she woke, Trace was already gone. She dressed hurriedly and went into the dining room, expecting to find him there. But the room was empty, except for one of the girls who was placing a pot of chocolate on the mahogany sideboard.

"Dimity . . . do you know where Mr. Hambleton is? Has he already had breakfast?"

"Oh, yes ma'am," the girl said. She bent her knees and bobbed, before continuing her work. "He already out and gone."

"Did he say where he was going?" Rachel's eyes darkened and her expression reflected her concern.

"No, ma'am," Dimity said. The young girl turned to face Rachel. She bit her lip and glanced down toward the floor.

"It's all right," Rachel said. Dimity always tried so hard to please. She smiled at the girl and walked to the sideboard.

"You go ahead with whatever you were doing. I'll just serve myself."

But when Rachel sat at the table, she didn't pour the hot chocolate, or place butter on the biscuit that sat on an elegant plate before her. Instead, she stared across the long table and out a window.

Dimity bit her lip again and then hurried from the room, going down the hallway toward the back of the house. In a moment, she came back, her face completely changed by a bright smile.

"Miss Rachel?"

Rachel shook herself out of her apathy and picked up a butter knife.

"Yes, Dimity."

"Mama Cleo said she seen Mr. Hambleton leave out the front door and strike out across the yard. Seems like he might have been headed toward the cemetery." The girl was immensely pleased that she could bring Rachel such important news.

"The cemetery?" Rachel said, frowning as she considered what the girl had said. "Why on earth would he . . . ?" She shook her head again, finally reaching for the chocolate pot. "It doesn't matter," she murmured to herself. "Thank you, Dimity."

Trace stood at the foot of the unmarked grave. His eyes were closed and softly he chanted beneath his breath, letting the sing song words and rhythms come from his chest until he could feel it in every pore of his body.

He could feel the spirit lifting him, moving him out of his earthly body almost until the peace he'd been seeking finally came, settling around him like a warm, sweetly scented blanket.

His eyes were still closed and he grew silent, letting every sense become keenly aware of every sound and scent. When he opened his eyes, he lifted his arms and spoke quietly.

"Are you here my father? Is this the spot where the soldiers dragged you, and buried you, unsanctified by the love of your family and known only to the Great Spirit? I think sometimes I don't really hear the answers anymore, Father . . . perhaps I make them be what I want them to be. Help me to listen . . . and to hear. I want to know . . . I need to know if you're here."

Trace stood for a long time, waiting, his body tense and

still. But there were no words, no sound except the wind in
the live oaks and the distant cawing of crows in the fields.

His shoulders relaxed and he sighed, looking up for a moment into the branches of the trees. When he saw the gray
dove perched on a low limb, he felt his heart stutter and then
begin to beat again. For a moment, he actually thought the
bird's eyes were looking directly into his, and it gave him an
odd feeling.

He closed his eyes and rubbed his fingers against them.
When he opened them again, the dove was still there, quiet
and peaceful and still seeming to look directly into Trace's
eyes. It was the sign he'd been waiting for. He knew it the
moment that he looked into the bird's tiny black eyes and saw
such silent contentment.

His father was like the dove—quiet and filled with a great
peace and dignity. He had not been a warrior, but a scholar,
a man dedicated to peace and to living in grace with all men
of the world, even though he was often criticized for it by his
own people. If Trace had looked up and had seen an owl or
a hawk, he would have thought little of it. But the dove was
a sign. He knew it.

He dropped to his knees beside the grave and prayed silently
for a moment. He felt as if some great stone had been lifted
from his heart. He knew where his father was. He could bury
his mother's brooch, reuniting his parents and insuring that
their spirits would be one.

If he achieved nothing else here, this one discovery was
worth everything he was doing and would do.

Rachel had finished breakfast and had just come out onto
the front porch with a basket of sewing. She saw Trace coming
across the lawn, his long legs reaching out like a man with a
purpose. His dark head was bent, his hair, untied this morning,
flowing out behind his shoulders. He had such dignity and
beauty that she couldn't take her eyes off him.

Just the sight of him made Rachel's heart turn over. Trace was not like any other man she'd ever known. Something seemed very different about the man she had married, something she had not been able to identify until this moment. He was like a soldier marching across a battlefield. A proud warrior with a purpose that nothing or no one could deter.

When Trace looked up and saw Rachel standing on the porch, her sewing basket in her hands, he hesitated, then continued on toward her. He took the steps two at a time and, reaching her, he bent to place a kiss against her warm skin.

"I missed you," she murmured. "I had hoped to have breakfast with my new husband."

"I'm sorry," he said. "I couldn't sleep and I didn't want to disturb you." He glanced at the sewing she held. "Here, what's this? Don't tell me that among your many talents you are also a seamstress?"

"I enjoy embroidery," she said. "I'm making a birthday present for Hallie." But Rachel was hardly interested in discussing her sewing. Why did it seem that many of their conversations were trivial and meaningless? As if Trace were trying to distract her. But why?

"Where did you go? To the cemetery?" Rachel's gaze turned briefly toward the stand of live oaks.

"No," Trace said, shrugging his shoulders. He sat in one of the porch rockers and crossed his legs. "Just walking."

When Rachel sat down beside him, she noted the grass and the faint stains on the knees of his trousers. She frowned, but said nothing.

She knew that Trace had no reason to lie to her. Certainly not about something so inconsequential as whether or not he'd been to the cemetery. And she had to admit, he seemed very happy this morning. There was a new contentment about him she thought. Perhaps he was getting used to his new home at Windridge.

* * *

That night, long after Trace had made love to his beautiful wife . . . long after she lay sleeping peacefully in their bed, he got up and dressed quietly. As he searched for his mother's brooch in the bottom of a bag, his gaze moved back to the bed where Rachel slept.

He knew she was growing more and more curious about his past. And he knew she didn't always believe the excuses he gave her about his moods and actions. Sooner or later, she would have to know what he was doing.

But not yet. Not just yet.

He told himself that it would take time to complete all his plans and that it was too soon to reveal his deception to Rachel. But, in his heart, he knew there was another reason: that Rachel would leave him . . . and that he wasn't ready for that to happen.

The small leather pouch containing the brooch fell onto the floor with a loud clunk. The sound caused Rachel to stir and murmur something in her sleep.

"Damm," he muttered.

Trace held his breath, watching her from the opposite side of the room. When he heard her quiet breathing again, he slipped silently from the room and out of the house.

It took only a few moments to dig a small hole with his knife and place the brooch in the dirt of his father's grave. He would come back when the moon was new and complete the more formal spirit ceremony. For an odd moment, he wished the charade with Rachel were real and that she could come with him, that this sacred burial of his parents could be done in the presence of a kind and loving family.

But that wasn't to be.

After a silent prayer, Trace stood staring down at the grave, though he could see little in the dark. Then he left the confines of the cemetery and ran back across the lawn.

Rachel noted a change in Trace the next few days. He discussed the idea of moving his office from Holly Springs to the plantation and Rachel, though a bit surprised, had no objections. In fact, she was delighted that he would be here all day, instead of going to town.

Their life should be perfect, she thought. And yet, she noticed that he seemed to grow even more distant. The only time Rachel felt he let her get close to him was in bed at night. Their lovemaking took her to heights she never imagined, and his responses were genuine and equally passionate. The way he kissed her and held her, the way he whispered hot words into her ear as their physical bodies soared.

She was especially puzzled about some of the words . . . strange, foreign sounding words that she'd never heard before. Her entire body flushed as she remembered last night and the words he had whispered to her while in the heat of the moment.

"What did they mean?" she had asked shyly, her face buried against his chest.

"What?"

She could feel his body tense . . . feel him distancing himself from her the way he did during the day.

"Those words . . . the words you said to me." Why was he making this so hard?

"I don't know," he murmured. "A man says many things when he's making love to a beautiful woman." He laughed, but she could still feel the tension in his big strong body.

To a beautiful woman, he had said. Not making love to the woman he loves. Rachel closed her eyes. She didn't want to think about that. She wanted to enjoy this moment, to savor his arms around her and the softness of his breath against her hair. For she knew, that no matter how wonderful their lovemaking had been, tomorrow would come.

And tomorrow, Trace would change back into that cool, distant stranger that she hardly knew.

Thirteen

The next morning, Trace waited in their room for Rachel to finish bathing and dressing. When she came back into the bedroom, he thought he'd never seen such a vision. In her white dressing gown, with her hair tumbled over her shoulders, she looked like an angel—a golden angel that had just stepped off a cloud to greet him.

Her eyes showed surprise, then quickly changed to pleasure when she saw him still in the room.

"I thought you'd be gone by now," she said.

He liked the way she stood away from him. Shyly almost, like a little girl waiting to receive an invitation.

"I wanted to have breakfast with my wife," he said. Slowly he stepped toward her and took her in his arms. The lingering scent of rose soap made him grit his teeth and take a deep steadying breath.

He turned her around and with a playful swat on her bottom, gently pushed her toward the armoire.

"So get dressed," he growled playfully. "Your husband is hungry."

Trace didn't like playing these games with Rachel. And he didn't like seeing that look of concern in her eyes when she asked questions about his actions or his past. He had put her off, offered excuses, even made love to her to distract her thoughts.

But he couldn't keep doing that forever.

They had just sat down for breakfast when Cleo came into the dining room.

"Rachel honey . . . Mr. Hambleton . . . they's a Indian man at the front door. Says he's lookin' for work. Says his family is hungry." Cleo sniffed and rolled her eyes. "Don't know why everybody comes to Windridge when they's hungry. Don't know why—"

"Cleo . . ." Rachel scolded. She folded her napkin hastily and pushed her chair away from the table. "Where is he?"

"Probably still standing in the front yard," Cleo said disdainfully. "Even tho' I told him to take hisself round to the back."

"Cleo, you didn't," Rachel said.

Trace was watching the entire scene with a hint of amusement. Cleo still wouldn't acknowledge that he was master of Windridge. She always deferred to Rachel when there was a problem that needed handling. He knew that Rachel, being kind and considerate, was troubled by that. And, as always, she turned to Trace to include him.

"Come with me, darling," she said.

Trace rose from the table, flashing a dark look toward Cleo that only seemed to heighten her disdain. She turned with a loud sniff and a whirl of black skirts, and hurried away toward the back of the house muttering something about Indians and poor people.

Trace let Rachel step first out onto the front porch. He kept his head bent, gazing beneath his brows at the man on the walkway below the steps. Did he know him? The Indian was dressed in denim trousers and a faded calico shirt. His feet were clad in moccasins that were dirty and worn with age. He didn't look much older than Trace himself, but there was a weariness about him that defied age. His dark face was lined and dark from the sun. And his eyes held a glint of pride and anger that Trace recognized all too well.

Trace thought it was probably the family that the men in town had been talking about that night before the wedding.

But Trace didn't recognize the man and so he stepped from behind Rachel and stood next to her at the edge of the porch.

"May I help you?" Rachel asked.

The gentleness in her voice made Trace glance sideways at her, and for one brief moment, he felt a great pride welling inside his chest. Almost as if he had a right to claim such pride for a wife who was kind and generous. When he turned his gaze back, the Indian was staring at Trace . . . looking right into his eyes.

"I am looking for work," the man said. "My wife is almost ready to deliver our child and the other two, they are very hungry."

Just then, as if receiving a cue, the man's wife and two little girls stepped out from behind the huge boxwoods that lined the front porch.

Rachel gasped when she saw them. The woman's bare feet were terribly swollen and her thin legs seemed hardly able to hold the weight of her protruding stomach.

Trace thought it was the sight of the children that brought Rachel's gasp of sympathy and made her start down the steps toward them. They were terribly thin, their clothes slick with dirt and grime.

"Rachel . . ."

Trace caught her arm and pulled her back. Both of the children had bright rosy cheeks and their eyes were glittering. Trace suspected they had a fever and he didn't want Rachel subjected to whatever they had.

"Sweetheart . . . give them food and send them on their way." Trace's voice was soft, meant only for Rachel. But from the corner of his eye, he thought the Indian somehow heard and understood his every word. "The children are ill."

Rachel's eyes flashed and her mouth flew open as if she couldn't believe what he had said.

"I will do no such thing," she said. She walked down the steps and took the woman's arm, then stretched out her other arm to include the children.

"Come," Rachel said. "Come into the house. We'll get you something to eat. Then we'll find a safe place for you to stay."

The woman and her children did not move, but she looked longingly toward her husband as if waiting his command.

"We do not seek charity," the Indian said, his eyes meeting Trace's with a hard, stubborn look.

"I prefer to call it neighborliness," Rachel said with a proud lift of her chin. Still, the gentleness had not left her voice. "After you've eaten and rested, then we'll talk about work and the wages you will receive." Rachel glanced at Trace.

His eyes were dark, brooding. He stood with his hands at his hips, shaking his head in disbelief.

"Rachel . . ." he said, his voice soft with warning. "You have no idea what you're getting yourself into here."

"Would you turn them away?" Rachel said quietly. "Leave this woman to deliver her child in the woods like an animal? Just look at her, Trace. This baby could come any day."

Trace had never seen Rachel like this—her cheeks flushed in anger, her eyes brightly defiant. Her beautiful lips were compressed into a line that told him she would not be opposed on this decision. Finally, Trace sighed and turned on his heel to walk into the house. He stopped at the dining room door when he heard Rachel come into the entry hall behind him.

The Indian and his family were with her. They looked decidedly out of place in the clean cool house, appearing shy and awkward.

The woman peered down at her dirty feet on the shining, spotless floors. She seemed ashamed.

Trace's gaze met Rachel's, and he found a stubbornness there that amazed him. *By God, she intended to bring them right into the dining room.*

He stood for a moment, stunned and puzzled by this petite, beautiful woman he had married. A woman, he realized, that he didn't know as well as he thought. He shook his head and with a slight grin of defeat, waved his arm gallantly toward the dining room.

With a self-satisfied look, Rachel moved forward, motioning the family with her.

The Indian woman stopped at the doorway.

"Dy you oo doe ho hist," she said.

Something about her shy words of embarrassment touched Trace and despite his hardened heart, he found himself wanting to reassure her and to make her feel welcome, too.

"Zah yoh shi hah?" he said, asking if she was hungry.

The woman nodded, her dark eyes moving toward her children with longing.

"Then please . . . eat." Trace said, waving his hand toward the table. *"Hut sty you hoo gah."*

Rachel stood staring at Trace, unable to understand his words and amazed that he was conversing in this woman's language. But whatever he said seemed to reassure the woman and she stepped into the dining room.

"It's all right," Rachel said. "You are welcome. We have plenty of food."

"It's the chairs," Trace said, motioning toward the rich upholstery that covered the seats. "She feels shame that they are so dirty. And that they haven't washed this morning."

"No . . . no," Rachel said. "It's all right. Come." She turned toward the hallway and called out. "Cleo! Dimity?"

Cleo came bustling down the hallway, her skirts rustling, her eyes wide with curiosity.

"Cleo, please have someone bring damp towels so that they might wash their hands. And have the cook send porridge and bread and soft scrambled eggs for the children." She smiled at the Indian woman who was looking at Rachel with awe and wonder.

"Is there anything special you would like?" she asked, her gaze moving toward the woman's enlarged stomach.

The woman couldn't seem to find her voice. She merely shook her head, her eyes wide with amazement.

Trace thought it was one of the most agonizing meals he'd ever endured.

The Indian man sat in his chair, arms crossed over his chest, refusing the food in front of him. Yet, his dark eyes, when they moved over his wife and children, were kind, urging them to eat.

Rachel seemed confused and hurt that the man would not eat. She kept glancing at Trace for some explanation.

The woman and children ate as if they were starving, which Trace suspected was close to the truth. The girls wolfed their food down like little animals, raking it from the plate with their hands and strewing it across the elegant white tablecloth and onto the carpet.

Cleo stood at the doorway watching with alarm, her arms crossed over her large bosom. She watched as if she couldn't believe her eyes. When one of the children sneezed and blew food across the table, Cleo moved forward with a shriek.

"Goodness sake, Miss Rachel. That chile don't got no business at this table. Look what she done to the—"

"That's enough, Cleo," Trace said.

It was the first time Trace had ever reprimanded anyone in the Windridge household. For a moment, Cleo seemed frozen to the spot and Rachel's eyes moved from her husband to the woman who had raised her. But she said nothing, deferring instead completely to Trace.

The room was completely silent. Even the children had stopped eating.

"It isn't necessary for you to stand here and watch them eat," Trace continued, his voice deceptively soft. "Unless of course, you'd like to join us."

"Join you?" Cleo said with a disdainful hoot. "Why would I wants to join you?" With a resentful look at Trace, she turned to go, muttering to herself as she hurried down the hall.

"Dirty little rascals got no manners. Messin' up this . . . messin' up that. Who gonna clean it? Ole Cleo, that's who. Sho, it's easy to be charitable if'n you don't gotta clean it up."

Rachel rolled her eyes, but she couldn't help smiling at Trace.

"It's all right," she said to the family. "Finish your meal and then we'll find you a nice cozy place where you can rest." Rachel's glance moved over the Indian man who sat stoically, still not eating.

There was a stubbornness, a fierce pride about him that reminded her of Trace. Why, she couldn't say. Heaven knew, Trace was nothing like this man.

After the family was fed, Rachel escorted them down the hallway and out to the back of the house.

"Where's Justus?" she asked at the kitchen door. She had made the twins' older brother her overseer not long ago and, although he had been raised here at the house, currently he was more often out and about in the fields.

"In the tobacco patch, most likely," Cleo said.

"Have the twins find him and when he comes, Cleo, tell him to find a suitable place for this family to stay. Perhaps the old shed out behind the stables. It's sturdy and it's big enough for a family. With a little work, it can be made into a very nice little house."

Cleo made her disapproval known by rolling her eyes and grunting loudly.

"Don't know why you wants to go to all that trouble. They ain't gonna stay. Gonna jes keep on wanderin', like they always do."

"Cleo . . ." Rachel said, giving her a stern look.

"All right . . . all right. Whatever you say. Ain't none o' my bisness."

Rachel turned to Trace just inside the hallway, where he stood watching her. His face looked no more approving than Cleo's.

When she walked to him, he took her arm and pulled him with her back into the house. They stood alone in the quiet hallway.

"You shouldn't have brought the family into the house. They didn't expect it, Rachel."

"I know they didn't expect it. But it was what I wanted to

do." She pulled her arm free of Trace's hard grasp and stood frowning at him. "I can't believe you honestly think I should have turned down their pleas for help."

"I didn't say that. Giving them food is one thing. But you shamed the man . . . can't you see that? It took everything he had to ask for a white woman's help in the first place, and then to be brought into this magnificent house and forced to sit and be insulted . . ."

Rachel's mouth flew open and when she clamped it back together, her lips trembled.

"How dare you say that to me," she whispered. "I would never . . . I have never . . ."

"Rachel . . . I know you didn't do it intentionally. But nevertheless, that's exactly what happened. Do you think just because they're Indians that they like living this way? Dirty and so poor that the man can't even afford shoes for his wife? By bringing him in here in the middle of all this . . ." Trace waved his hand about the beautiful surroundings. Rachel had never noticed the look of loathing on his face until now. She had thought he loved Windridge as much as she did.

"Trace, what are you saying?" She seemed incredulous that he could berate her for doing what was right.

"I'm saying, dammit, that the man was ashamed because they were dirty, because he has not been able to care properly for his family. And by flaunting this in his face, you made him feel even more shame. That's why he didn't eat."

Rachel clamped her teeth together and took a long, steadying breath.

"And how is it that you know so much about Indians? How did you know what the woman said earlier?"

Trace had not thought twice about his reaction to the Cherokee words. He had simply answered the woman—it had come as instinctively as breathing.

"I told you before. I drifted around a bit before I came to Holly Springs. These are just things I picked up."

"I don't care what you've learned Trace. I say the man didn't eat because he's stubborn," she said. "Pure male stubbornness and false pride—that's all it is. And that trait, my dear husband, is not exclusively an Indian one."

Trace wanted to shake her. He'd never realized before just how willful and hard-headed she was. But before he could respond, they heard a noise behind them. Both of them turned to see the Indian standing in the hallway, watching them. Obviously, he had heard every word they'd said.

"Excuse me," the Indian said. "I wanted to thank you for your kindness. And to tell you that I will do work to repay you for the food my family has eaten." He stood erect, shoulders back. And there was a fiercely determined gleam in his black eyes. The pride Trace had just spoken of was blatantly obvious now.

"That's not necessary—" Rachel began.

"Thank you," Trace said. He practically pushed Rachel aside as he stepped to the man and nodded his acceptance. "There's wood to be chopped for the kitchen. Ask Miss Cleo to show you to the woodpile."

"But . . . but, he can't chop wood without eating . . . Just look at him, he's—"

"Rachel . . . be quiet," Trace said between gritted teeth.

But this time, the Indian seemed less stubborn. He did not smile, but he looked toward Rachel more kindly.

"I will eat," he said. "And I will cut twice the wood."

"No . . . I didn't mean . . ."

The man turned silently, his moccasin clad feet making no noise in the hallway.

"Trace, I intended to let the family stay. To live here."

"I know," he said.

"So . . . why should he chop wood for his meal if he's to be living here and working here? I take care of all the people who live at Windridge."

"This man is different. He wants to take care of his own and he doesn't mind working to accomplish that."

"Trace," she hesitated, choosing her words carefully before

she continued. "Darling, you are my husband, and I want to share everything with you. This is your home now, and I mean that with all my heart. But I am used to doing things my own way here at Windridge. I am not used to being dictated to . . . not even by my father."

Trace stared into her glittering eyes. Her outspokenness surprised him. And her independence irritated him more than he wanted to admit.

"Then I suggest you get used to it, my darling wife," he said sarcastically. His voice was low . . . menacing almost. The resentment he'd felt for years welled up inside him. This was his home, dammit. It had been his long before Senator Townsend ever set foot on the place. And he wasn't about to let this slip of a woman run his life, now that his goal was almost in his grasp.

Trace could see the change in Rachel's eyes. Surprise and defiance, blended in those sparkling blue depths.

"You are my wife now," he continued. "And I don't consider it proper for my woman to work with the fieldhands like a man."

"Your . . . your *woman?*" she asked, practically sputtering.

"From now on, Rachel, you will do as I say. And that includes staying here in the house like a lady. You are better suited to playing hostess." His dark eyes glittered dangerously. "And to warming your husband's bed."

"Oh!" Rachel said. A dark flush sprang to her cheeks. Her chin quivered with fury.

Trace turned away from her and walked toward the back of the house.

"Trace! Come back here."

He didn't falter, didn't hesitate, but kept walking, going out the back door and slamming it hard behind him.

Rachel stood trembling. She could not believe what she had just heard. And she couldn't believe that the man she loved had spoken to her in such a harsh, condescending manner. If there was one thing she had been certain of when they married, it was that Trace was different. And that he would not hold her to the same rigid standards as most men did their wives.

This was a side of him she'd never seen. And she had no idea what she could do about it.

Fourteen

Trace stayed away all that day. He didn't even come home for dinner, and by then Rachel's anger had turned to concern. She sat alone at the long table, the candlelight gleaming against the elegant Venetian crystal and English dinnerware. The roast duckling was perfect, prepared just the way Rachel liked it.

Still, she hardly noticed any of it. Her mind and her heart were filled with longing, and she worried about Trace's behavior.

"He be all right," Cleo said once when she came in and found Rachel staring at the candles' flickering light.

"What?" Rachel asked, glancing up as if she'd been in a deep sleep.

"I said Mr. Trace gonna be all right."

"I can't understand why he hasn't come home," Rachel said. Small worry lines appeared between her brows. "Perhaps he's had an accident, or . . ."

"Ain't had no such thing," Cleo said. "Though Lord knows why he wants to waste his time out there. We got people to do that. He don't have to do it."

Rachel shook her head. "Cleo, what are you talking about? Doing what?"

"Helpin' them Indians, that's what. He's out there now, sleeves of that fine silk shirt you bought him, rolled up like a field hand." Cleo snorted and refilled Rachel's water glass.

"Lord a mercy." Cleo grunted and moved her big body around to whisk nonexistent crumbs from the table.

Rachel pushed her chair back and stood up.

"Now jes a minute, missy. You can't go out there," Cleo said, her eyes growing round with indignation.

"And why can't I? As you so often point out, this is my house."

"That shed is a pigsty, that's why. Why look at this here fancy silk dress you got on. One swish against that filthy floor and it be ruined for sho." Cleo's gaze moved with appreciation down the pink material trimmed with rose colored lace.

Rachel bit her lips. It wasn't the dress that bothered her. She disliked the fact that Trace had been gone all day without telling her where he was. Was he truly that angry at her? Merely because she had disagreed with him about the Indian and about her role as a wife?

"He seemed so against the Indians staying," she said, almost to herself.

"Well, he don't seem agin it now," Cleo muttered. "You through eatin'? Lord, chile, you didn't eat enough to keep a pigeon alive."

"I'm not hungry," she said, turning from the table. "I'll eat later. I promise," she added over her shoulder as she hurried toward the back of the house.

It was dark outside. There was no sign of a moon tonight and the clouds blotted out the stars. The only light came from the kitchen where Lula and the girls were still cleaning up.

Rachel hurried past the kitchen and along the stone walkway toward the stables. She could see lights in the second floor of the stable building, where the twins lived with their brother Joshua.

Beyond the stables she saw the outline of the old shed. Light barely filtered through the dirty windows, but what there was let Rachel see the shadows of people moving about inside. As she grew closer, she could hear two men talking.

They were not speaking English, but the same language she had heard Trace and the woman use. She recognized Trace's distinctive deep voice and she could hardly believe what she was hearing. It seemed that he had learned more than a *bit* on his travels, as he'd told her earlier.

He was speaking their language fluently.

"I knew you didn't recognize me," the Indian said in his native tongue. "But I knew you right away. I remember the last night I saw you. It was the same night my brother and I ran away. I never saw my mother and father again after that. They encouraged us to run. I thank you for sharing with me what happened to them. I can hardly believe my mother is still alive and well."

"She's very feeble, White Feather," Trace said. "She always worried about her sons and then after your father died, she was never the same." Trace tapped a finger against his chest. "Her heart was broken."

"I will go to see her," White Feather said. "As soon as we are able, I will go to this place called Ok-la-ho-ma."

"I know you long to see your mother. But you would do well to stay away from the plains. It is not a welcoming place for the Cherokee. They might even imprison you there."

White Feather frowned, his gaze falling on his children where they slept on low cots, and then his wife, who even now worked tirelessly, though her body was awkward and heavy.

Hummingbird had been pleased beyond reason by the little house. She had seemed hardly able to believe they were lucky enough to find a woman like the mistress of Windridge who would give them such a fine place to live. And she could not believe her husband, White Feather, had found his cousin whom he had spoken of all these years.

"Now that the white man has possession of all our lands here, they might not be so quick to imprison us," White Feather said. "I am but one solitary man. How could I possibly threaten a sea of white eyes?"

"I don't know," Trace said. He sighed and turned around to look out the windows. What he saw made him catch his breath and frown.

"Look, I have to go," he said, turning back to White Feather. He took his cousin's shoulders and embraced him. "Tomorrow we'll get this place repaired and cleaned until it looks like new. Hummingbird will have a clean house in which to deliver her child."

White Feather saw what had made Trace so anxious to leave. He saw his cousin's bride, the beautiful white woman called Rachel standing outside, gazing in through the dirty windows.

"You should tell her the truth," White Feather said softly.

Hummingbird stopped her sweeping. Her dark eyes turned toward Trace, urging him to listen to her husband.

"I can't," Trace said. "Not until the deeds to this place are in my hands for good."

"And what then, my cousin? Will you seek your revenge on her—turn her out the way the whites did you and your family? Or do you intend to let her stay and be your slave?"

Trace grunted softly.

"Rachel would hardly be any man's slave," he said. "She'd probably die first."

"Do you love her?" White Feather asked softly.

"No," Trace said quickly. "I told you—I married her because it was the quickest, easiest way to get Rosewood back."

"But there is something between the two of you. I saw it earlier when you were speaking in the hallway. It is lust then?" White Feather asked with a knowing smile.

Trace frowned. It surprised him to learn that his intimate relationship with Rachel was not something he was willing to discuss. Not even with his long-lost cousin.

"Sometimes lust turns to love, is that not true Hummingbird?" White Feather looked with a teasing smile toward his wife. She grinned and went back to sweeping, yet her dark eyes flashed back to her husband again and again.

"The little mistress," White Feather said, nudging Trace. "I think she loves you already."

"She says she does," Trace admitted. He lowered his head thoughtfully. "But she doesn't yet know what I've done."

"Be careful," White Feather said. "That in seeking your revenge, you don't lose your heart in the process."

"That's not going to happen, cousin." Trace nodded solemnly and turned to go.

Rachel was surprised to see him coming out of the house. Though she hadn't understood a word the two men were saying, she felt she could have stayed there listening all night. There was such beauty in their words, a power and grace that moved her and made her want to hear more. Hearing Trace speak the language gave her a tingle in the pit of her stomach that traveled up to her chest, spreading warmth upward to her face.

"What are you doing out here in the damp air?" Trace asked. He glanced up at the sky. "It's going to rain."

"I . . . I wondered where you'd been all day. Cleo said you were out here . . . helping the Indians . . ."

Trace couldn't see Rachel's eyes. But he could see how she looked up at him and he could hear the hurt and puzzlement in her soft voice.

"I suppose I felt a little guilty about them," he said blithely. "So I decided to help. I'm afraid I lost track of the time. Come on, let's go inside."

Dinner was still on the table so they went in and sat down.

"I can have Dimity bring warm dishes from the kitchen," Rachel said. "Ours have grown cold."

"This is fine," Trace said. He placed his napkin in his lap without looking at Rachel. There was a dark, brooding look about him—a troubled, almost angry look that puzzled Rachel even more.

He hardly spoke during the entire meal, except to answer Rachel's questions with polite, often curt answers. Whatever was bothering him, she thought he wasn't about to share it with her.

Later, in bed, Trace lay unmoving beside her. He didn't offer to make love to her, or even to hold her in his arms. He wasn't asleep; she could tell by his breathing. She could feel the tension in him as he lay there so quiet and still.

Rachel stared into the darkness, listening to the night sounds of the house. A wind began to stir and murmur around the eaves and in the big trees outside their bedroom windows.

Something was wrong. Rachel wasn't sure what it was. She wasn't even sure if it had to do with Trace. Perhaps this was the way marriages were. Perhaps, after a period of time, a man became less interested in his wife and settled down more to the routines of his work and caring for his home.

All Rachel knew was that those little nagging doubts in the back of her mind wouldn't go away. In fact, they were becoming stronger and more persistent. It was as if her heart spoke to her, telling her that love was not supposed to be this way. Her husband had no reason to pull away from her, to distance himself from a wife who loved him tenderly, who gave herself to him body and soul. And yet who never seemed to receive the same thing in return.

Rachel vowed that she would find out exactly what was wrong. But, if she learned that Trace didn't love her . . . could never love her, then she wasn't sure what she would do. She was awake long after Trace's body had relaxed in sleep and she moved closer beside him. She was still awake when the rains came.

Fifteen

Rachel slept very little that night, and when she woke it was mid morning. She wasn't surprised to find that Trace had already left, but she was surprised at just how irritable that fact made her.

She hurried from bed and dressed, calling to Dimity when she heard her passing in the hallway.

"Yes'm, Miss Rachel?" the girl said as she stepped gingerly into the doorway.

"Dimity, help me with these buttons."

"You sho look mighty fetchin' in this ridin' outfit ma'am."

"Thank you," Rachel said tersely. She could hardly keep still until all the buttons were fastened. She whirled around to the armoire to find her riding boots.

"Is somethin' wrong, ma'am?" The young woman stood with wide eyes, watching Rachel.

"No . . . nothing. Is Mr. Hambleton in the dining room?"

"Why, no ma'am . . . Mr. Hambleton—he done be long gone this mornin'. Out to help the new family movin' in, I heard Mama Cleo say."

Rachel gritted her teeth and pulled her boots on. She wasn't about to sit in the house all day waiting on her husband to come home.

"Please have the twins saddle my horse. The tobacco plants need to be checked."

"In this rain?" Dimity asked, rolling her eyes toward the darkness beyond the windows.

"Because of this rain," Rachel said impatiently. "I have rain gear."

"But ma'am, you still get wet." Dimity gestured toward the windows. "It be pourin' down outside. Maybe I should tell Jared to hitch up the little buggy . . ."

"Lord, Dimity, you sound like Mama Cleo." Rachel stood up and lifted her skirts, flouncing them back over her boots. "If I'd wanted the buggy I'd have asked for the buggy. Its wheels will get stuck in the mud, and I can hardly take it into the fields. Now please . . ." Rachel's voice softened a bit as she saw the chagrin on Dimity's sweet face and the frown that wrinkled her normally smooth brow. "Please . . ." she said, forcing herself to smile. "Just ask them to saddle a horse for me."

"Yes'm."

Rachel stopped in the dining room long enough to pour herself a cup of strong coffee and take a few bites of biscuit. She wrapped several biscuits and pieces of salty ham in a cloth and pushed it beneath her riding jacket. She then hurried out of the house, not bothering to tell anyone else where she was going.

She needed to get out, to find her good humor again in the fresh scent of rain and the smell of the wet flowers and grass. Being outdoors always helped when she was troubled or angry.

Besides, she knew Mama Cleo and Lula would only try to persuade her not to go. This morning, she wasn't in the mood to be persuaded about anything. Once she was covered by a long hooded rain cape, she ran out to the barn, saying little to the twins as they held her mare and helped her into the saddle.

She told them where she was going, too. She might be angry, but she wasn't foolish enough to ride out alone, without letting someone at the house know where she would be.

"Tell Mama Cleo I'll be back by afternoon."

As she rode past the small house where the Indians were, she saw some of the Negro men working in the covered shed that was attached to the building. But she didn't stop, or even let her eyes try to find Trace.

If he wanted to ignore her . . . if he wanted to put this silent distance between them, then she would not beg or plead with him. Did he think he was the only one who had pride? Rachel had infinite patience and understanding, but once it was breached, it was gone completely. This morning for some reason, that moment had come.

She rode slowly, letting the little mare pick her way through the mud and muck. The field where the tobacco plants had been planted was sandy and well drained, but she had to see for herself that they weren't flooded. Tobacco was an important crop for Windridge, and Rachel often supervised it personally.

The wind was blowing fiercely, and by the time she left the tobacco field, her skirts were wet, despite the rain cape. She could feel the dampness seeping into her very bones. But she rode on, past the orchard and out toward the work village. She would go to the cabinetry shop and check on the armoire while she was out and spend a few pleasant moments inside. She could get warm there before she started back to the house.

When she reached the village, her eyes turned instinctively toward the grove of trees that sheltered the spring. Today in the rain and fog it was almost lost to her sight. Rachel's heart actually ached as she thought of that day when she and Trace had made love there.

Was that the day that things began to change between them? Did her passion that day . . . her bold wantonness have anything to do with Trace's behavior of late?

She gritted her teeth and pulled her mare into a lean-to next to the cabinetry shop. Stepping inside, she found it was as cozy and warm, as she hoped it would be. She hadn't realized how cold she was until she was out of the wind and rain.

"Lord, Miss Rachel," Mr. Copeland said. "What are you doin' out in weather like this?

Marshall nodded his agreement, then laughed.

"Jes like when you was a girl. Better watch out—old Mama Cleo come barrelin' in here in a minute. Grab you by the ear and take you back to Windridge like a scolded kitten."

"Come in, take off that wet cloak. We even have a little fire in the stove, although I suspect it will be so hot in a while that we'll have to let it go out. Just built it to take the chill off the air."

He pulled a straight, cane bottomed chair up to the stove and urged Rachel to sit. She was trembling as she reached her cold hands toward the warmth and sat huddled, waiting for the heat to permeate her frigid skin.

"Oh," she said, her teeth chattering. "I can hardly believe it's so cold. The rain feels almost as if it has a bit of ice in it."

"Could be," Mr. Copeland said. "Spring is a mighty funny time of year for the weather. Here, let me get you a cup of coffee. It's strong enough to walk, but—"

"Please . . . that sounds good," Rachel said, managing to nod. "Here," she said, reaching inside her jacket, "I brought some of Lula's ham and biscuits. Please share them with me."

The two men looked at each other and grinned.

"Shore ain't about to turn down Miss Lula's cookin now, are we, Marshall?"

"Huh uh," the Negro man said, eyeing the biscuits hungrily.

They pulled chairs up around the stove and Rachel divided the food. Then they sat eating in amiable silence, listening to the sound of rain on the tin roof.

When they'd finished, Rachel realized that she was finally growing warm. She was more relaxed, and some of her anger had left, too.

"I do love it here," she said, glancing about the room and breathing in the scent of all the different woods. "How is the cherry armoire coming?" She nodded toward the back of the building.

"Wait til you see it," Marshall said proudly. "It's the prettiest piece I ever made. All we's waitin' for now is the drawer pulls that you ordered from New Orleans."

"If I go into town this week, I'll stop by the general store and see if they've come in." Rachel stood up, intending to go to the back and see the piece of furniture.

Just then the door burst open and she turned, hardly comprehending what was happening.

Trace stood in the doorway, his eyes riveting her to the spot. In a black greatcoat, he looked big and broad, almost frightening in his intensity. He stood with his legs apart, black boots reaching almost to his knees. His hands were at his hips as he stood glaring at his wife.

"Trace . . ." Rachel felt a mixture of emotions boiling inside her. Pleasure that he was here, and fear at the look in those black fathomless eyes . . . then anger because he made her feel that way.

"What are you doing here?" she asked, finally finding her voice.

"I've come to take you home."

Rachel heard Marshall mutter something. Both of the men moved away, as if to separate themselves from what was happening.

"I'm not ready to go home," she said, her voice turned cold. As cold as his eyes. "Besides, I have the mare. I can—"

"Your mare is already tied to the back of the buggy. So I suggest you get in and let me drive you home."

Rachel felt her anger turning quickly to fury.

"To begin with," she said, trying to keep her voice quiet and reasonable. "I don't need you to drive me home. I'm perfectly capable of driving myself . . . when and wherever I please." Rachel turned with a haughty look and moved toward the back of the building even though the other two men didn't move.

"Marshall, I'd like to see the armoire now, if you don't mind."

"Rachel . . ." Trace's voice was loud, booming almost in the room. "You and I have a few things to discuss."

"Then discuss them," she said. She turned back to face her husband, tapping one foot impatiently as she stared into his eyes across the room.

"This is hardly the place," he said, letting his gaze move pointedly over the two men who stood with such awkwardness.

"Well, I disagree," she said coolly. "If you have something to tell me, any place is suitable. I've known these men all my life. If you have something to say, just say it."

"Rachel, dammit . . ." Trace gritted his teeth and shook his head. It seemed he'd gotten more than he bargained for when he wed this woman. A woman, he reminded himself, that he had thought as sweet and pliable as any he'd ever met.

It was one of the few times he'd ever been so wrong.

Rachel's left eyebrow arched and she lifted her chin. She didn't look away from his gaze for one second.

"I told you that I will not have my wife going to the fields like a farmhand," he said, his voice quiet and menacing. "And I hardly think it proper for you to be spending time alone here with two men. Nothing personal, gentlemen," he added with a curt nod toward Mr. Copeland and Marshall.

Marshall lifted his shoulders and smiled sheepishly. Mr. Copeland scratched his head and shuffled his feet. But neither of them said anything.

"And I told you," Rachel said, "that I am not used to being dictated to by any man. And since you do not deem it necessary to tell me where you go during the day, I cannot see the necessity of my telling you where I go."

"The necessity," Trace said through clenched teeth. "Is that you are my wife now. And you will do as I say."

The room was completely, eerily silent.

Marshall rolled his eyes first toward Trace, then back toward Rachel.

Rachel lowered her eyelashes as if she might acquiesce. Then with a slow, deliberate move, she turned her back on

Trace and his demanding look and started to walk toward the back of the building.

Trace could feel his blood boiling. Never in his life had he had a woman openly defy him before other men. And never had he been so wrong in his judgment of a person, as he'd been about this woman. His fury caused him to act as he often did, without conscious thought, but rather from some deep ancient instinct.

With a low growl he took three long steps across the room. Rachel let out a yelp as he ducked his head beneath her left arm, then with his arm beneath her hips, scooped her up and across his shoulder. It all happened in a matter of seconds.

"Put me down," she hissed. "Damn you, Trace Hambleton, you put me down this minute."

Marshall's mouth was open wide as he watched the unbelievable scene and saw the usually dignified young mistress of Windridge being carried toward the front door like a bag of flour. Mr. Copeland stepped forward and opened the door for Trace, causing Rachel to gasp in disbelief.

"Don't help him, for goodness sake," she sputtered. "Tell him to put me down."

"I don't think he's gonna listen to anything we have to say, ma'am," Mr. Copeland said with a wide grin. "Good day Mr. Hambleton . . . Miss Rachel," he said, as Trace carried Rachel out onto the wooden walkway in front of the shop.

He carried her out through the silver curtain of water that dripped from the tin roof. And he unceremoniously dumped her small frame into the front seat of the covered buggy. Then with a glance back at the two men in the doorway, he nodded and tipped his hat before climbing up onto the seat beside Rachel.

She was in the process of going out the other side. Trace grabbed her and pulled her back with one hand while with the other, he flicked the reins across the horse's wet back.

As the buggy moved down the rain soaked streets, Mr. Copeland turned to the Negro man beside him.

"Well, well. What do you think about that, Marshall? Mr. Hambleton came for Miss Rachel just like old Mama Cleo used to do. And the young mistress didn't seem to like it any more now than she did then." He laughed quietly and shook his head.

"Naw, she didn't. What do you think?"

"I think, my friend, that Mr. Trace Hambleton is much of a man. Yessir, a mighty much of a man."

Marshall snorted and grinned as he watched the buggy move out of the village and back toward the main house. They could see Rachel flailing about and hear her indignant shrieks.

"Well sir, I knowed Miss Rachel since she was no more'n a pup. And I say that man done bit off more'n he can chew."

Sixteen

"How dare you!" Rachel shrieked as they drove down the street. "How dare you treat me in such a manner in front of my friends."

"They aren't your friends, Rachel—they work for you. There's a difference." He didn't look away from his driving, but sat very straight, his face partially hidden beneath the black hat he wore.

"You are no longer a child, to run to this place and hide from the world and your responsibilities."

"You . . . you know nothing of my responsibilities," she sputtered. "Or why I come here."

"You're a grown woman." For the first time, he turned to gaze at her, letting his black eyes rake over her face and down to her breasts. "And I don't think it's appropriate for you to spend time alone with Mr. Copeland and Marshall, or in the field like one of the slaves."

"You don't think? And since when it is your place to tell me how to behave?"

"Since the day we married," he growled. He flicked the reins against the horse, causing it and the carriage to jump forward.

"Oh, I see. It's perfectly acceptable for you to come and go as you please and yet I must define my days by your terms?"

"You're being childish," he answered.

"And you are disgustingly overbearing. Not to mention your penchant for secrecy."

Trace only gritted his teeth and drove on, refusing to acknowledge Rachel's accusation. He should have seen this confrontation coming and he should have been better prepared to handle it. But he had to admit, her behavior took him completely by surprise.

"Look," he finally said. "Let's both just calm down. It's not as if I'm asking for much. You play your role as a dutiful wife and I'll play mine as a responsible husband."

Rachel might have been tempted to give in to him until that moment.

"Play?" she gasped. She felt her cheeks growing hot, felt a tingle of alarm race from her neck down her spine. "Play?" she asked again. She couldn't even think of an appropriate response.

Trace shook his head and frowned, then he pulled the horse to the side of the road. The rain that blew into the carriage caused Rachel to shiver as it made loud plopping noises against the carriage's leather top.

He might have taken her in his arms and tried to distract her had it not been for the look of fury in her eyes.

"That was the wrong word," he said, "I didn't mean it the way—"

Rachel looked at him through narrowed eyes.

"No," she said softly. "I think perhaps you did mean it. Mama Cleo always said it best—sometimes if we're not careful about the words we choose, our feelings speak for us."

"No, Rachel, it isn't like that. Of course it isn't. How could you even think such a thing?"

"How could I think you married me for some reason other than love?" she asked bluntly. Only her trembling chin gave away her true feelings. Otherwise, she was resolved and strong as she faced him with the things that troubled her.

"Well, now let's see," she drawled sarcastically. "Maybe it's because you have never once said you love me. Or perhaps it's because the only place you seem to want me is in your bed . . ."

Trace saw the first moisture in her eyes. And, if on other occasions he might have seen that as an opportunity, today the sight of tears in those beautiful eyes brought a sharp ache to his heart.

"Rachel," he said. He pulled her into his arms and although she didn't resist, her body was tense. "I didn't know . . ." But he did know—he had seen the longing, the questions in her eyes long before this. Somehow, this was the first time he hadn't been able to think of a quick response.

Rachel pulled away, glancing briefly at him and trying to disguise the hurt she felt.

"Please," she said. "Let's just go back to the house." She shivered. "I'm cold."

He looked at her for a long time, wanting to hold her, wanting to explain. Hell, he even thought for a minute of telling her the truth. But in the end, he picked up the reins and drove toward the house.

In the stables, Rachel didn't wait for him to come around and help her down. She jumped out of the buggy, pushed past him and ran through the rain into the house.

"Dimity," she called in the hallway.

The young woman came into the hall from one of the rooms and took Rachel's rain cape, holding it away from her and watching it drip onto the honey colored floor.

"I'd like a hot bath and I don't wish to be disturbed by anyone."

"Anyone . . . ?" Dimity said. "Not even—?"

"Not by anyone," Rachel repeated with a lift of her brow.

Her skirts, wet and limp, dragged the floor as she turned and walked away.

In the small room that Rachel used for bathing, she lit candles, placing them everywhere. She even lit a small fire in the fireplace, more for comfort than for warmth. When the copper tub was filled with soapy hot water, she locked the door and undressed and then stepped gingerly into the water.

It wasn't long before she heard footsteps in the hallway, then the sound of someone trying the door.

She heard Trace's voice, quiet and cajoling.

"Rachel," he said. "Let me in."

"Go away."

"Rachel . . . open this door."

She heard the determination in his voice, and that slight hint of danger she sometimes heard but didn't quite understand.

"I said go away."

She needed to think, and she found that hard to do when Trace was near. He made her forget everything except her senses, everything except the taste of his mouth and the feel of his strong arms around her.

She held her breath for a moment, then relaxed when she heard his footsteps retreating down the hallway.

Trace stalked down the stairs and into the parlor across from the dining room. Dimity and another young servant woman scurried out of his way like frightened chicks. From the doorway, they watched him, saw the angry, stormy look on his face before backing away and hurrying down the hallway.

Trace's hands were shaking when he removed the top from a crystal decanter and poured himself a large shot of the senator's best bourbon. He tossed it down his throat, coughing and wiping his hands across his watering eyes before filling the glass a second time.

He sat in a damask-covered chair, propping a long leg across the chair's arm as he sipped the second shot of bourbon more slowly. His eyes stared hard across the room, though there was nothing in his vision except Rachel's image.

A more stubborn, willful woman he'd never met.

And he'd be damned if he was going to let a bossy little woman dictate to him in his own home. This *was* his home, dammit. And it was about time he let her know that.

Rachel stayed in the bath for a long time. Until the heated water warmed her skin and turned her cheeks rosy. Until it grew tepid and the candles in the room began to melt away.

She thought about Trace. About the first time she saw him. She thought she had fallen in love with him at that very moment. She could hardly believe her luck when he'd shown an interest in her, too.

No one had ever made her feel the way Trace did. And no one had ever treated her the way he did.

She reflected that most men she'd known had given in to her every whim. Her father could deny her nothing and the beaus she'd had seemed to treat her similarly. Was that why Trace's demands disturbed her so?

"No," she muttered, frowning thoughtfully. It was more than that.

Edmund had loved her. He had wanted to marry her. And she had no doubt that he'd have been just like her father, spoiling her and letting her continue to run things at Windridge the way she'd always done. But she hadn't loved Edmund and she knew now she could never love him the same way she loved Trace, with this perplexing, turbulent intensity.

She didn't regret that it was Trace she loved, despite his sometimes odd behavior and his coolness toward her. She could never love anyone else and she knew that in her heart.

Finally as the water grew cooler, she sighed, having come to a conclusion.

She believed that she could have her independence and his love, too. She had to believe that or she wasn't sure she could go on. She'd make Trace love her, dammit. She'd always believed that love and goodness could conquer anything and could melt the coldest heart. It wasn't necessarily something she'd been taught. It was just something she knew down deep inside her soul.

Just then she heard footsteps again. Harder this time and more urgent.

"Rachel, open the door this minute."

Despite her resolve to let things be, the tone of his demanding voice made her clamp her lips together in a straight, stubborn line.

She refused to answer. It might do him good to wait a while.

The door flew open with a bang and slammed back against the wall inside the bedroom. Rachel shrieked in surprise and her actions caused the soapy water to splash over the tub and onto the floor.

He stood there in the doorway, larger than life, looking like a man with a terrible purpose.

"Don't ever lock the doors in this house against me again, Rachel," he said. His strong body was shaking with anger.

Rachel thought she'd never seen him this way, with this terrible fury in his eyes. But as he stood staring at her, slowly the look changed.

Trace's gaze moved from her wet, bedraggled hair, down to her startled eyes and softly parted lips. To her rosy cheeks and pale shoulders, gleaming in the candlelight. The still agitated water lapped at her full breasts. The sight mesmerized him— the water covering her pink nipples, then in a silent, teasing rhythm, uncovering them again.

She was the most beautiful creature he'd ever seen.

Slowly he reached behind him and closed the door. His black storm eyes raked over her as an odd choked sound came from deep inside his chest.

There was a tap on the door and they heard Cleo's voice outside.

"Rachel honey . . . you all right in there?"

Rachel's eyes met Trace's, questioning and filled with a quiet longing.

"Everything . . . everything's fine, Cleo," she said, her voice trembling.

Trace didn't even wait for Cleo's footsteps to fade away before slowly stepping to the tub. He bent and placed his hands beneath Rachel's arms and pulled her warm, water soaked body up. He jerked her hard against him and buried his face against her neck as his hands possessed every inch of her body.

Rachel's senses were being assaulted, overwhelmed by the sheer strength and desire she felt rippling through him. She gasped as his teeth and lips ravaged her neck. She clung to him, fearing she might actually fall if he let her go. When his head dipped and his mouth trailed hot kisses across her skin, down to her soapy breasts she gave a quiet little cry of ecstasy.

A cry of surrender.

Trace felt small ripples of delight race through his body. She was always so open and loving . . . more giving than he deserved. And, God help him, despite his earlier anger, he couldn't seem to keep himself from wanting her.

He pressed his face against her trembling belly, feeling her hands in his hair, her breath feathering against the side of his face.

He lifted her from the water and took her mouth in a hot kiss that sent molten fire through his veins.

"I'm sorry," he muttered against her lips. "So sorry . . ." The words were foreign to him and hard to say. They were words he'd sworn never to say to a person like Rachel.

But this was different. *She* was different.

"Oh, Trace," she sighed, melting against him and lifting her hands to his face. "Trace . . . I'm sorry, too."

If there had been the slightest resistance in her heart, the slightest holding back, his words now whisked them away. The light in his dark eyes made her tremble with wanting. He lay her on a rug in front of the fireplace, then fairly ripped away his clothes and took her in his arms again.

He began to make love to her with slow, sweet deliberation and with an intensity that shook both of them and sent them spiraling too soon toward the edge of completion. Again he whispered those guttural, erotic words to her. This time, the sound of them whispered against her face, against her ear, made Rachel feel wild . . . insane with some ancient longing she'd never experienced before. Her body responded with surprising intensity until she was gasping for breath, until her fingers dug into his shoulders, and she cried out against his heated skin.

Afterward, it took a while for their breathing to return to

normal. They held each other tightly, as if reluctant to ever part. Rachel caressed his bare skin and snuggled against him.

Trace stared with disbelieving eyes into the darkening room, feeling as if he'd just been struck head on by a cannon blast.

"My God," Trace whispered. His voice was filled with wonder . . . and with undisguised amazement.

What was he doing? What on God's earth did he think he was doing?

This wasn't supposed to happen. This woman wasn't supposed to make him feel such forbidden ecstasies. She wasn't supposed to make him forget his purpose, lose his resolve, his very soul even, when he made love to her.

He had been in complete control. When had all that changed?

He turned his face and looked into her eyes. For a moment, he saw his destiny in those beautiful depths. He saw life and love, waiting for him, pulling him in as surely as if he were an animal caught in an unrelenting steel trap.

He felt different when he was with her. Softer . . . more vulnerable.

Weaker.

And he knew if it was the last thing he ever did, he had to put her away from him. He had to end this thing, before it was too late for them both.

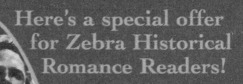

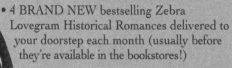

4 FREE BOOKS

These books worth almost $20, are yours without cost or obligation
when you fill out and mail this certificate.
*(If the certificate is missing below, write to: Zebra Home Subscription Service, Inc.,
120 Brighton Road, P.O. Box 5214, Clifton, New Jersey 07015-5214)*

Complete and mail this card to receive 4 Free books!

YES! Please send me 4 Zebra Lovegram Historical Romances without cost or obligation. I understand that each month thereafter I will be able to preview 4 new Zebra Lovegram Historical Romances FREE for 10 days. Then if I decide to keep them, I will pay the money-saving preferred publisher's price of just $4.00 each...a total of $16. That's almost $4 less than the regular publisher's price, and there is never any additional charge for shipping and handling. I may return any shipment within 10 days and owe nothing, and I may cancel this subscription at any time. The 4 FREE books will be mine to keep in any case.

Name _____

Address _____ Apt _____

City _____ State _____ Zip _____

Telephone (___) _____

Signature _____ LF0897
(If under 18, parent or guardian must sign.)

Seventeen

The next morning, while Rachel and Trace were at breakfast, they heard a carriage drive up to the front of the house. Moments later, Dimity came into the dining room with Hallie behind her.

"Hallie," Rachel said. She jumped up from the table and went to embrace her friend. "Heavens, you're out early. Won't you have breakfast with us?"

"No," Hallie said. "Just tea, Dimity, if you have it."

"Yes'm." With her polite little dip, Dimity scurried from the room.

As Hallie untied a gauzy scarf from beneath her chin and removed her hat, she could hardly contain her enthusiasm.

"I have the most wonderful news," Hallie said. Her bright gaze moved from Rachel to Trace, who sat watching her with an amused look on his handsome face.

"What?" Rachel asked. "Here . . . sit."

"Shall I go?" Trace asked, still smiling. "Is this going to be one of those female conversations that a man is not privy to?"

"No . . . no," Hallie said. "I want you both to hear. Oh . . . I never dreamed I might one day find someone . . . that I could have a chance at being as happy as the two of you."

"Hallie . . . ?"

"It's happened, Rachel. Roland Saunders has asked me to marry him."

"Oh Hallie . . . that's wonderful." Rachel stepped to embrace Hallie and as she looked over her shoulder, she noticed a strained look on Trace's face. Was it Hallie's comment about the two of them being happy that made him so uncomfortable?

She brushed her apprehension aside. After yesterday and last night, nothing could ever convince her that Trace didn't care for her. Not even his brooding silences and distant looks.

"We must give you a party," Rachel said. "Yes, that's just the thing . . . don't you agree?"

"An engagement celebration," Hallie said, clapping her hands and bouncing with delight.

"Trace, isn't it wonderful?" Rachel asked.

Trace lowered his gaze and picked up his coffee cup.

"Yes, wonderful," he said. "Congratulations, Hallie. Roland is a lucky man." He stood up then, his expression cool and unreadable. "I'll leave the two of you alone to plan your party. I need to see to the renovations on the house for White Feather's family."

Trace stepped toward Rachel. For a moment, he allowed himself to take in all her beauty, from her sparkling eyes to her soft pink lips, parted in anticipation of his kiss. He looked directly into her eyes, then brushed a kiss across her mouth.

"White Feather?" Hallie asked when Trace stepped away from Rachel.

"He's an Indian who came here with his family a few days ago," Rachel said. "They have two beautiful little girls and his wife is expecting a third child soon. We've given them a place to stay, and Trace has become quite involved in helping with the renovations."

"Well, I truly do admire a man who has such a compassionate nature," Hallie said, fairly simpering.

Trace smiled and took Hallie's hand, encased in lacy gloves, and placed a soft kiss against it.

"Good day, Miss Hallie."

Hallie sighed as she watched him leave the room.

"Oh, Rachel. That man actually gives me goose flesh, just looking at him. He's so . . . so masculine." She turned to Rachel, her eyes sparkling. "And when he kissed you a moment ago . . . oh, I could just feel the excitement between the two of you. You must tell me about him . . . about everything. It's one of the reasons I came. I need you to tell me everything about being married, Rachel. Everything."

Rachel laughed and pulled her friend back toward the table.

For the next few days, Rachel was so busy she hardly had time to think about any of the doubts she was having about the mysterious man she'd married.

He was busy and seemed content. Rachel told herself that everything was fine . . . that their life was normal.

The work on the shed was completed, the small house transformed into a sweet, cozy home. The Indian woman, Hummingbird, fairly glowed with happiness. She was friendly and smiling, always working, despite her approaching delivery.

One day, Rachel was in her rose garden at the front of the house when the woman brought a gift to her.

"To . . . thank . . . you," she said, her English halting and uncertain. "For your . . . kindness."

"Oh, Hummingbird," Rachel said softly. She opened the small package, wrapped in soft deerskin and tied with a leather thong. Inside was a comb carved from shell and decorated with feathers and tiny beads.

"Oh," Rachel said, glancing from the beautiful comb, back into Hummingbird's warm eyes. "It's beautiful . . . just lovely. Did you make it?"

"Yes," Hummingbird said, nodding. Her face glowed with happiness that the little mistress, as she'd heard the slaves call her, liked her gift.

Rachel stepped forward and embraced the woman. Just then she saw Trace coming toward them. He stopped, seeing Rachel and Hummingbird embrace. And when his eyes met Rachel's, there was such a look in them that it almost took her breath away.

It was a look of tenderness. His black eyes sparkled with it, and his lips curved upward in a sweet smile that Rachel had never seen before. For a moment, she thought there might even be some other, deeper emotion in his beautifully expressive eyes.

Then Hummingbird stepped away, and nodded shyly before going back toward her house.

"Look," Rachel said as Trace approached. "Hummingbird made it for me. Isn't it beautiful?"

Not nearly as beautiful as you, he wanted to say. This woman had mesmerized him, bewitched him. Taken his very soul and turned it inside out. And that was the reason he couldn't allow himself to say those words to her. He had cautioned himself a hundred times, especially since that day when he'd forced his way into her bath. And found himself involved in more than he had bargained for.

"Yes . . . very," he said.

The date of Hallie and Roland's party was fast approaching, and Rachel had little time for wondering or worrying about anything except that. The weather was mild and beautiful, the house cleaning going well.

Trace spent his days either seeing clients in the study, where he'd made his office, or riding over the plantation, checking on crops. There were no more confrontations about her involvement with the field hands or man's work, as he called it. But she suspected that was only because she had been too busy to spend as much time outdoors as she usually did.

Rachel hoped Trace was happy. She was surprised at how little he knew about crops and other plantation duties. But he seemed eager to learn everything, and when he came home in the afternoon, there was an intensity, and excitement about him that pleased her.

The Indian, White Feather, was with him constantly. And when Trace and he weren't out in the fields, he was at White Feather's house. The entire household talked about it, about how the new master spoke the Cherokee language so well, as if he'd been born to it.

Rachel had actually heard someone say that Trace and White Feather seemed more like brothers than strangers sometimes when they were talking and laughing.

Trace rarely laughed that way with her. And he certainly wasn't as animated. In fact, if she would admit it, she thought he had grown even more distant from her than he had been before. Sometimes she watched him from across the yard or out a window, noting the way he cocked his head to one side, the way he brushed his hair back when it came loose from the leather thong that held it. He spoke to White Feather with such interest, such intensity.

And the way White Feather looked at her was even more puzzling. There was something in his eyes. Sympathy, she thought. And at other times, she thought it was something secretive, something that he and Trace shared that she did not.

But at night, everything changed. When they were together in their room and the house was quiet, Trace was hers completely. He couldn't seem to get enough of her or she him. Rachel had the feeling that his desire for her was something he couldn't contain or control. And when he seemed distant or strained during the daylight hours, that need he seemed to have for her was the one thought she clung to.

The morning before Hallie's party was particularly chaotic in the house. Trace laughed at her as she rushed from one room to the other, running her gloved hand over the lampglobes and tabletops. Or fussing over the flowers to make sure they were just the way she wanted them. She was with him in his study when they heard riders approaching the house. She glanced out the windows and gave a quiet murmur of surprise.

"Oh heavens," she muttered. "Soldiers. What on earth could they want here at Windridge? And why does it have to be on this day?" Smiling at Trace, she hardly noticed his look of concern.

"Since you're the master of Windridge, I presume you'll

want to see what they want." She loved teasing him when he was serious and she loved seeing that little spark leap into his black eyes.

Trace shrugged and shook his head.

"Really . . . if I don't get these papers drawn up soon . . ." He turned away from her, pretending to be busy as his mind turned and twisted.

The soldiers were looking for him. He could feel it instinctively in every pore of his body.

"Oh, all right, I'll do it," she said. She touched him lightly on the shoulder before turning with her skirts awhirl and headed toward the front door.

Trace could hear the conversation from where he sat. Small beads of perspiration lined his brow and though his hands remained perfectly steady, he could feel his heart beating heavily in his chest.

"Miss Townsend," he heard a male voice say.

"Why, Major Nelson. How nice to see you again. My name is Hambleton now—I was recently married."

"Ah . . . congratulations."

"Thank you. What brings you and your men all the way out here to Windridge?"

"Call me Thomas . . . please," the man said.

"Thomas, then," Rachel said.

"We received a telegraph recently from one of our outposts in the Oklahoma territory."

Trace closed his eyes, waiting for the fatal blow to come. His fingers tightened around the pen in his hand.

"Seems an Indian . . . a man named Sun Killer, escaped there several months ago. And after a search of that area, they've come up with nothing. They thought he might have headed this way . . . to Holly Springs."

"I see," Rachel said quietly. "And so you wanted to warn us . . . ?"

"Actually, it's more than that," Major Nelson said. "It's

probably a very remote possibility, but we have to check it out nonetheless. It seems this Indian once lived here."

"In Holly Springs, you mean?"

"No ma'am. I mean here. Right here where we're standing . . . at Windridge."

The pen in Trace's hand snapped, part of it flying across the room with a clatter.

"I . . . I'm afraid I don't understand."

"This was his home, ma'am, before the government confiscated it. You mean you didn't know this house belonged to a man of Cherokee descent?"

"No . . . confiscated . . . ? What are you saying? My father has the deeds to Windridge—I've seen them." She remembered the deeds he had given her before her wedding. They still lay in her father's safe. She hadn't even thought to take them into town as he instructed and have Trace's name put on them.

"Oh, the house is his, ma'am. It's legal. As I understand it, President Van Buren granted the house and all its acreage to the senator soon after the Indian evacuation." The man paused for a moment. "You do realize that it's a common practice . . . there's nothing illegal or—"

"Yes . . . yes, of course I've heard about things like this happening. I just didn't realize . . . I had no idea that's how Father received Windridge. I . . . I can hardly believe it."

Trace stood up and stepped behind the door. He could see the soldiers through the crack. He could also see Rachel's profile and how troubled she was by what the major had just revealed.

"This Indian . . . this Sun Killer," she said. "You say Windridge was his home. Are you also telling me that he wants it back?"

Trace gritted his teeth. He should be there with her when she heard. She should be able to look into his eyes and see the truth when the words were actually said. Kiss her sweet mouth when it gasped in disbelief and wipe away her tears of sorrow and betrayal.

"Dammit," he muttered, stepping away from the door and back into the room.

"Well, ma'am, there's that possibility, although I think it's highly unlikely. I mean, what can one man do against all the occupants of this place? Or against my men here? They seem concerned that he might be out for revenge . . . might even try and burn the place down. My opinion is that the man's long gone—probably out to California or even up to Canada where he'll never be found. But my orders were to come here and warn you and that's what I've done."

"Major . . . I mean Thomas. Was this Indian alone? I mean does he have a family or—?"

Trace stood very still, his body rigid, his eyes narrowing with concern. He hadn't considered that Rachel might think the army was looking for White Feather.

"Don't, Rachel," he whispered to himself. "Don't tell him about White Feather . . ." Trace wasn't sure what the army would do with someone like White Feather—a man who had been on the run since he was sixteen. But knowing their cruelty and lack of respect for the red man, he doubted they would let any Indian stay here in Alabama.

In his heart, he knew the reservation would kill White Feather. It would kill his very soul. He might have been an outcast from the whites and on the run most of his life, but he had never been imprisoned—kept in a cage like an animal. Even if Rachel only casually mentioned White Feather's presence, it would insure his capture by these soldiers. And Trace thought his cousin and family would not survive that.

"He's alone, ma'm. From what I hear, Sun Killer is a man who prefers being alone. But that doesn't make him any less dangerous."

Trace held his breath, waiting.

"Well, there's been no one here like that," Rachel said.

Trace could hear the relief in her voice even though he was sure the major could not.

"In fact, there's no one here at Windridge except family."

"And your slaves, ma'am," the Major corrected with a laugh.

"They're my family too, Major," Rachel said, her voice quiet.

"Huh . . . yes ma'am. Well, just tell your men to keep their eyes open. And if you see this Indian lurkin' about, just send word to our headquarters over at Greensboro."

"Yes, I'll do that."

Trace stood waiting for Rachel. He had no idea if she had guessed the truth.

When she came back into the study he looked deep into her eyes. For a moment, she stared back at him, her look troubled.

Trace opened his mouth to speak, and Rachel walked to him and put her arms around his waist, laying her head against his chest.

"He said that this house once belonged to a Cherokee family, Trace. It was taken from them."

"I know," he said. "I heard."

"My father knew it," she said. "He had to have known."

Trace frowned as he felt her body shudder. He had half expected her to ask if he were Sun Killer. And he had been braced to tell her everything. What he had not expected was this pain in her voice as she acknowledged what her father had done.

"Does that bother you so greatly?" Trace asked. He held her, until the trembles that rippled through her small frame finally stopped.

"Of course it bothers me," she said, frowning at him.

He had never felt such a need to protect anyone this way, except perhaps his mother. And some of the younger children on the reservation in Oklahoma.

But this was different.

Rachel pulled back and looked up at him. Her blue eyes, usually so bright and happy, were filled with anguish.

"He had to know," she whispered. "My father always talked

about how he loved this place. How he wanted it, coveted it from the very moment he saw it."

Trace clenched his teeth together. Rachel was realizing what he had known all along. That a white man had only to covet a thing to make it his. Senator Townsend had been kind to him, and he had seen that the man wasn't an evil person as he'd always thought. But that only made his frustrations worse.

Yet, if he could not hate the man who took his parents's home and ultimately was responsible for their deaths, then who could he hate?

"I have to know," she said. She pulled away from Trace and walked about the room. Her eyes roamed over the expensive wallpaper and furniture, over all the small imported items her father had filled the house with over the years. "I have to write to him and find out if it's true."

As Trace watched her leave the room, he didn't know if he should feel relief for his reprieve, or heartache for his young bride.

Eighteen

Trace knew that Rachel sent her father the letter, but beyond that, he had no idea what she'd told him. It wasn't a subject he wanted to pursue, even though White Feather warned him that he was making a mistake.

"Now is the time. She is obviously troubled by what her father did. Her sympathies are bound to be with you. Why not tell her now?"

"No," Trace said tersely. "Not yet."

Trace thought of his father's grave and his mother's brooch that he had placed there in the ground. He had been waiting for the appearance of the new moon to perform the sacred burial ceremony that would insure his parent's rightful place in the spirit world.

Tonight would be the new moon. When the guests were gone and the house was quiet, he would slip away and fulfill this ancient, most sacred of obligations. He had already told White Feather and Hummingbird.

They understood his need to do this. But Trace could sense Hummingbird's disapproval about his continued secrets from Rachel.

"She is good, Trace. And she loves you. The longer you continue to keep these things from her, the more she will be hurt when she finds out, and the more resentment she will feel toward you."

"That can't be helped," he said. "I have to do this in my own time, and in my own way."

"You are a stubborn man, Sun Killer," she said with a disdainful groan. "White Feather . . . speak to your cousin." She turned and left the men alone in the front room of the newly renovated house.

White Feather watched his wife leave, then turned accusing eyes toward his cousin.

Trace lifted his hand, warning away the other man's words.

"I want you to come with me to my father's burial site," Trace said. "Tonight when the moon is new, I intend to perform the ceremony of the spirits. It's only right that another of my father's family is there with me."

"I will be honored," White Feather said with a solemn nod. "And I will speak no more of your actions toward the little mistress. You are your own man and you must do what a warrior's heart dictates he should do."

"Thank you." Trace shook hands with his cousin and left the house.

That evening when the carriages began to line the circular driveway and the house filled with guests, Trace stood with Rachel at the doorway.

Hallie and Roland were there as well, greeting family and guests. Practically everyone in Holly Springs had come to wish them well.

Trace supposed it was only natural that Hallie's brother Edmund would be there. It was the first time he'd seen the man since that day he'd overheard the man's profession of love to Rachel. Against his will, he tensed, and he could feel Rachel's hand come to rest reassuringly on his arm.

He relaxed and shook Edmund's hand, even though the look in the man's eyes told him he might prefer striking him rather than shaking hands.

"I'm so glad you came, Edmund," Rachel said.

Edmund took her hand and bent gallantly to place a kiss there.

"I am ever and always your servant, Rachel," he said, his voice deep with emotion.

"Well," Trace said beneath his breath as Edmund walked away, "I see the young beau is still in love with my wife."

"You sound very possessive when you say such things," Rachel murmured in return. She was smiling and nodding as the guests came through the door and passed on into the house.

Trace thought she had never looked more beautiful than she did tonight. Her shimmering iridescent gown looked as if it had been made by pressing very sheer pieces of gold into cloth. The color reflected against her face, making him want nothing more than to touch her and test the warmth of her sun-kissed skin.

"I *am* possessive," he said. He looked at her from the corner of his eyes, his gaze dark and inscrutable.

"I am not a piece of furniture or a prized horse," she said. Her voice was as sweet as honey, yet there was a glint of warning in her sparkling eyes.

"You are my wife," Trace said, following her lead and smiling at the guests, even though Edmund's words still rang in his ears and still seethed in his gut. "Edmund may have forgotten; I hope, my dear, that you do not."

"Perhaps you should remind me later tonight." Rachel's eyes changed, her irritability with him replaced by a sparkle of mischief, a challenge as bold as any he'd ever received.

Trace felt his body growing warm, felt the spiral of desire rising in him the way it always did when he was near her.

For a moment, he wished he had not planned to do the ceremony of the spirits tonight. He wished, instead, that he was taking his beautiful, desirable wife straight to bed after the party.

As the night passed, Trace found that he was enjoying the party more than he'd ever have thought possible. Despite Edmund's brooding stare at Rachel from across the room, or the way he seemed to want to touch her whenever he passed, Trace was enjoying the music and the company very much.

When Edmund asked permission to dance with Rachel, Trace gritted his teeth and nodded his acquiescence. But his dark eyes were seething as he watched Edmund move about the room with her in his arms.

"Damned pompous little bastard," Trace muttered beneath his breath.

On the dance floor, Rachel pulled away from Edmund's tight embrace and gazed up at him. Her look left no question about how unsuitable she found his attention.

"I've never seen you looking more beautiful, Rachel," Edmund said.

"Thank you, Edmund," she replied.

"Are you happy?"

Rachel laughed lightly. "Of course, I'm happy. I have everything I've ever wanted. What woman wouldn't be happy?" For a moment her eyes sought her husband's. And when she found him, a tiny pleasurable shock raced through her at the look of intense disapproval she saw on his face.

"Hallie tells me you were upset that you knew so little about your husband."

Rachel stepped back in surprise, stumbling a little as she missed the music's beat.

"I wish she hadn't done that," Rachel said. She frowned, glancing toward her friend Hallie as if she'd like to reprimand her. "That was a while ago, right before the wedding. I hardly feel that way now."

Edmund's eyes were cool and his lop sided grin seemed more like a smirk.

"Perhaps you'd be interested in hearing what I've learned about the man you know as Trace Hambleton."

"I . . . what on earth do you mean?" Rachel hardly knew how to respond. She couldn't just walk off the dance floor. Everyone would notice, including Trace.

Edmund's voice grew softer, more urgent as he leaned forward to whisper in her ear.

"He is not from Tennessee as he claimed," he said, seeming very pleased with himself.

"That . . . that's hardly important."

"Oh, but I think it is. He's lied to you Rachel. About more than one thing. His name is not Trace Hambleton. I admit I have no idea who he really is, but I can tell you that there is no census record of anyone by that name."

Rachel felt a rush of weakness move over her, down her arms and legs. She felt cold all over as she heard his words and heard the ring of truth in Edmund's self-satisfied voice.

"How dare you," she whispered. There were tears in her eyes as she stared at Edmund. At the man she'd once thought loved her. "How could you do this? Go behind my back this way and try to—"

"Because I still love you," he hissed, pulling her tighter against him. "If you weren't so besotted by this man, if he hadn't pulled you so completely into his web of deceit, you'd know how much I love you."

Rachel could hardly breathe. The sound of babbling voices, the music . . . it was all becoming oppressive.

"Ask him, Rachel," Edmund urged. "If you don't believe me, ask your husband why there is no record of his ever having lived in Tennessee. And while you're at it, ask him what his name is and why he *really* came here and married you."

She stopped abruptly and when Edmund tried to pull her back into his embrace, she turned and walked quickly away, not caring now what others thought.

Trace was coming toward her, obviously intending to rescue her from what he probably thought was a rude proposition. There was fire in his dark eyes as he glanced from her to Edmund, who still stood in the center of dancers, looking as if he'd been wounded to the very core.

Rachel wanted to run to her tall, handsome husband, throw herself in his arms and beg him to tell her that what Edmund said was not true. And at the same time, she wanted to run in the other direction and not have to hear his answers to her questions.

"Rachel," Trace said, taking her arm and leading her toward

the hallway, "What's wrong? Did that little bastard say something . . . do something to upset you? If he did, I swear I'll—"

"No," Rachel said. She looked deep into his eyes, wanting to see the truth. Wanting to find some reason why he would lie to her and to everyone else in town.

Was she even legally married?

"Really, I was just feeling a little dizzy," she said, pulling her gaze away from his. "It's so hot in here." She lifted her hand and flipped open the little fan that hung from her wrist.

"Let's go outside." Trace reached out to a passing servant and lifted two glasses of champagne from the tray he carried. "Have you eaten? Cleo said you were too busy to eat much today."

His concern touched her and made her think that Edmund was crazy. He'd only made up those things to try to turn her against the man she loved. He was jealous . . . that's all it was.

Trace led her to the edge of the porch, away from the side of the house where the music and noise were loudest. Here it was cooler and the light was dim. He held her arm protectively as she sat down in the large white chair, then he pulled another close and handed her the glass of champagne.

"Here . . . drink this. You look very pale."

"I'm all right," she said. But she took the champagne and drank a sip, then let the breath out of her lungs with a loud sigh. "I'm fine," she said.

"I don't believe that for a minute. And I don't believe that you rushed away from Edmund because you were feeling ill. I think he said something to upset you . . . and I want to know what it was."

"Trace . . . leave it," Rachel replied. Suddenly she was overwhelmed with fear that she might never be able to hold him again, that she might never kiss him and have him look into her eyes as he made love to her. Everything was changing. She could feel it in her very soul.

"Tell me, dammit," he said. "Or I'll find Edmund and make him tell me himself."

The look in his eyes actually made Rachel shudder.

"Is Trace Hambleton your real name?"

The words were so quiet that Trace could barely hear them, but their desperation made his heart skip a beat.

"Who are you really?"

Trace took a deep breath and bit his lower lip.

"Who does Edmund say I am?" he asked, his voice cool.

No denial. No anger about some false accusation. Just a soft question.

And Rachel knew. All those times she'd wondered. All the questions she'd asked only to receive an amused reply, or no reply at all.

Rachel gave a little cry and closed her eyes. The champagne glass dropped from her fingers with a crash that shattered the quietness around them. Her head bent as she covered her face in her hands.

Trace put his fingers beneath her chin and forced her to lift her head and look at him.

"Tell me who he says I am," he demanded.

"He doesn't know," she said, tears streaming down her face. "Only that you never lived in Tennessee and that your name isn't Trace Hambleton."

Trace shook his head as he looked into eyes shattered by betrayal. He felt her body trembling and moved his hand up to wipe away the hot tears on her cheeks.

"Shh," he whispered. He should have felt some relief that at least she didn't know who he was yet. But he could feel nothing except a deep, excruciating guilt.

"Is Edmund lying?" Rachel demanded, looking into his eyes only inches away from hers.

Trace leaned back in his chair, distancing himself from her. He raked his hand down his face and rubbed his eyes.

"No," he whispered.

He thought he'd never forget the sound of her soft little

gasp. Or the look on her beautiful face as he pushed his chair back and stood gazing down at her in the shadows.

"I'm . . . sorry." He turned and walked away, moving quickly down the steps and out among the carriages before Rachel could respond or move to stop him.

"Trace . . ." she called. But her words were choked with tears and the sound went no more than a few inches past her.

"Oh, Trace," she repeated, bending to press her tear stained face against her trembling fingers. Her body ached, as if his admission had been a fist, slamming into her heart.

Nineteen

Rachel sat in the shadows of the porch for what seemed like hours. Finally she wiped her eyes and took long slow gulps of air, trying to compose herself. She had to go back inside. The guests would be wondering about her. So would Hallie.

She found Hallie and Roland near the front door, bidding good night to some of the guests. Rachel paused for a moment and ran her hands down the waist of her shimmering gold dress, then lifted her chin and smiled brightly.

"Darling . . ." Hallie turned to Roland. "Would you get my wrap?"

When Roland left, Hallie said, "What's wrong? You haven't been crying, have you? Where's Trace?"

"For heaven's sake, Hallie," Rachel said. "Which do you want me to answer first?" The effort of remaining cheerful was wearing on her nerves and she wasn't sure how much longer she could keep up the pretense.

"You have been crying," Hallie said, looking into Rachel's reddened eyes.

"Of course, I haven't been crying. What would I have to cry about on my friend's happiest of nights?"

Suddenly, from the corner of her eye, Rachel saw someone moving nearer. It was Edmund who stood leaning against the stairrail watching and listening to her and Hallie.

"Your eyes are terribly red," Hallie said. She was frowning as if she couldn't quite decide whether to believe Rachel or not.

"It's the weather. I always sneeze and have red eyes when the trees and shrubs are blooming." Rachel glanced at Edmund and shot him a look of pure resentment.

"Well, I thought perhaps since Trace wasn't here . . ."

"He's probably out in the drive, seeing to the carriages and sending everyone on their way."

Hallie's mouth pursed, then she smiled.

"I'm sorry. It was silly of me to think you might have had a quarrel. But when I saw him earlier, he was watching you dancing with Edmund. He didn't seem to like it very much."

Edmund walked forward, making his presence known with a discreet cough.

"Edmund," Hallie said with a bright grin. "I was just talking about you."

"So I heard, little sister." He might have been addressing Hallie, but his eyes were for Rachel alone.

The intensity of his gaze made Rachel blush.

It was a relief when Roland came back with Hallie's evening wrap. She never thought the day would come when she would actually be happy to see Hallie, or any of her friends, leave this house.

But she wanted nothing more than to be alone. And to find Trace.

"Thank you again, Rachel," Hallie said, embracing her. "The party was perfect. It's a night we'll remember for the rest of our lives." She gazed into her fiance's eyes and together they walked out onto the front porch.

Edmund lagged behind.

"From the way you look I assume you confronted your husband," he said. "Whoever he is."

Rachel didn't want to admit it to him. Didn't want to give him the satisfaction of being right. But she took a deep breath and faced him.

"Yes," she said. "I did."

"And?"

"You were right," she said. She could feel her cheeks growing warm as she faced him. She refused to look away from his smug gaze. "Trace Hambleton is not his real name. But that hardly means he's done anything wrong."

"Did he tell you that?"

"He didn't have to tell me."

"Ah." Edmund's look was so self satisfied that Rachel actually had to clench her fists to keep from slapping him.

"Edmund, you say you did this because you care about me—"

"More than care," he said fiercely.

"Then if you do . . . care," she said slowly and deliberately, "I ask that you let me handle this on my own. And that you not tell anyone else in Holly Springs about this until I've learned more."

Edmund stepped back and let his eyes move over Rachel's golden gown that clung to her luscious figure. When his gaze moved back to her face, his eyes were dark and shining.

"If I were anything other than a gentleman, I might demand your favors for my silence."

"But you are a gentleman," she reminded through clenched teeth. She had known Edmund all her life, but at the moment she thought she almost hated him. "And even if you did propose such a thing, I think you know what my answer would be."

He dropped his gaze.

"Yes," he said. "I know." He seemed a little embarrassed.

"Will you promise me, Edmund?" she asked, her voice soft. "As a friend?"

Finally a weak smile appeared on his face and he took her hand in his.

"You make it very hard for me to refuse you anything," he said. He bent and kissed her hand, then shot her a knowing look. "But if he hurts you . . . if he does anything to cause you pain or distress, you've only to come to me and I'll take care of it. I hope you know that, despite my sometimes less than gentlemanly behavior," he added with an apologetic grin.

Rachel swallowed and for the first time her chin trembled. "Yes," she whispered. "I do know that."

"All right, then," he said. "I won't do or say anything until you tell me differently."

"You promise?"

"Yes . . . I promise."

"Thank you."

As soon as Edmund left, Rachel pulled up her skirts and ran toward the back of the house. She had to find Trace. There would be no sleep for either of them tonight until this was settled.

She finally found Cleo in the parlor where the musicians were putting away their instruments and preparing to leave.

"Cleo," she said. "Have you seen Trace? He was on the porch earlier, but I haven't seen him since the guests began leaving."

"No," Cleo said. She looked long and hard at Rachel's reddened eyes. "You look tired," she said.

"I am," Rachel said. "I'm going out for a bit of fresh air, then I'm going straight to bed." It was better to lie to Cleo than to upset her, she thought.

Rachel stood on the front porch, letting the breeze cool her heated skin. Her eyes scanned the darkness beyond the front lawn. All the guests were gone and there was no one else in sight.

"Where are you?" she whispered. She thought of all the time Trace had spent with White Feather lately.

"That must be it," she muttered.

She didn't want to go past Cleo again so she ran down the steps and around the house, beneath the wisteria bower and out toward the small house.

When she knocked on the door, it seemed to take forever for Hummingbird to answer.

"Oh, I'm sorry," Rachel said, seeing Hummingbird's drowsy

eyes and tired appearance. She glanced past her to the empty room and the quiet house. "You must have been sleeping. I hope you're feeling well." Her glance moved down to Hummingbird's large stomach.

"It's all right," Hummingbird said. "Come in . . . is anything wrong?"

"No . . . nothing. I . . . I thought perhaps Trace was here."

Hummingbird bit her lips and her dark doe eyes darted away from Rachel's gaze.

"No," she said. "He isn't here."

"Hummingbird," Rachel said, stepping closer. "Do you know where he is? Do you know what's happening? Please . . . if you do . . . can you tell me?"

"My husband would not be pleased," she said.

Rachel saw the sympathy in the woman's eyes and she reached to take her hand.

"I have to know," she said.

The young woman hesitated a moment and when she spoke it was with a quiet reluctance.

"I'm sure the little mistress would not choose to visit the cemetery on such a dark night. But if she did, she might be surprised by who she found there."

"The cemetery?" Rachel frowned at the woman and saw her imperceptible nod. She squeezed Hummingbird's hand. "Thank you, Hummingbird."

Rachel hurried back around the house so that Cleo and the others would not see her. Once past the lights, she turned across the wide lawn and ran toward the cemetery. By the time she reached the stand of live oaks, she was panting for breath and the hem of her golden gown was soaked from the dew.

She could see a light flickering within the fenced area. She moved cautiously from tree to tree, shielding herself from the two men until she was closer. Her heart was pounding at her throat and she felt a little dizzy from trying to breathe quietly when her body actually longed for a gulp of air.

Even in silhouette she recognized Trace as one of the men.

The other must be White Feather. As she drew closer, she could not believe her eyes. This couldn't be her dashing, sophisticated husband.

But as she gazed at the bare-chested man, dressed and painted in Indian fashion, she knew it was him. And even more unbelievable, he seemed to be engaged in a strange religious ceremony.

Her ears roared as she stood very still and strained to hear every word.

White Feather stood aside, holding a burning torch in his right hand as Trace stood at the foot of the unmarked grave. His hands were lifted, his bare chest gleaming and muscular in the dim light. His hair was loose and in the light it looked as black as White Feather's.

Both of the men chanted softly.

Rachel's eyes widened, reflecting both horror and fascination at what she saw and heard. Trace's words were foreign, but she knew them immediately as the Cherokee language she'd heard him speak to White Feather.

And at night when he made such wild, passionate love to her.

She almost gasped at the ripple of alarm that raced through her body.

Trace's head was tilted back, arms raised as he seemed to direct his words to the moon and stars. Then she heard him speak quietly in English.

"For you, Mother, because as a woman three quarters white, you never learned the Cherokee language so well."

Rachel thought she'd never heard such tenderness in his voice, or that little hint of affectionate humor, either.

"O Spirit of the Cherokee Wind, present here in this hallowed place, take the spirit of my mother and by this token which I have placed in the ground, reunite her at last with her husband, my father. Grant them peace and everlasting love."

Trace's arms fell and he bent his head. For a moment, all

was quiet and yet Rachel's mind was ajumble with thoughts and questions. She was touched by his words and his gestures, moved by the magnificence of him. And yet, she wanted to scream at him and demand to know who he was and why he had posed as her husband, when obviously he was nothing like the man she married.

Just as White Feather and Trace were turning to leave the enclosed area, Rachel managed to stumble out of her hiding place.

They saw only a blur of white and gold as she raced around the fence and barred their exit.

"How dare you?" she screamed. "How dare you come here in the middle of the night, dressed like some . . . some wild savage and say these heathen things at my mother's grave?" She knew her words didn't make sense. It wasn't even what she was feeling.

Trace stared at Rachel. Her eyes were wild and frenzied, her hair tumbled from its pins down around her face and shoulders. Her body was trembling with anger.

White Feather groaned and glanced at Trace. It was plain he wanted to leave, but Trace held his hand toward him, silently asking him to stay.

"It is also the grave of my father," Trace said, his voice quiet and solemn.

Rachel seemed stunned and for a moment her eyes darted to White Feather. He nodded.

"I . . . I don't understand," she whispered. "I don't understand any of this."

"I am not the man you thought you married, Rachel," Trace said. "I am Cherokee and this is my father's land."

"No," she whispered. Her heart ached with betrayal as she realized in one blinding moment why he had come here. And why he had married her.

"You . . . you're the man Major Nelson was looking for. This man . . . this Sun Killer." Her voice was a hoarse whisper of disbelief.

"Yes."

For a moment there was only the guttering sound of the torch that White Feather held.

"But . . . but you can't be. I just heard you say that your mother was three quarters white." Her eyes were questioning.

"That's true. Although it didn't seem to make a difference to the men who came here all those years ago and took this land so your father could have it." Trace's jaw clenched and unclenched. Now that he was actually saying the words to her, he found himself growing more angry, more resentful that he'd had to resort to such deception to regain what was rightfully his.

"It didn't make a difference," he continued, his voice hard and cold, "when they dragged my father into the yard and killed him like an animal. Or when they took my mother from her home and forced her to go to a place she hated . . . a place so bare and lifeless that every day of her life was torture. She prayed every night to come back to Alabama. Then when she finally realized how futile her hopes were, she prayed to die . . ." Trace's voice choked and he stopped, clenching his teeth and leaning his head back to take a breath of air.

Rachel's lips parted as she stared at him. She'd never seen him this way. She had seen the anger in him, the danger even. But she had never seen past that to this terrible pain that burned in his eyes and seemed to eat away at his very soul.

"Trace . . ." she said, taking a step toward him.

"No," he growled, shaking his head. "Don't. Don't come any closer. And don't tell me you understand. Because people like you and your father can never understand . . . never!"

His words, hard and bitter, struck her like a fist. She backed away from him and from that terrible look glittering in his eyes.

She didn't know him at all. He was a stranger. A fierce, dangerous stranger who had purposely betrayed her and who seemed to hate her and all she stood for.

With a choked sob, she turned and ran from those eyes. Back to the safety of her home. A home that didn't really belong to her, after all.

Twenty

"You were too harsh with her, cousin," White Feather said.

They both watched as the gold of Rachel's dress glimmered in the lantern light, then disappeared into the darkness that surrounded the cemetery.

Trace sighed and closed his eyes.

"I know," he said. "None of this is her fault. Her father is the one I should be dealing with." He shook his head, trying to clear away the vision of Rachel's beautiful face and the hurt he saw reflected in her eyes. "It didn't turn out the way I intended." His voice was soft, reproachful.

"It isn't too late," White Feather said.

"You're wrong," Trace answered. "It is too late. Rachel has been betrayed by her husband . . . by a man she thought she loved—"

"She does love you."

Trace shook his head and went on as if his cousin had not spoken.

"Didn't you see the look in her eyes?" he asked, his voice bitter. "Surely you heard the disgust in her voice when she realized she was married to an Indian." His lips curled in sneering disdain.

"You are seeing things that are not there," White Feather said. "Rachel loves you . . . the man, not the color of your skin or the sorrows you have endured. And if you go to her . . . speak to her—"

"It's too late. I'll just have to petition the courts for a divorce. I'm sure, when they find out the wedding was carried out in deceit, there will be no problem."

"And in the meantime?"

"In the meantime, there's no reason why both of us can't live here in the same house until this is settled. We're both civilized adults, regardless of what she thinks about me. It's a big house." Trace lifted his chin and his eyes glinted with determination. "But make no mistake about it, this house and this land are mine. When I petition for the divorce, I also intend to file formal claim for this land. One thing I did learn in the Oklahoma territory is the law and this country's Bill of Rights. I will fight as long as I'm breathing. I'll take my case to the highest court in the land, if need be. And when it's over, Rosewood will be mine in every sense."

"It will not be easy," White Feather said. "Especially if you intend to divorce Rachel."

"No," Trace said. "I expect this will raise the biggest uproar this side of the Mississippi."

Rachel sat shivering in their darkened bedroom. She felt lifeless . . . spent, as Trace's words raced over and over again in her mind. She knew she should change out of her evening gown—the wet skirt lay uncomfortably against her legs and coldly down over her feet.

But she couldn't move. She couldn't seem to make herself do anything except sit and stare into the darkness.

She couldn't even cry.

It was almost dawn when Trace opened the bedroom door. Rachel had fallen asleep in the chair and now she roused herself and stood up, facing him rigidly, her heart pounding in anticipation.

She heard him mutter and curse as he ran into a chair in the darkened room. Then there was a flare of light and the faint whiff of sulfur as he lit one of the lamps.

She could see him clearly now, his hair still loose, his appearance as pagan and primitive as before. But the paint was gone from his dark skin and a white shirt covered his chest.

She watched as he glanced toward the neat, unrumpled bed. Seeing she wasn't in bed, he turned and found her.

They stared at each other across the room. She thought the anger seemed to have left him somewhat—but not the resentment and the fierce pride. It was still there in his dark eyes, as strongly as ever.

"You should be in bed," he said. He shook his head, thinking how stupid and benign those words sounded under the circumstances.

"We have to talk, Trace," she said. "I have to know what you intend to do."

He sighed and came slowly toward her. When she took a step backward, he laughed, the sound harsh and loud in the room.

"What's wrong?" he asked. "Afraid I'll touch you? Dirty you somehow? Don't you think it's a little late for that? Or are you forgetting that I know every sweet, luscious inch of your body?"

Rachel gritted her teeth and her small body trembled with anger.

"You bastard," she whispered, tears sparkling in her eyes.

"Be very careful what you call me," he said, his voice low and dangerous. "My patience is not without limits."

"I hate you. Do you know that?" Tears spilled down her cheeks, but she made no effort to wipe them away. Instead, her eyes blazed into his, searching and desperate.

"I'm used to hatred," he said coldly. "So why should yours surprise me?"

"Why Trace?" she asked. For the first time, her steely resolve broke and her voice trembled with pain. "Just tell me why you did this to me."

Despite his attempt at coldness, Trace could hardly bear the look in her eyes, or the way her voice shook when she asked the question. And despite all the times he had tried to tell himself that he could never truly have this woman for his own, he found his hardened heart beating just a little faster when he looked at her and saw her anguish.

"Why?" he asked, ignoring the ache in his heart. "Why not? You're beautiful, rich . . . *white.*"

Rachel's chin trembled and Trace found himself wanting to cut out his deceitful tongue.

"Oh, I see," she whispered. "Is that one of your savage fantasies? Is it the way everyone says it is? That an Indian would kill to lie between a white woman's thighs?" Her voice, angry and bitter, practically spat the words at him.

"Such language is not worthy of you, Rachel."

"Oh," she scoffed. Angrily, she wiped her hand over her face as she continued to glare at him. "Yes, the high and mighty Rachel Townsend. Such a good Christian woman. So kind and loving. Do you think I don't know what everyone says about me? Do you think I haven't tried with every ounce of my being to live up to those expectations?"

Tears ran unchecked down her face now and still Trace could not move. He would not allow himself to go to her and comfort her.

"But everything changed when I met you, didn't it?" she cried. "Perhaps if I had not been so in love with you, I'd have been more of a challenge for your savage conquest. You didn't even have to resort to rape as most of your kind do, did you? Because I made it so easy for you. I jumped at the chance to be your wanton little—"

"Rachel." Trace's warning was a low growl.

"Whore . . ." Though her eyes still sparked, the word came out a quiet, pitiful little whisper.

Trace took a deep breath and expelled it loudly.

"Rachel . . . this has nothing to do with you. I came here with one purpose in mind—to get back my father's land and to restore Rosewood to my family's name."

"Rosewood," she said blankly.

"It's the name my mother gave the house."

"I see."

"I intend filing a claim to have the property returned to me. It's what I would have done anyway, except that I met you and—"

"And it was much easier just to marry me," she whispered. "In Alabama, a woman's property belongs to her husband."

Trace chewed on his bottom lip.

"Yes," he said finally.

"And I was such a fool that I fell easily into your plans."

"I never meant to hurt you," he said. He hesitated a moment, looking deeply into her eyes. "When I file the claim for the house, I'll also place a petition for divorce. There's no reason you can't stay here in this house until the decree is final."

"Oh . . . how very kind. To let me stay in my own home until everything is nice and neat for you."

Trace cursed beneath his breath and took another step toward her.

"Don't," she warned. "Don't you dare touch me. Ever again. Do you hear me? I don't ever want to feel the touch of your hand on me again. I hate you for what you've done to me. And I will never forgive you. Never!" Her small body was shaking uncontrollably.

Trace was afraid she might actually faint.

"Get out," she said, her voice a fierce hiss. "Get out of this room . . . out of my sight!"

He walked toward her and even though she backed away from him, this time, he stalked her. Rachel stood against the windows. She could feel the windowsill digging into the back of her thighs. She had no idea what he intended to do.

He took her wrists, dragging her up against him until his face was mere inches away from hers.

"I know you're angry and hurt. And I will leave this room. But only because I want to, Rachel. This house and everything in it belongs to me now. Do you understand? If I wanted you, I would have you . . . right here and right now."

He turned away, kicking a chair as he stalked from the room, leaving Rachel breathless, her eyes wide as she watched him go.

She hesitated only a second before racing across the room and locking the door. Then, sobbing quietly, she slid down the wood panel and collapsed onto the floor.

Trace stood outside her room, his breath hard and labored as he tried to control his anger. When he heard the door lock, he gritted his teeth, tempted for a moment to kick the door in and let her know that no lock would hold him if he wanted in.

But he heard a quiet thump against the door, and then the sound of her crying, muffled and soft.

"Christ," he muttered beneath his breath. He wasn't sure if his reeling mind meant it as a curse or a prayer.

Rachel lay crumpled against the floor, her fists clenched tightly against her pain and anger.

"Damn you, damn you, damn you," she whispered.

She was hot and her face felt swollen from all the tears. Suddenly, rebelliously, she pushed herself up from the floor and began unbuttoning her dress, finally ripping the delicate gold material and pushing the offending garment off her body.

When she flung herself naked onto the bed, the sun was just rising over the trees to the east. She heard the birds in the live oaks begin to twitter and sing their morning song, and then she remembered nothing.

Trace lay in one of the other bedrooms near the back of the house. He couldn't sleep and as a distraction he let his gaze wander over the not unfamiliar room. If he recalled correctly, this small room had once been his mother's sewing room. He could remember coming here on rainy afternoons to watch her sew. It was one of those memories that had brought warmth and comfort to him those long terrible nights on the reservation.

He had often thought that it would be a relief, finally having Rachel find out about the charade he was living. He'd told himself he wanted her out of his life, out of his thoughts for good. He had too much work to do, too big a battle to fight to be burdened with a woman like her . . . a woman who hated him now with all her being.

Now it was done. Legally obtaining Rosewood might be a long, drawn out procedure. But once it was legal, he would do as he pleased with it. Perhaps he could find more of his lost family and bring them to Rosewood.

He could plant whatever crops he wished, destroy the work village by the old springs and restore the meadow to its sacred purpose. He could even free Windridge's slaves, if he wished.

He lay on the bed, his arms folded behind his head. He closed his eyes, intending to sleep. But behind his eyelids, there came again and again, the vision of Rachel. A realistic reminder of this beautiful woman who had been his for a while. His wife . . . his lover, as sweet and wild as mountain honey.

He opened his eyes and glanced to the side of the bed where she normally would be sleeping. He felt the muscles in his stomach tighten, felt an aching warmth in his chest. Inexplicably, the scent of mock orange came to him and the remembrance of their first wild, sweet night together. The feel of her body, the touch of her hands, her mouth . . .

"Dammit!"

His hands moved from behind his head and he rubbed his fingers across his eyes. He was weary . . . bone tired. And yet, he could feel his desire for Rachel growing even now, against his will. This part of his body, he couldn't seem to control—not when it came to her.

He sat up suddenly and slid his legs over the edge of the bed. He stood up and slipped his trousers back on and walked to the single window in the small room. Raising the window, he could hear the birds singing. He was in a part of the house that overlooked the kitchen and now he could see and smell wood smoke rising from that building.

He took a long deep breath of fresh air, letting it wash over his heated body, willing his treacherous flesh to return to normal. His lips twitched into a bemused smile and he shook his head with a mixture of regret and amazement.

Now that it was done, why was he feeling such regret? He'd done what he had to do to survive, what he'd been taught to do.

His eyes darkened and he muttered a quiet curse. He knew why: Rachel. Just as his body remembered every inch of her body, his heart just as vividly remembered the love and goodness she'd given him so freely.

But he couldn't have her. Ever again.

He might as well get used to it.

Twenty-one

It was fairly early next morning when Rachel stepped out of her room, considering she hadn't gone to sleep until dawn. She was struggling with a pair of gloves and had taken no more than two steps when she realized someone else was in the hallway.

She turned and stared in Trace's eyes and immediately her cheeks turned crimson. He seemed perfectly at ease and not concerned at all about her anger, or the awkwardness of the situation. For a moment, Rachel wanted to confront him. She wanted to slap that cool, impassive look off his face. Her eyes bored into him for a moment before she whirled back around and hurried ahead, running down the stairs and out the front door.

Trace stood for a moment at the top of the stairs and watched her go. This morning he felt cooler, more in control than he had last night. He had thought about this very moment—the first time he'd see Rachel after their bitter confrontation. He had heard her crying last night through the door and he knew she felt hurt and betrayed. And despite his sleepless night and his guilt ridden conscience, he had told himself it couldn't be helped.

But if he'd expected her to still be in tears this morning, he was mistaken. She was as beautiful and composed as ever. It was only that little spark deep down inside those lovely eyes that told him her pain and anger were still very real.

She covered it well. Even now, his breath had not returned

to normal after being the target of those snapping eyes. Trace did not like admitting that she could aggravate him so. Or that he had such little control over her effect on him.

Slowly, he descended the stairs, bypassing the breakfast that waited for him in the dining room and going instead out the back of the house.

He intended on going to Holly Springs today and filing the paper for the divorce decree. It would only be a matter of hours before the entire community knew what was going on between him and Rachel.

Jim and Jared were just going into the stables. Trace smiled despite himself when he saw them wrestling and laughing. They straightened immediately when he called to them.

"I need a horse, boys," he said.

"Where you be goin', Mr. Trace?" Jared asked. "Why didn't you jes ride with Miss Rachel?"

"Miss Rachel? Where was she going?"

"Into town, suh."

"Damn," he muttered.

"What's that, suh?"

"Nothing Jared, nothing. Just bring the roan around, would you?"

They were just saddling the horse when Justus came riding into the stable and jumped down from his horse. He didn't seem to notice any of them for a moment. When he did he nodded to Trace, but addressed his brothers.

"Boys," he said. "Go fetch Miss Rachel. They be trouble in the quarters—Mose has got some liquor from somewhere and he's threatenin' to whup everybody. Hurry now."

Trace frowned and stepped forward. He hated to delay his trip into town—he had no idea what Rachel was up to. But this was something that couldn't be ignored. It still irritated him that Justus always deferred to Rachel on matters relating to the plantation.

"Miss Rachel has gone into town," Trace said. He placed

one of the stirrups atop the saddle and tightened the cinch before pulling himself up onto the horse. "I'll take care of it."

Justus bit his lip and there was a worried look on his face.

"Well?" Trace snapped. "Is there something else?"

"No suh," the young man said. "Nothing else. Just Mose."

"Get on your horse then. You'll have to show me where he is."

They rode together around the stables and past White Feather's house. Within seconds they were entering the wide road that lay between the row of slave houses.

Trace could see a crowd of Negroes in front of one of the houses and two men struggling on the ground.

As they approached, some of the women backed away. Others scurried back toward their own houses. But the two men fighting seemed oblivious to anything or anyone else around them.

Trace swung down from the big roan and marched toward the group.

"Suh," Justus called, getting down from his horse as well. He caught up with Trace, matching his long steps stride for stride. But he wasn't watching his steps, he was watching Trace and the hard, determined look on his face. "Suh . . . you might should oughta—"

"What?" Trace snapped. "Wait until the little mistress gets back? One of these men could be dead by then."

Justus opened his mouth to speak again, but Trace pushed his way through the crowd of men. Most of them were as tall or taller than he was and some of them were more muscular. But he seemed not to notice as he marched through them and bent to grab the shirt of the flailing man who was on top of the other.

"Get up," he demanded. "Stop this."

Trace could smell the heavy scent of liquor on the man he held and he could see the crazed look on his face. Mose's fist came back and he flailed wildly, trying to free himself from Trace's grip.

Trace shook the man like a puppy, even though Mose was a huge, well-built young man. He pushed him back through the circle of men, and slammed him with a bang up against the house.

Mose shook his head, dazed and disoriented as he stared curiously into Trace's eyes. Trace slammed him again until finally the big man's knees almost buckled.

The circle of slaves behind him gave a low collective groan, a mutter of disapproval. And for the first time, Trace realized just how alone he was, and how much in danger.

"There will be no fighting here," he told Mose, who had now settled down and stood quietly with his back against the shanty. Only his eyes reflected his resentment. "Do you understand me?"

Mose hesitated and when Trace's fist tightened on his shirt once more, the man nodded.

"Where did you get the liquor?"

The men gathered behind them were silent and still.

Mose shrugged his massive shoulders and dropped his gaze toward the ground.

Trace let him go and took a step backward. He sensed someone behind him and whirled to find Justus standing there. In his hand was a whip which he now handed toward Trace.

Trace frowned, glancing from the whip into the eyes of the Negro men who stood watching and waiting. He took a deep breath as he gazed into Justus's eyes.

"I wasn't aware that Miss Rachel allowed whippings at Windridge."

"She don't," Justus said, his voice very low. "But I thought . . ." He pushed the whip toward Trace in a kind of sheepish offering.

"You thought wrong," Trace said. He turned and glanced over his shoulder at Mose. "Mose, is there any liquor left? You'd better tell me the truth. I'll find out sooner or later."

"No, suh," Mose said. "Ain't no mo. I drunk it all."

"That wasn't real smart was it?" Trace muttered. "It doesn't seem to agree with you."

"No, suh," Mose agreed.

"Justus, get the man something to eat. Is there any coffee?"

A girl standing at the open doorway of the house called to him.

"I got some."

Trace glanced up at the girl. She couldn't have been more than fifteen, but she was pregnant and from the concerned way her eyes kept darting toward Mose, Trace assumed he was the father.

"Is this man your husband?" he asked.

"Yes, suh," she said. For the first time, she smiled, showing even white teeth. "He be a good man mos the time, suh."

"I'm sure he is," Trace said. He raised his hand in a helpless gesture and started to walk away.

"Suh," the girl said. "Mr. Trace . . ." she added shyly. "I gots plenty o' coffee if'n you be needin' some. The little mistress, she be mos' generous with rations."

Trace opened his mouth to speak, then closed it. He glanced toward his horse, then toward the west where Holly Springs lay. Then he shrugged his shoulders, nodding his agreement.

"Coffee sounds good," he said.

The girl's eyes brightened and she clasped her hands together. Then she hurried inside, returning only minutes later with two cups of paper thin china, sprinkled with tiny blue flowers. They were rimmed with gold and though there were chips on them, they were still beautiful and obviously the pride of the young woman's household.

One of the men pushed forward a short log of unsplit wood and set it on end to make a seat for Trace while Mose took his coffee and stood a few feet away. None of the men made an effort to leave.

Trace sipped the strong hot coffee, then nodded his approval toward the girl. She was grinning broadly, and when Trace glanced toward the men, most of them were grinning, too. What was intended as only a few moments, lasted most of the day.

After an initial period of silent awkwardness, some of the men began to talk. Trace learned their names and what their jobs were on the plantation.

He found it amusing that Justus, who always before had shied away from him, now seemed to present himself as Trace's staunchest ally.

"Mr. Trace here is a fair man," he boasted once. He stepped closer as if he might clasp Trace on the shoulders, but Trace's lifted brows and look of amusement stopped the young man in his tracks.

"Mr. Trace," Mose said. The man seemed sober now. "We sho could use some repairs to the house. Rats, they get into the house, bes' my Belle can do to keep 'em out." He leaned forward and spoke softly to Trace, as if he didn't want the others to hear. "She be worried 'bout it with the baby comin' and all."

"Show me," Trace said.

After that, Trace found himself pulled from one house to the other, making mental notes and also reminding Justus of all the repairs that needed to be done.

When he rode back to the house it was mid afternoon and he was weary and dirty. But he had to admit he'd never felt a stronger sense of contentment.

What had started as a troublesome day had turned out to be one of the best he'd had since coming back to Rosewood. For the first time, he truly felt that he was home.

He saw that Rachel's carriage was back in the carriage house beside the stables. But inside the house she was nowhere in sight.

Dimity brought his supper and he could see by the look in her eyes that she knew something was wrong between him and the little mistress. The house was eerily quiet. The other servants spoke in whispers and glanced at him from the corner of their eyes. And Mama Cleo seemed reluctant to even come near him.

After dinner, he went into his study. It was almost dark when he heard someone step into the room behind him. He turned and saw Rachel standing just inside the doorway, her chin held high, and a look of cool disdain in her beautiful eyes.

Trace stood up and nodded stiffly. They were like two strangers who'd just met under suspicious circumstances. Cool and polite, one studying the other, until Rachel stepped into the room and held a paper toward him.

"What's this?" he asked.

"The deeds to Windridge," she said. Rachel held her teeth tightly together, willing herself not to cry in front of him. She would not let him see how badly his betrayal hurt, or how much it had cost her.

She should hate him for what he'd done. And just when she thought she did hate him, she saw something sweet and vulnerable in him—something decent. Like the stories she'd heard today from the house servants—about how he had tamed a drunken Mose, then had coffee with Mose and Belle in front of their house. How he had walked through the entire quarters with the slaves and listened to their concerns.

He was staring at her as if he hadn't heard correctly.

Rachel pushed the papers forward, urging him to take them. When he didn't, she stepped past him and dropped the packet onto his desk.

"My father deeded the house to me before our marriage. I went into town today and had it changed legally to your name. So it's yours now. There's no reason to file a claim that could take years to settle. And no reason for anyone to know who you are until you decide you're ready for that to happen. The house, the acreage, all the outbuildings and the slaves, are yours." She spoke stiffly, as if she could barely move her lips.

"I also took the liberty of freeing Mama Cleo, Lula, Dimity, Justus and the twins. It would be less embarrassing to me if you could delay the divorce until I can make arrangements to leave for Washington to live with my father. If there's a problem with my staying here until then—"

"No," he said quickly, shaking his head. He looked at her and then at the papers lying on his desk. "No, of course not," he said. "I . . . I hardly expected this."

"Didn't you?" she asked, her voice and eyes cold as ice. "You thought that I'd fight you? I don't know why you'd think such a thing, Trace, knowing how easily I fell under your spell before. You should be feeling very smug about just how simple that was."

He didn't feel smug at all, dammit. And he didn't feel good about what he'd done.

"Rachel . . . I . . ."

"Well, it's yours now. See . . . no screaming or fighting, no struggles." She didn't say the words, but Trace knew that once again she was talking about more than just the deeds to Windridge.

"The thing is," she added, her voice very soft in the quiet room, "Your deceit was really quite unnecessary. You see . . . I'd have given you anything Trace. Willingly. All you had to do was ask."

For the first time since she came into the room, there was a glint of moisture in her eyes. She turned quickly and left the study, her skirts rustling, the scent of her perfume stirring the air behind her like flowers in a warm summer breeze.

Trace closed his eyes and shook his head, then muttered a low growl as his hand reached out blindly and swept everything from the desk with a crash.

Twenty-two

That night Trace lay restless in the small bedroom at the back of the house. His conversation with Rachel kept running again and again through his mind. He couldn't get her face out of his head, or the way she had looked when she'd handed him the deeds to Rosewood.

He couldn't understand why she would do anything to make his possession of Rosewood easier. To save face perhaps? To delay having everyone find out that their "perfect" marriage was a farce? Perhaps just to give her time to get away to Washington before the news spread.

She'd be humiliated when everyone learned the truth. Ridiculed and scorned for having been tricked into a red man's bed.

Trace kicked his feet against the bedcovers.

How different she was than he had expected. Not many women raised like Rachel—wealthy, beautiful young women who had lived all their life surrounded by people who wanted only to take care of them—were so kind, or so loving. Rachel had everything yet her blessings had not spoiled her or made her aloof to the troubles of other people. He had seen for himself that she gave not only of her wealth, but of her time and herself.

But no one gave away a plantation as vast as Rosewood. No one.

Trace shifted his weight and sighed heavily as he continued to stare into the darkness.

Rachel could also be stubborn and willful. It was a trick, he decided. A calculated little trick to make him feel guilty. He hadn't bothered to look at the deeds. Perhaps she hadn't really changed anything. Perhaps she only wanted to make him think she had.

Trace cursed and pushed the covers off his feet. He pushed his legs into his trousers, and without bothering to put on his shirt, yanked open the door and headed downstairs toward his study.

The house was quiet. There was only the glow of a lamp from the ladies parlor across from his study. He paid no attention to it, but instead hurried into his study, his bare feet making no sound against the floor.

Rachel hadn't been able to sleep. She'd gone out to the kitchen to see if there was still hot water in the kettle over the fireplace. Then she'd made herself a cup of tea and had taken it with her into the small parlor at the front of the house.

She couldn't bear lying sleepless in that bed, alone but for the memory of Trace's hard body against hers, making her feel more secure than she'd ever been in her life. She thought of the sound of his breath, quiet and steady in the room and how she would lie there listening to his breathing, amazed at how much pleasure one could derive from so simple a thing as that. Hardly able to believe how lucky she was to have found a man like him.

She groaned quietly and closed her eyes against the pain. It was best not to think of him. Best to keep busy, even if it meant she had to stay up reading night after torturous night.

She thought she heard a noise in the hallway and she turned her head to listen. There was only a whisper of sound, perhaps a creaking of the wood floors.

Then out of the corner of her eye, she saw a light come on and she realized it was from Trace's study across the hall. She laid her book aside and gathered her voluminous dressing gown about her.

Trace found the deed. It lay atop the pile of papers he'd

gathered from the floor after sweeping them off in frustration this afternoon. Turning up the wick of the lamp, he sat behind his desk, intending to read every word. Just to make sure this wasn't some game Rachel was playing.

Rachel stood watching him, letting her eyes move over his bare muscular chest and arms. God, but she wanted to touch him, to feel those arms around her again. Silently, she cursed herself for being such a fool where he was concerned.

"I assure you, everything is legal," she said.

Trace's gaze moved slowly up from the papers to the doorway where Rachel stood. Her eyes in the shadows were unreadable, her expression cool and composed.

Yet, even in the shadows, he was well aware of the outline of her tempting curves beneath the white dressing gown. The sweet swell of her breasts, the pale column of her neck so graceful and slender.

Trace pulled his gaze away from her all too provocative figure. Ignoring her, he read the deeds quickly, but carefully, before opening a drawer and placing the papers inside.

"Do you believe me now?" Rachel asked.

Only then did he stand to acknowledge his wife's presence.

"What are you doing up?" he asked, his voice as cool as her eyes.

She laughed softly, a sound that was anything but humorous.

"Why don't you ever say what you mean, Trace? Or would you prefer that I call you by your real name? Sun Killer." Her eyes didn't flicker as they stared into his. "Somehow that name does seem much more appropriate."

Trace said nothing. As much as he would like to shake some sense into her, he wasn't about to let himself get pulled into another argument.

"When will you be leaving for Washington?" he asked.

"Ah," she said. Her white teeth flashed in the dimly lit room. "Here's the truth at last. When will I be out of your house and out of your sight, you mean?"

Trace thought he'd never heard such an edge to her soft voice, or such sarcasm pass her lips.

"Is my being here in this house making you uncomfortable, dear husband?" she asked provocatively. She moved farther into the room, coming closer to the light and not bothering to cover her breasts where her dressing gown draped open.

"Don't play these games with me, Rachel. I'm warning you."

"Warning me?" she asked. She laughed again, but this time tears glittered in her blue eyes. "Well, it's a little late for that, isn't it? The warning should have come long ago, *Sun Killer.*" She practically ground the words out between her teeth. "The first day you stepped onto this property. The first time you kissed me . . ." She broke off her words with a choked little sob before taking a deep breath and gritting her teeth. "Before I went to bed with a man like you who had the power to change my life forever."

"A savage like me, you mean," he said, his voice quiet and steady.

"Yes, damn you," she whispered fiercely, her eyes snapping. "A savage with no heart and no conscience."

Trace looked across the desk directly into her eyes. The spark that was always between them threatened to explode. Both of them could feel its electricity in the air.

"You're wrong about that part, Rachel," he said. "I do have a conscience. And I regret—"

"Oh, do you?" she spat. She laughed again as tears trickled slowly from her beautiful eyes. "Do you want me to tell you about regrets?" she murmured. "About humiliation."

Suddenly, Trace could no longer contain his frustration. He stepped forward quickly, taking her chin in his hand and forcing her to look into his eyes.

"I wish you could ask my mother about humiliation," he said. "And ask her how it felt to have her husband murdered before her eyes. Then to be ripped from the home they'd built together and to be made to feel like dirt beneath the feet of the white soldiers!" Trace's face was very close and his eyes sparked with fury. "Ask her how it felt for a woman who lived much the way you do to be marched a thousand miles with little food and water, with no place to bathe or change clothes. To be ridiculed and spat upon. To be taken by the soldiers whenever they pleased . . ." His voice choked and he stopped.

The revelation made Rachel's eyes darken and she gasped.

He'd never told anyone that part before. And he didn't quite know why he was telling Rachel now.

When he continued his voice was softer, huskier.

"Ask a twelve-year-old boy who had been raised with love and consideration how humiliating it is to be beaten and kicked. To be told day after long, torturous day that he is worthless . . . that he is trash. No more than a animal."

Abruptly Trace released her, then moved across the room. He didn't trust himself to be this close. Not when his feelings about her were so confused.

He was stunned that the touch of her had sent a wave of desire ripping through his entire body. And yet he felt such resentment and frustration. The shocking realization that he wanted to make love to her and punish her at the same time made him back away, disgusted with himself.

Rachel's lips trembled as she stared at him. She could feel the pain in his voice reaching out, touching her in the deepest, hardest part of her heart.

"They . . . they raped your mother?"

"It's something I swore I'd never talk about. I didn't intend to—"

"I'm sorry . . ." she whispered.

"I don't want your pity, dammit," he snapped.

Rachel shook herself, willing her insides to stop quivering. Somehow the fight had gone out of her and she wanted only for this terrible agony to end.

"You have your home back," she said, her voice soft . . . kind even. "I hope having that is a consolation to you, Trace," she added. "And I hope that, one day, by being here, you'll be able to recapture some of the peace you knew as a boy. But whether you want to hear it or not, I am sorry. I hate the role my father played in all of this, and I grieve for your father's death and for all the terrible things that happened to your mother. But most of all . . ." She hesitated as he turned and looked deep into her eyes.

"Most of all, I'm sorry for that little boy, and all he saw and endured. And for the bitterness that changed him too soon into a man who hates everyone and everything."

For a moment, they looked at one another in silence. When Cleo came bustling into the room, her voice shattered the quiet and caused both of them to turn toward her.

"Rachel honey . . . Mr. Trace . . . what you two doin' up this time o' night? You ain't sick, too, are you?" Cleo's eyes were wide with alarm.

"No," Rachel said. She went across the room and put an arm around Cleo's ample shoulders. "What do you mean . . . sick, too?"

"It's the twins," Cleo said.

Rachel rarely saw weakness in this woman's eyes. Or heard any hint of fear. But she heard it now.

"What is it?" Rachel turned at Trace's question and saw that he had immediately come to join them, their differences apparently forgotten.

For now.

"I don't know," Cleo said. "They both gots a fever. A real bad fever. Summer sickness ain't good," she muttered beneath her breath. "Death and destruction lingers in hot air, they say."

Rachel frowned at Cleo.

"Don't say such things," she said. "You know how I feel about all those superstitious beliefs of yours. Go wake Dimity and Lula. Tell Lula to bring the fever medicine and clean clothes. Is Justus all right? He isn't sick as well?"

"No," Cleo said, shaking her head. "He's the one woke me and told me about the boys. He looked to be all right. But livin' with 'em, he bound to get it, too. When your poor mama died, the fever spread through the quarters like wildfire. Twenty souls died that summer. Your papa thought you'd die, too."

"It doesn't mean the same thing will happen now," Rachel said, trying to brush aside Cleo's fears. If she appeared calm, perhaps it would transfer over to Cleo and the others.

But calmness was far from what she was feeling. Summer fevers *could* be devastating. They sometimes wiped out entire families in only a few weeks' time.

"I'll get dressed," Rachel told Cleo. "Then I'll be right there."

"Lordy, no," Cleo said, her eyes glowing with alarm. "Ain't no need fo you to put yoself in danger, too. You know very well if it's yellow fever it could—"

"Nonsense," Rachel said. "You don't really think I'm going to sit in this house and do nothing when the twins are sick do you? I'll be there in a few minutes."

Trace stared hard at Rachel as she turned and hurried up the stairs.

"Can't you talk no sense into her, Mr. Trace?" Cleo asked.

For a moment, he wanted nothing more than to do just that. To forbid her to help, if necessary. He felt a deep, weary sense of foreboding stirring somewhere deep inside him. And he felt something else as well.

Fear . . . an emotion he thought he had conquered many years ago. Fear that something might happen to Rachel. And that he would be absolutely powerless to do anything about it.

"She won't listen," Trace said. "If there's one thing I've learned about my wife, Cleo, it's that she's going to do what she thinks is right, regardless of what anyone else says."

As Cleo shook her head, muttering, then hurried toward the back of the house, Trace stood, still staring at the empty stairway.

He hurried up the stairs to put on his shoes and shirt. He might not be able to persuade Rachel to stay out of harm's way. But at least he could go with her and offer what help he could.

Twenty-three

Trace dressed and came into the hall at the same time as Rachel. She glanced at him, not meeting his eyes, then without speaking hurried on down the stairs. He walked into the room over the stables just behind her. The stench of sickness was heavy in the still, lifeless air.

Rachel hurried to the bed where both the boys lay.

"Jim?" The boy did not speak, but moaned quietly, moving his head back and forth against the pillow.

Jared's eyes were open, but he was very weak, barely able to speak.

"Jared, honey, can you talk to me?" she asked.

"Huh uh," he said, shaking his head. This little boy, who was so fearless, had dark eyes filled with fear.

"It's all right," she said, smiling at him. "Just tell me where it hurts." Rachel touched cool fingers against his forehead and he nodded. "Your head hurts?" Again Jared nodded, his eyes wide as he stared up at her.

Slowly, she touched his arms and legs, then his stomach. He told her with his eyes and with his nods that he hurt in every part of his body.

Rachel bit her lip, and when she turned to the others, concern was etched in her eyes.

"We have to separate them. Jim's fever is much the worse. Justus, get someone to help you—go to the storeroom in the attic and find us another bed to set up on the other side of the room."

Justus nodded and hurried away.

"Cleo, would you please open the door. It's stifling in here."

"Lordy, chile," Cleo said, her eyes wide and disapproving. "We can't do that. Them mosquitoes eat us up. They been swarmin' everywhere since the rain."

Rachel's eyes were filled with frustration as she looked thoughtfully from the boys toward the door.

"We have to have some fresh air. Ask Lula to bring that new bolt of mosquito netting. We'll have to drape it over the beds, though heaven knows that won't help much."

Trace felt a sense of awe at Rachel's ability to put aside her own troubles and take charge so quickly and with such efficiency. His eyes were filled with quiet respect as he watched her.

He'd seen career officers who didn't possess half the leadership abilities of this small, soft-spoken woman.

"Rachel," he said, stepping toward her. "White Feather and I used netting as screens for the windows in his house. We could do the same here if you think it would help."

"Oh, yes," she said, practically sighing with relief. "That would be perfect. We'd have fresh air as well as protection from the mosquitoes."

"I'll get a hammer and tacks."

"Trace," she said, as he walked toward the door.

He turned and looked into her eyes.

"Don't bring White Feather," she said. She saw the beginning of resentment and a questioning glint in Trace's eyes and she hurried to explain herself. "If this is yellow fever . . ." Her glance darted toward Cleo and she lowered her voice slightly. ". . . I wouldn't want him to carry it back to his own children."

Trace felt his resentment melting away and he nodded.

"I think you're right."

"Oh Lord, it's the Yellow Jack . . . I knowed it!" Cleo cried, hearing Rachel's words. "Lord have mercy. Oh, sweet little Jesus baby, not our twins."

Trace touched Cleo's arm sympathetically as he left the room.

"We don't know that yet, Cleo," Rachel said. "Why don't you have Dimity wake some of the men—send someone into town to bring the doctor."

Cleo swallowed hard and backed out of the room. She still had on her nightgown and an old robe and when she opened the door, the wind blew the material about her. She looked like a large ghostly spirit.

"I do that right away," she said. "Right away."

The doctor still hadn't arrived at dawn. Rachel could hear the sounds of the plantation coming to life outside. The roosters crowed as if it were any normal day. Children squealed and ran in the area beside the kitchen.

Inside the room above the stables, it was quiet. Jim had hardly stirred except when Rachel tried to spoon liquids into his parched mouth. Jared was the one they had moved into the new bed and he lay restlessly, kicking at the sheets and mumbling in his sleep.

Trace and Justus had finished hanging the netting across the windows, holding it in place with tightly fitted strips of wood. Rachel went outside to see.

"You know," she said, as she nodded her approval. "Perhaps we should let Mose and some of the men do the same with the houses in the quarters. If this fever spreads . . ."

"That's a good idea. I'll take care of it," Trace said.

Rachel smiled with gratitude, and for a second, they looked into each other's eyes. Then Trace pulled his gaze away and began to gather his materials.

Justus followed him, and Rachel couldn't keep from smiling as she watched them go. She knew he had regarded Trace with a bit of jealousy at first—perhaps even resentment that this strong young stranger had come to take care of the plantation . . . and her. But Trace's concern and hard work had quickly turned the young Negro man into a loyal friend.

When the doctor arrived moments later, Cleo and Lula followed him up and stood with Rachel at the door, watching and listening as he examined the boys. Rachel saw him shake his head when he left Jim's bed and went across the room toward Jared. She bit her lip and prayed silently.

When the doctor straightened and came to Rachel, she held her breath. His eyes were grave and she warned herself that the look she saw there didn't necessarily mean what she thought it did.

"I'm sorry, Rachel," he said. "There's nothing else to be done. You and Cleo have already done as much as I could. We'll just have to wait and see. In the meantime, I think it would be wise to keep all your people here on the plantation and not let them mingle with folks in town."

"Then . . . then you think it's yellow fever?" she asked, her voice filled with horror.

"I think it might be," he said.

"I knowed it," Cleo wailed softly. "Oh Lord, I done knowed it."

Lula put her arms around Cleo and they stood like that, their eyes filled with sorrow as they looked into the room at the two slight figures on the separate beds.

Rachel walked out with the doctor and down the stairs into the yard. As he drove away, she saw Hummingbird coming across the yard, her gait slow and awkward.

"Hummingbird," she called. "Don't come any closer. We can't take a chance on your being exposed to the fever."

Hummingbird stopped and held up her hand. In it was a small jar which she placed on a nearby fence post.

"I bring medicine for the children," Hummingbird said. "Earth medicine."

"Oh," Rachel whispered, her eyes suddenly filling with tears. "How thoughtful . . . how sweet of you to do that.

Thank you." Rachel wiped her eyes and smiled across the yard at the young woman.

They were probably close to the same age and their dispositions were alike in many ways. For a brief moment, Rachel realized how different their relationship would be if she weren't white and Hummingbird weren't Indian.

They probably would be the dearest of friends.

"How are you?" she called as the woman turned to go.

Hummingbird turned back and with a sweet smile she nodded.

"I am well. The baby will come soon."

"And the girls?"

"They are happy and healthy," she said. "Enjoying the first home they've ever really known."

"I'm glad," Rachel said. "Really glad."

It was hours later when she heard footsteps on the landing outside the door. She looked up and saw Trace coming in the doorway.

"We've finished several of the houses and warned everyone about being out at night. We're going to burn the marshy area behind the quarters tonight. Justus has gone out to the village to tell everyone there."

Rachel wiped the back of her hand across her brow.

"What time is it?" she asked wearily.

"Almost noon," he said, stepping closer. "Have you eaten? You look exhausted."

"No, but I will . . . later," she said.

"I think you should come now," he said.

Rachel looked at him with a bit of surprise. Rarely had she heard his voice so gentle or so coaxing. He was a man who tended to give orders rather than ask for something.

"Well . . . I . . ." She glanced at the boys.

"I've already asked someone to stay with them," he said. He walked across the room and the look in his eyes warned her that he would not hear any further protests. "Dimity is preparing a bath for you, then you can eat."

She nodded, a little surprised that he had taken care of everything. She was really too tired and weary to argue with him, and her stomach grumbled hungrily.

"What about you?" she asked.

"I'll eat in the kitchen," he said with a shrug of his broad shoulders.

"You don't have to do that," she said. Her eyes held a self-conscious glint as she frowned at him. "Surely, under the circumstances, we can be civil enough to eat in the same room."

"That's entirely up to you," he said.

Rachel pushed her hair back from her eyes. She was having a hard time believing that this was the same man she had battled with earlier. He was calm . . . passive even, and there was the oddest look in his eyes. Tenderness, she'd have thought, if she didn't know better.

She frowned and shook her head against the feelings he stirred inside her. She had to remind herself that he had betrayed her. He broke her heart into so many pieces that she was certain it would never be the same again. And it had all happened because she was too trusting, too anxious to believe that those looks he gave her really meant what she wanted them to mean. Her mistake had been in believing something that was never there to begin with. And in believing it, she had only fooled herself.

She couldn't afford to let it happen again.

When she answered him her voice was cooler, more thoughtful.

"I have no objections." She brushed past him, going down the steps and toward the house, without giving him a chance to say anything else.

Trace walked out onto the landing and watched her go. If not for his pride, he could have kept his secrets and continued to lie to her about who he was. His heart told him that she would have believed him.

He could have pretended the rest of his life to be fully a

white man. He would have had the plantation, even if it wasn't in his family's name.

And he could have had Rachel, for the rest of his life.

"Sun Killer," he muttered, his eyes stormy. "You are a damned fool."

Twenty-four

The tureen of hearty chicken soup that Cleo placed on the table smelled delicious.

"Cleo," Rachel said, as the woman turned to go. "Have you eaten yet? Why don't you come eat with us? I don't want you getting sick."

"Oh honey, I ain't got time," Cleo said with a wave of her hand. "That Dimity is jes about the puniest little thing I ever seen. I gots to help her turn the mattresses, then I'm goin' to stay with the twins awhile. Might be a good time for you to get some rest."

"All right," Rachel said. She almost laughed at Cleo's look of surprise. She obviously expected an argument. But Rachel knew that she'd probably stay up all night and she wasn't foolish enough to think she could keep this up night and day.

Trace watched her while she ate. She had been so warm and natural with Cleo, and yet, as soon as they were alone, she changed. He could almost feel a wall descending between them. Not that he should expect anything else under the circumstances.

He just couldn't explain why it bothered him so much.

"You don't have to do this, you know," he said.

"Do what?" she asked.

"Take care of the twins every minute. Oversee the housecleaning . . . take care of Cleo and every detail of work on the plantation."

"I see." She wouldn't look at him at all.

"What does that mean?"

"I suppose I should apologize," she said. "I certainly didn't mean to usurp your . . . authority. It's just that I've been taking care of this household for most of my life. It's a little hard to forget that."

"Dammit," he muttered. He put his spoon down and leaned toward her. "That's not what I meant, and you know it."

"Oh? Then exactly what did you mean?"

"I meant . . ." Seeing the stubborn glint in her eyes, Trace shook his head and muttered a quiet curse. He ran his hand over his face and pushed his chair back from the table.

"Hell. Forget it," he said. "Do as you please. Think anything you wish. You will, anyway."

Rachel clamped her lips together as she watched him stalk away from the dining room. The sound of his boots was loud as he went down the hallway and out the back of the house. Her appetite was gone. She sat motionless, her eyes vacant and sad. She felt as if she didn't have enough strength to climb the stairs and go to bed.

She was still sitting there when Dimity came to her with the mail. On the silver tray was a letter with her father's handwriting. It was the first time she'd heard from him since she wrote asking him how he obtained Windridge.

She opened the envelope anxiously and quickly scanned the opening amenities until she reached the part about the house. Her eyes grew dark as she read his words:

"I assure you darling, my possession of the plantation was completely legal. There is nothing new about land grants received from the government. Was I to turn down the president's gift? I am concerned that you ask such questions and am anxious to know where you heard such stories. As to your other questions, I did know that the property was owned by a man of Cherokee blood. As soon as the Senate concludes, I will make my way home to Alabama as quickly as possible so that we might clear up this matter. You may expect me in about a month's time. In the meantime, I hope you and Trace and the household are well. All my love, Father."

A month. She could hardly go to Washington if her father was coming home in a few weeks. But, at the moment, a month seemed like an eternity. She wasn't sure she could bear to be in the same house with Trace for another month.

And yet in her heart, she dreaded the day she would have to leave Windridge for good.

"Rosewood," she murmured, testing the name on her tongue.

But it was only because it was her home that she hated to go. Her sadness had nothing to do with Trace Hambleton—or whatever his name was. She despised him for what he had done to her.

Rachel went up to her room and collapsed onto the bed. She didn't expect to sleep, not with all the thoughts running through her mind. But she was surprised when she woke later to find it was almost dark.

She hurried downstairs and saw Dimity clearing supper dishes from the table.

"Oh . . . Miss Rachel. Mr. Hambleton done ate. You want I should leave these for you?"

"No, Dimity. That's all right—I'll get something later. Where is Mr. Hambleton?"

"Oh he gone out to the quarters. He say they gonna start burnin' the marsh soon as it's good and dark."

When Rachel reached the twins' room, she found Cleo there, sitting near Jim's bed and changing the cool cloth on his forehead.

"How is he?" She didn't know why she asked. She could hear the sound of the boy's labored breathing as soon as she walked through the doorway.

Cleo shook her head.

Rachel walked across the room to Jared's bed. He seemed to have lapsed into the same state of unconsciousness that Jim had been in since the beginning.

Rachel moaned and changed the cold compress on his head.

"Oh, Cleo," she said. "What are we going to do?"

"We gonna pray," Cleo said. "The hoo-doo man say we gots to sacrifice somethin'. He gonna throw a gris gris charm into the marsh fires tonight."

Rachel clamped her teeth together and pretended not to hear. Cleo knew perfectly well how she felt about such nonsense. But if she believed it and if it made her feel better, then she would not argue about it.

Rachel walked to the window. From here she could see the glow of the fire in the marsh and the silhouette of men moving back and forth.

Trace was there. Working on land that was as familiar to him as it was to her—and just as precious. That seemed odd somehow, even a bit comforting. If she had to give up her beloved land, at least it would be to someone who loved it too.

It was a long night. A terrible dark night filled with the sound of Jim's breathing. It rattled in his throat and chest with agonized labor. By morning, Rachel wasn't sure how the frail little boy's heart continued to beat.

When the rattling sound of his breathing stopped suddenly, the room was completely quiet. And then the sound of Cleo's wails filled the air.

"Oh, Lordy," she cried over and over again. She fell against Jim's still body, then raised herself up again, throwing her arms into the air as she grieved.

Rachel was crying, too, as much for her Mama Cleo as for the boy. At least Jim's suffering was at an end, while theirs had to continue.

"Mama Cleo," she whispered, going to her and touching her trembling shoulders. "Oh sweetie, don't grieve so. You're breaking my heart," she cried. She felt Cleo's hands clasp hers and both of them cried together.

"We . . . we have Jared to think of now," Rachel said when she finally stopped crying.

"Yes . . . you right," Cleo said with a sniff. She took a

handkerchief out of her apron and blew her nose. Her gaze moved across the room to the other bed. Then with more sobs, she pulled the sheet over Jim's face and stood up.

"Jared gonna want to go with his brother," Cleo declared. "When he finds out, he gonna want to go, too. You know he never went nowhere or did nothin' without Jim bein' right there with him."

"Then we won't tell him," Rachel said, her voice steady. "Do you hear me, Cleo . . . we mustn't tell Jared what's happened to his brother. Not a word of it."

"He gonna have to know sooner or later."

When Cleo was so pragmatic, Rachel wanted to shake her. Part of it was the voodoo culture, instilled in her from childhood. And part of it was simply Cleo's practical nature.

"Well, he doesn't have to know now," Rachel said. "Cleo, we'd better send someone out to the quarters where the fires are, to tell Justus what's happened. And tell him if he wants to speak to his other brother, he'd better hurry."

She could hear Cleo's sobs as she left the room.

In truth, Rachel wanted to cry, too. She wanted to fall onto the floor and rant against fate for taking this poor sweet little boy from them. But there wasn't time. Jared needed her now, more than ever.

Trace was with Justus when he came. The scent of smoke that clung to them quickly filled the room. Rachel stood with Trace while Justus went to Jim and turned back the covers. He cried like a child, holding his little brother's hand and rocking back and forth in grief.

It was Trace who finally stepped to him and quieted him. He waited beside Justus until he seemed ready to part with his dead brother, then he walked with him toward the door. As they passed Rachel, Trace touched her shoulder and whispered quietly to her.

"I'll see to a coffin and the burial. Are you all right?"

"Yes," she said. "Just tired. Trace . . . I'd like Jim buried in the family cemetery, not in the quarters. Next to my mother . . . if Justus has no objections."

Trace only nodded his agreement. He could feel the grief emanating from Rachel, although outwardly she appeared calm.

"Don't worry," he whispered. "You stay here . . . take care of your family. I'll see to Jim's burial. When this is over, we'll call the pastor and have a ceremony, if you like."

"Thank you," she said.

Several times during that day Rachel thought they would lose Jared, too. He seemed to stop breathing at times, then he would rally.

After seeing to Jim's burial, Justus had come back and he hadn't left Jared's side. When Rachel went to eat supper at Trace and Cleo's insistence, Justus was asleep in a chair beside Jared's bed. When she came back, he was still sleeping. Cleo was kneeling at the side of the bed, and for a instant Rachel's breath caught in her throat.

When she saw the subtle rise and fall of Jared's chest, she breathed a sigh of relief. But the moment had left her so weak and shaken that she steadied herself against the doorframe. It was then she heard Cleo's muttered words.

"Take this old woman, Jesus," she said. "If'n someone in this house gots to die, jes take this old woman. This boy is young and one of our brightest. He could do some great good for our people, Lord. I always said he gonna be somebody, and he got a chance here with Miss Rachel and Mr. Trace. Don't take him now—jes take me, instead."

Rachel's blood ran cold when she heard the words. Nonsense or not, what Cleo was doing frightened her beyond words. Rachel had seen and heard for herself how Cleo's prayers were usually answered. All her life, Cleo's faith had been a comfort to everyone, especially Rachel. Rachel's childhood fears always seemed to vanish once Cleo said that she'd pray about it. And hearing what she asked for now, Rachel felt shivers crawl over her flesh.

"Cleo," she whispered as she walked to the bed. "Don't do this." She reached beneath the woman's arm and tried to lift her from her knees, but Cleo pulled away, her eyes sparking with disapproval.

"Leave me be," she said.

"I won't. You get up this instant and stop saying these things." Finally, seeing Cleo was not going to budge, Rachel fell on her knees beside the woman who had raised her from childhood.

"Mama Cleo," she whispered tiredly, looking into the woman's grief stricken eyes. "I want Jared to live, too. But I don't want to lose you, either. Do you hear me? You have been like a mother to me and I love you. Please . . . don't do this."

"Child," Cleo said softly. Her eyes sparkled with tears and her look was as gentle as Rachel had ever seen it. "I know you do. I know that. But I'm an old woman now."

Rachel muttered a soft disavowal, but Cleo stopped her.

"Listen now. Jes cause I asked it don't mean He gonna say yes. Don't mean I'm goin' nowhere," she assured Rachel. "But I gots to ask, don't you see? I can't let this little boy die, too. I gots to offer something in return for his life."

Rachel sighed and sank back onto the floor. It was no use talking to Cleo once she'd made up her mind about something.

"All right," she sighed. "All right, Mama Cleo. Whatever you say."

"Besides," Cleo continued with a soft smile. "You gots Mr. Trace now. You two gonna have a fine life, whether I'm here or not. I know how much you love him. I can see it in your eyes. And he loves you, too."

Rachel felt a tingle race through her and she stared hard at Cleo.

"Why do you say that?"

"What? That he loves you? Well, Lordy child, anyone with eyes and half a mind can see that. Don't he always come and fetch you when its time to eat? Don't he ask Dimity to fill your bath and make you rest? And when you be sleepin' I seen him tiptoe into your room to see if you're all right and cover you up when you're cold. If that ain't love, then I don't know what is."

Rachel bit her lip. She wished it were as simple as Cleo made it out to be.

Dear God, how she wished it were that simple.

Twenty-five

By morning, Jared seemed to have passed the crisis. He opened his eyes, recognizing all of them. But he was still very sick. Too sick to ask about his brother, which Cleo declared was a blessing.

But they hardly had time for elation before Lula came to tell them that Dimity had also taken ill.

"Her fever so high, she be talkin' out of her head," Lula said, her eyes wide with fear.

"Oh no," Rachel said.

The next few days were long, bone weary days spent going from Jared to Dimity's room in the big house. The fever had also spread to the quarters despite all their precautions.

Jared was sitting up in bed, being fed broth when Rachel came in. The first thing she noticed was the sheen of perspiration on Cleo's face.

When she placed her hand against Cleo's brow, her heart began to beat rapidly.

"My God, Mama Cleo . . . you're burning up. It's too hot in here, that's all it is." She turned to Justus who had just come in with a fresh bucket of water. "Justus, leave the door open." But she was shaking and afraid. She knew with a dark dread that it wasn't the heat.

When she looked back into Cleo's eyes, she saw a look that terrorized her. It was a quiet, peaceful look of resignation.

"It's just the heat," Rachel repeated.

"The Lawd has answered my prayer," Cleo said quietly. "You've only to look at the boy to see what's happenin'."

"No," Rachel cried "No, do you hear me . . . no!"

"Child," Cleo said with a smile.

"Justus, find Mr. Hambleton. Tell him I need him."

When Trace came, he looked concerned as he glanced toward the bed. When he saw that Jared was all right, he frowned and stopped.

Rachel jumped up and ran to him.

"Trace," she said, her voice quivering with anxiety. "Mama Cleo is sick. I'm afraid it's the fever. You have to send someone for the doctor. Please, Trace . . ."

"Angel . . ." he said almost beneath his breath. "Calm down." He turned to Justus who was already heading for the door.

"I get the doctor, Mr. Trace," he said.

Trace ran his hands down Rachel's arms and touched the back of his hand lightly to her brow. He frowned into her eyes.

"I'm not sick," she said. "It's Cleo."

"Just let me be, Mr. Trace," Cleo said. "The Lawd gonna take me in his own sweet time. Might as well be settin' here tendin' to this little boy as layin' in bed waitin'."

Trace heard Rachel's quiet sob and saw the distress in her eyes. Jared also seemed afraid, though he was too weak to say anything. Trace stepped to the bed and placed his hand gently under Cleo's elbow.

"Mama Cleo," he said. "Let's get you to your room. Rachel will feel better if you rest. Besides . . ." He nodded toward Jared's wide eyed stare. ". . . you don't want to alarm the boy."

Cleo frowned and looked at Jared.

"Why, no sir, I shorely didn't intend to do that," she admitted.

"Well, then?" Trace lifted his brows and nodded to her, urging her silently to go with him.

Cleo placed the bowl of broth on a table and she bent toward Jared, enveloping him in a massive embrace.

"God love you boy," she said, tears sparkling in her eyes. "You gonna be all right. You hear? Now I want you to promise Mama Cleo that you will learn a trade and that you'll be a good boy for Miss Rachel and Mr. Trace."

Jared hardly seemed to know what was happening. That much was apparent in his uneasy glances at Trace and Rachel. But, as if he sensed it were a very serious moment, he nodded and placed his thin arms around Mama Cleo.

"I will," he said.

With a loud sniff, Mama Cleo stood up and walked out the door. She patted Rachel's face as she passed.

"I can see my own self to my room," she said.

Trace walked outside to stand beside Rachel.

"What in the world was that all about?"

Rachel told him quickly about Cleo's prayers and her offer to sacrifice herself for the boy. She had expected Trace to understand her concern, to laugh even and agree that it was a ridiculous notion. She wanted him to tell her not to worry. Instead, his eyes grew distant and he frowned.

"Trace . . ." Rachel said. "You . . . you don't believe in such superstition do you? Please, tell me you don't."

"Rachel, listen to me." He took her shoulders and held her steady as he looked into her eyes. "Whether you choose to believe it or not is immaterial. It's what Cleo believes that matters. With my own people, I've seen old men and women will themselves to die when they think they're no longer useful."

"But Cleo *is* useful. I love her! She's like a mother to me. She can't die, Trace. Not like this . . . not because she wills herself to die, or because of some crazy idea that she's sacrificing her life for Jared's. She can't. I won't let her."

Her fingers had clamped about his wrists and she held onto him as if she might die if she let him go.

"Angel . . ."

Rachel heard the tenderness in his voice. Somewhere in the back of her mind, she knew it was the second time he had called her by that name in the last half hour. But she was too distraught to even wonder about why he'd said it or if it had any real significance.

"It might not be up to you," Trace said, his voice soft with sympathy.

"No, I can't accept that." Rachel was shivering, shaking her head against his words and against the terrible fear in her heart.

"Look, let's go make sure Cleo is in bed. The doctor will be here soon, and if it is the fever, perhaps it's early enough to . . ."

He couldn't finish—he couldn't lie to her anymore. Not about something as important to her as this. There'd been too much deceit between them already.

"I promise you," he said steadily. "I promise I'll help you. We'll do everything we can to make her want to live. All right?"

Rachel could only nod. She was so tired . . . so completely exhausted by all that had happened.

Cleo died three days later. Peacefully, smiling at Rachel, and holding her hand until the last.

Rachel had been so strong until that moment when she realized that her precious Mama Cleo was gone. Since the very beginning—from Jim's death and Jared's miraculous recovery, and when four children had died in the quarters and many others became ill—Rachel had held on. Even when the doctor had said that, though Dimity would recover, she was so weak that she might never be the same.

But with Cleo's death, Rachel's strength finally deserted her. When she collapsed, Trace was there, catching her in his arms and carrying her with great tenderness to her room and placing her on the bed.

Beneath his breath, he alternately cursed and prayed, touching her over and over again to make sure she didn't have the fever, too. He quickly stripped off her clothes and threw them into a heap outside in the hallway. He bathed her tenderly, like she was a child, and covered her with freshly laundered sheets. He left a lamp burning and stepped out into the hall to find one of the servants.

"Take these clothes and burn them, along with every piece of linen in Mama Cleo's room. Then ask Justus to have Marshall and Mr. Copeland at the cabinetry shop fashion a fine coffin of cherry wood for Miss Cleo, even if it takes all night. It was the only thing she asked for."

"Yessir," the young man said.

When Trace stepped back into the dimly lit bedroom, Rachel was still sleeping. Her exhaustion had finally caught up with her.

Trace regretted that it was necessary to bury Mama Cleo so quickly and with such apparent coldness. But it couldn't be helped. Only one more reason for his beautiful wife to resent him, he supposed.

But his concern now was for Rachel's health. That was all that mattered to him. He sat beside her, his eyes watchful and dark. By morning, she was still sleeping, although she had stirred several times in the night and called out in her sleep.

When the doctor came early that morning and examined her, he turned to Trace with a weak smile.

"It's not the fever," he declared. "Just pure exhaustion, I'd say. She needs rest and nourishment. I can actually feel her bones through her skin."

Trace nodded, his look solemn.

"I'll see to it."

"I'll leave some laudanum in case she needs it for rest later. She's going to be pretty upset about Miss Cleo. That old woman was everything to Rachel."

"I know."

Trace had expected Rachel to cry or even to be angry when she woke. Instead, she was oddly quiet and passive, her beautiful blue eyes lifeless and dull.

He told her as gently as he could about the necessity of having Cleo's funeral quickly.

"So . . . it's already done?" she asked.

"Yes."

"Did you bury her with Mother and Jim?"

"Yes, we did," Trace replied.

Rachel nodded, but her thoughts seemed to be elsewhere.

Her frailty touched Trace as nothing or no one had in years. He wanted to hold her, to gather her close to him and hold her until that terrible pained look in her eyes disappeared. But he was helpless. He could do nothing to ease her pain.

Even days later when she was up and about and when she was regaining some of the strength and weight she had lost, she still seemed consumed with grief. There was a quiet, haunted look in her eyes, as if she had lost everything that was important to her.

Trace felt guilt ridden, blaming himself for his part in her grief. If he hadn't betrayed her, hadn't shaken the very foundation of her beliefs and security, she might not have taken Cleo's death quite so hard. Yet nothing he said or did seemed to matter to her. She would only look at him, her eyes lifeless as though she didn't even hate him anymore.

And he hated himself more.

Twenty-six

It was late when Trace came in from the fields, but it had been a glorious summer day and the sun was still visible through the line of trees to the west. The roof of the house and the outbuildings were cast in gold and long streaks of light mingled with cool shadows across the lawn.

No sickness had occured in the quarters or the big house for three days, and Trace was convinced that the fever had finally run its course. He should have felt some elation, yet every time he walked into the beautiful house and found it quiet and still, the pleasure seemed to vanish from his very soul.

He met Dimity in the hallway.

"You're looking well, Dimity," he said. "How are you feeling?"

"Feelin' fine," she said with a dip of her knees.

"Where's Miss Rachel?" he asked.

"She done gone to bed," Dimity said, motioning toward the upper floor.

Trace gave a quiet grunt of frustration and bounded up the stairs two at a time.

He understood that Rachel was still grieving for Cleo. But she should be awake, filling the house with her warmth and light. She should let her laughter spill into the hallways and out the open windows as she bantered with Dimity and the other house servants.

She was like no one he'd ever known. Her outward beauty

belied an inner strength that he could only marvel at. In her absence, he had also discovered that he missed her.

Trace stood outside the door, allowing that thought to sink into his brain. He frowned as he reached out and slowly turned the doorknob, and let himself into Rachel's darkened bedroom.

Thin slivers of sunlight managed to find their way past the drawn curtains, falling across the floor and the foot of the bed. In the light, small particles danced in the still air over the bed, like fairy dust sprinkled over a slumbering princess.

Rachel was sleeping peacefully, her skin looking very pale in the dim light, her auburn hair resting against one hand that lay beneath her cheek. Trace noted a slight frown on her beautiful face.

Trace's eyes were troubled as he stood watching the woman whose ivory skin was gilded by the soft afternoon sunlight. She seemed unreal . . . too beautiful to be a living, breathing woman.

But she was real. And she was here, so close and yet so very far from his reach. Every long night without sleep reminded him of that with great clarity.

It had been weeks since he'd left this room and her bed. His eyes were not privy to this sight anymore. He let his gaze take in every luscious curve, every line of her face, like a man too long without life-giving water. Her long dark eyelashes closed out her innermost thoughts to him and made him want to wake her.

But he knew all too well what he'd see in those eyes if he did.

He had accomplished his goal, the possession of Rosewood, with swiftness and surety. It would have taken much longer without Rachel. Trace still found it hard to believe that she had so willingly handed over the deeds to the plantation—as willingly as she had given him her body.

At first, he had reasoned that she was only the senator's daughter, a spoiled little rich girl, as deserving of punishment as her father.

This guilt he was experiencing now made him confused. He could feel his chest tightening. With a quietly muttered curse, he turned away from the bed and walked to the window. For the first time in years, he was feeling remorse for something he'd done. And he was realizing that he might have been wrong in his methods.

He had used her—swiftly and with no thought for tomorrow. And when she had come to him so eagerly, he had reasoned that it was all right. His deceit was necessary, after all, for her benefit as well as his.

Trace shook his head.

He turned back toward the bed, the muscles in his jaw working as he became more troubled, more guilt ridden. It was his fault that the spark had gone out of her, his fault that the house no longer rang with her laughter, or was warm with happiness.

He had his house and his land, but that was all he had.

Trace caught his breath and moved back to the bed.

Carefully, he lifted a strand of her hair, watching as it curled around his finger—almost as if it had a life of its own. He shuddered and took a deep breath. Then he let his hand move toward her bare shoulder, tracing the outline of her delicate bones with the tip of his fingers.

Rachel's eyes flew open and she gasped, then sat up in bed, pushing herself away from him as if he were some evil entity come to possess her.

"What . . . what are you doing?" she asked.

In the dimness, he couldn't see her eyes clearly. But he could hear the distrust in her voice.

Dear God, that was the last thing he wanted her to feel.

His first instinct was to gather her into his arms, hold her against her will, if necessary, until she realized that he had no ulterior motive for being here.

He pushed that instinct away and put his hands at his hips. Where they couldn't reach for her. Touch her.

"Get dressed," he said. "We're going for a carriage ride."

"What?" Her voice was sleepy and now she rubbed her

fingers against her eyes. "I'm not going anywhere with you," she muttered. "I'm sleepy . . . just leave me alone." She scooted back down beneath the sheets and turned her back on him.

Trace frowned and stepped to the bed.

"Why are you so sleepy at this time of day?" His gaze fell onto the bedside table where a dark green bottle sat on a silver tray. He picked up the bottle, and held it toward the light from the windows.

"How much of this have you taken today?" he asked, his voice harsh and demanding.

Rachel turned over slowly and pushed herself back up in the bed. She brushed her hair out of her face and stared at him through languid, dazed eyes.

"As much as I needed," she answered sullenly. "Why do you care?"

Trace ground his teeth together. His hand clenched around the bottle as if he might crush it.

"My God," he muttered angrily. Without another word he marched to the window and pushed it open.

Rachel shrieked as she watched him turn the bottle up and pour the contents out the window.

"Stop," she cried, stumbling from bed and across the room. "What are you doing?"

"Is there any more?" he demanded, his voice cold.

She stood looking at him as if he'd lost his mind. She looked like a wild little wraith, standing there in her crumpled cotton gown, with her hair tumbled about her face and shoulders. Her eyes were crazed but she was wide awake now.

"Answer me, Rachel," he growled. "The doctor left one bottle of laudanum. Is this it? Or have you sent for more?"

Rachel had seen anger on his face before. But she thought she'd never seen such a look as the one she saw now.

He was frightening. His skin had grown dark from working in the sun. His black eyes bored into her, and his long sun-gilded hair made him look like some primitive warrior come to do battle.

"I . . . no, there's no more," she replied stiffly.

"If you're lying to me . . ."

"I'm not lying, damn you," she said. She whirled away from him and marched across the room.

He watched her climb into bed. She looked like a small, petulant child.

"Get out of my room."

"You're going to get dressed," he said, moving steadily toward the bed. All the while, his eyes did not leave her face. "And we're going for a ride in the fresh evening air. Then we're going to have a nice, pleasant dinner in the dining room."

"I'm not hungry. And I'm hardly able to go for a ride."

"You are able and you will go—even if I have to drag you out of that bed and dress you myself."

Her eyes grew wide and she seemed to be holding her breath.

"You wouldn't do that."

Trace's body relaxed. His eyebrows lifted and a slow smile moved, almost imperceptibly, over his sensual lips.

Rachel's eyes blinked and she bit her lower lip to keep from screaming at him.

"I hate you," she said finally. There were glints of tears in her eyes.

"Good. Now, shall I send Dimity to help you dress? Or . . . would you prefer your husband's help?"

Rachel wasn't sure which infuriated her most, his sarcasm or his amusement.

"Damn you," she muttered.

Trace stepped toward the bed and Rachel pulled the covers up to her chin, her eyes warning him not to come any closer.

"All right, all right," she said. One slender white hand moved from beneath the sheet and pointed toward the door. "Send Dimity to help me."

"I'll bring the carriage around to the front in fifteen minutes. If you're not there, I will come back up here and carry you out myself. I don't care what state of dress . . . or undress you're in." He let his gaze move slowly over her face and down to the curve of her body hidden beneath the sheets.

Rachel's eyes darkened and she lifted her chin, challenging him with a look that told him all too well what she thought of his threat.

When he went into the hall and closed the door, he heard her voice, muffled and angry, then a loud thump on the wooden panel of the door behind him.

He smiled and for the first time in weeks, his dark eyes sparkled with pleasure.

She was waiting on the steps of the front porch when he drove the carriage around the drive. Trace let his gaze rest on her before he got out of the carriage, and later, as he threw the reins over a nearby shrub, he glanced from beneath his brows at her.

Her hair was tied back with a ribbon, more casually than her usual style, and beneath a simple filmy cotton day dress, she wore no layers of stiff petticoats, and obviously, no corset.

There was no artifice, no applied rouges or lip color. And yet, he thought she looked more beautiful than ever, as ethereal as an angel. For a moment he was tempted to walk up those steps, pick her up in his arms and carry her out to the carriage.

But, as if she sensed his innermost thoughts, she hurried down the steps and got into the carriage without waiting for him to assist her. She sat stiffly, looking straight ahead, chin lifted, lips pressed into a thin, disapproving line as she waited for him to untie the horse and get back into the carriage.

As they moved out the drive, Rachel still sat silently, staring straight ahead. It was almost dusk and only a faint glimmer of gold remained in the sky and on the highest tops of the trees.

The day's wind had died down until now there was a calmness, a peace that for one moment, reminded Trace of all the other days like this in the past. He remembered those moments when his father had come in from the fields, and his mother would be seeing to last minute details before dinner—perfect days that brought a security and contentment Trace thought never to experience again.

And yet today, with Rachel beside him, he felt that peace, if only for a moment.

"Where are we going?" Rachel asked. There was still a hint of resistance and stubbornness on her face.

"To the cemetery."

Her eyes changed. She looked toward him like a stricken, helpless doe, pleading and fearful.

"No," she cried. She reached for his hand upon the rein, as if for a moment she contemplated pulling the horse to a stop.

"All right," he whispered, seeing her agitation. He pulled the carriage to a stop at the side of the road.

"Please, Trace," she said breathlessly. "I'm not . . . I can't do this . . . not yet. Don't make me go there."

Trace took a deep breath, wanting to be very careful about the words he chose.

"Rachel, you haven't been since Cleo died."

"I know . . . I know, but I—"

"Look," he said. "I thought it would be good for you to get out of that house. To breathe some fresh air and hear the birds . . . watch the sun go down. And at the same time, I thought it might be easier to come here if you weren't alone." He hesitated for a moment, gazing at her face.

She held her hands tightly in her lap. Her head was bent, her face very pale as she sat trembling with dread.

"For many years . . ." he began quietly. ". . . All those years of not knowing where my father was buried ate away at me. As hard as I tried, I couldn't remember everything about Rosewood." His voice was soft, his eyes distant as his gaze took in the land that was so familiar, and yet so new. "And I couldn't visualize him anywhere." He turned to look at her. "You can't imagine the relief . . . the peace I had when I knew

I'd found him at last. And when I buried my mother's brooch in the same ground where he lay, I knew I could put it behind me finally."

Rachel shuddered as a quiet sob seemed to come from her very soul. She looked up at last and turned to meet his troubled gaze.

"Do you understand what I'm trying to say?" he asked. His brow wrinkled, his gaze intense as he looked into her eyes. "Sometimes we have to accept the pain in order to ever feel happiness again."

Tears streamed down Rachel's face.

She nodded.

"Cleo's gone, Angel. You need to say goodbye."

Again Rachel nodded, but she continued to tremble.

"I would never make you do something you don't want to do. But I think—"

Rachel turned quickly, the look of devastation in her eyes stopping his words.

"You made me love you," she whispered, her eyes stricken. "You made me feel all the peace and security in that love that a woman could ever experience and then you wrenched it away from me without a moment's hesitation."

All the breath seemed to leave Trace's lungs. For a moment, he couldn't speak and couldn't breathe as he gazed into those tortured eyes.

"No . . . Rachel . . ." he whispered. He bent toward her, wanting more than anything in the world to explain. Yet he wasn't sure that he understood himself all the driving forces behind his need for revenge.

And now, looking at her, he couldn't believe that anything in the world was worth the look of anguish he'd seen in those beautiful eyes.

With a cry, Rachel turned in the seat, then leapt down from the carriage, gathering her skirts about her and ran across the grass toward the cemetery.

Trace cursed quietly as he watched her go. But he didn't try to stop her or call out to her.

Wearily he picked up the reins and drove the carriage around the road toward the cemetery. He watched her from the carriage, when every fiber in his body screamed to go to her.

But he knew she wouldn't welcome him—not now and not here.

Silently, he watched her at Cleo's grave, her slender shoulders trembling with grief. His eyes burned from staring so hard, from watching for any tiny, telling movement that would be a sign he should go to her.

The sun set behind the trees at last, leaving the earth dark and immeasurably cooler. Insects began to stir in the grass and trees and just when Trace was thinking of going into the cemetery after Rachel, he saw the white blur of her dress as she came toward him.

When she got back into the carriage, it was too dark for him to see her face. But he could sense that she was as stiff and unyielding as before. The only difference was she was no longer crying or trembling from grief.

"Thank you," she said.

Her voice was as cool and polite as that of a stranger.

Twenty-seven

It was very late, probably after midnight, and still Trace lay awake in the cramped little room. It was too hot and he seemed to hear every creak, every sound in the big house that night.

A few moments earlier he'd heard someone talking in the yard near the kitchen. Then he thought he heard a bump, as if a door opened and closed. And now he heard footsteps in the hall. He was just about to get up and investigate when his door opened.

Rachel stood there holding a small lamp. The light from the hallway turned her hair into a gossamer cloud about her head.

Trace sat up in bed.

"Rachel . . . what is it? Is something wrong?"

For a second, Rachel found it hard to breathe, much less speak. The light from the hallway spilled across Trace's bed, illuminating his face and body. His long naked frame was covered only by a corner of the sheet. His hair fell, straight and silky, down his back.

The light from the doorway glinted on leanly muscled arms and chest. His skin was smooth and dark, and the sight of his bare muscular thighs against the white of the bed made Rachel long to touch him.

She had called him savage. But he was like a chieftain, primitive and beautiful. And sometimes, when he appeared so arrogant and overbearing, he was all those things. But he was more than that. He was the man she had loved and married. The man she had hoped to spend the rest of her life with.

"Rachel?" he repeated.

"I . . . it's Hummingbird," she said quietly. "Her time has come and White Feather asked that you wait with him."

"I'll be right there." He swung his legs over the bed, seemingly without modesty and unaware of his nakedness. Rachel spun away from the doorway and from the vision of his strong muscular body. The same body she had held, clung to, moved with during those nights of passion when she had discovered what it was like to love a man.

She still loved him. God help her, but in her heart she still loved him and longed to feel his arms around her, longed to see the look of bitterness in those black eyes vanish.

She'd seen tenderness in his eyes before. He couldn't deny that it had been there during those terrible heart wrenching nights when he had stood in Jim and Jared's room. His helplessness and frustration showed on his face. Then he looked after her on days when she was bone tired, too tired to eat and he looked across the dining room table at her and urged her with those expressive eyes to do just that.

And when Cleo died—how sweetly and tenderly he had scooped her up and carried her to her room. She remembered it even though he might have thought she did not. And when he had insisted that she go to Cleo's grave to help end her terrible grieving. She might accuse him of being dictatorial, of being hard and overbearing. But she felt in her heart that he was not that way at all.

Rachel took a deep shuddering breath and hurried down the stairs. She couldn't think about this now. Hummingbird needed her, and that was all she could let her mind worry about.

Lula was already there when Rachel arrived. Dimity, now completely recovered from the fever, had taken the children into the kitchen and made beds for them in the pantry where they'd be near the cooks and wouldn't feel afraid.

It was moments like these that Rachel missed Cleo most of all—when the entire household came together. It seemed that Mama Cleo should be here, giving orders and being her loving self.

White Feather was in the bedroom with Hummingbird, holding her hand as he knelt beside the bed. Rachel saw the look of worry on his face.

When Lula turned and flapped her hands toward him, shooing him away like a wayward chick, Rachel smiled.

"She's right you know," Rachel said. "Trace is on his way. Perhaps you and he might have breakfast together while you wait."

White Feather bent toward his wife, looking into her dark, pain-filled eyes. She managed a smile and reached up to touch his face.

"Go," she said. "I will be fine. When our new son is born, they will send for you."

White Feather smiled wistfully and held her hand against his lips. "You have always been so certain it will be a boy. How can you know such things?"

"Because it is what you wish, is it not? Have I not always given you everything you asked for, husband?"

Lula, who stood listening with her hands on her wide hips, gave a low grunt of humor.

"Lordy, Lordy," she said, turning to gather up clean cloths. "I sho do wish it was that easy, don't you, missy?" She rolled her eyes toward Rachel, who smiled.

White Feather kissed his wife and left the room.

Rachel went to take his place, holding Hummingbird's hand and looking into her eyes. From the pain she saw on the young woman's face, she thought it must have taken sheer willpower for her to smile and reassure her husband earlier.

Her grip on Rachel's hand was numbing. The strength in the small hand surprised Rachel.

"Lula," Rachel said, looking over her shoulder. "She's in terrible pain. What shall I do?"

"Jes hold onto her. Ain't nothin' else to be done 'cept that." Lula placed her hands on Hummingbird's stomach and when the woman groaned and writhed, Lula nodded as if her question had been answered.

"Comin' soon," she said to the laboring woman. "Third baby always comes quick," she added with a knowing shake of her head.

Hummingbird was gasping for breath and her skin shimmered with perspiration. Yet she managed an answering nod and there was a look of determination and satisfaction in her eyes.

It was the first time Rachel had ever witnessed a human birth. There had been many children born in the quarters, and of course, she remembered when Jim and Jared were born. But as much as she had begged and pleaded to see what was going on, Cleo had not allowed it. She'd declared it not fitting for a young, unmarried girl to witness such things.

As Rachel sat holding Hummingbird's hand and trying to reassure her, she thought of Trace and her own dream when she married him, of one day having his children. Beautiful dark skinned children with black eyes and a smile that would melt a mother's heart.

She'd often wondered if a man could still find his wife beautiful and desirable when her stomach was large with child. Would he still love her and want her the same way again.

Seeing White Feather and Hummingbird had answered that question for her. The way he had looked at his wife made Rachel's throat tighter, until she actually ached with longing to know and to have such love.

Rachel shook her head against such thoughts. It didn't matter. That dream of having Trace's children would never come true now.

It was just over an hour before Hummingbird's pains began to come in one long continuous surge. She clenched her teeth against the pain, gripping Rachel's hand so fiercely that Rachel was certain her fingers would break. The young woman writhed in the bed, digging her heels into the mattress.

When the time came, Lula stood at the foot of the bed,

ready to deliver the child. Suddenly, Hummingbird let go of Rachel's hands and threw her arms above her head to grasp onto the bed frame. Her eyes rolled back in her head and she could no longer contain the scream that seemed to come from the deepest core of her body.

Rachel stood up, her eyes wide with fear and sympathy. She'd never felt so helpless in all her life. Nothing she could do or say seemed to make a difference to the struggling woman. The only thing that would stop this pain was the child's entry into the world.

"Get one o' them blankets ready," Lula said to Rachel.

Rachel stood holding the blanket. Hummingbird screamed several times and just when Rachel was convinced that the young woman could stand no more, she saw Lula reach down to grasp the baby's head and help guide it from the mother's body. With hardly a glance at Rachel, Lula placed the child in the blanket that she held, then bent to tie the umbilical cord.

The child, a little boy, wasn't moving or breathing.

"Turn him over," Lula urged, though her hands were still busy with Hummingbird. "Make sure ain't nothin' in his little mouth. Give him a swat on the bottom."

Rachel was trembling, but she did as Lula instructed. She thought her heart might actually stop beating, she was so frightened.

As soon as she cleared the child's mouth and turned him over, he began to cry. His loud, lusty cries filled the small room and brought a smile and a sigh from Hummingbird.

"You was right, Miss Hummin'bird," Lula said, reaching toward Rachel for the baby. "Got that handsome husband o' yours a fine baby boy."

They heard footsteps coming toward the bedroom and Lula called to White Feather at the door.

"Now you wait jes a minute there. We ain't through in here yet. You just march yoself right back outside til we calls you."

Hummingbird looked past Rachel and Lula, smiling toward her husband.

"It's a boy," she whispered, her voice weak. "We have a son."

"Go on now," Lula urged. "Git."

White Feather backed reluctantly out of the room and when Hummingbird closed her eyes, there were traces of tears on her lashes.

Later, when the sheets were changed and mother and child were dressed in clean white cotton gowns, Lula turned toward the bed with a tired groan.

"Well now, that wasn't so bad was it?"

"Thank you, ma'am," Hummingbird said. She held her son tenderly in the crook of her arm and now she gazed down at him and touched a finger to his tiny nose and mouth.

"Why chile, you don't have to thank me. You be part of our family now, and we take care of family here at Windridge, ain't that right, Miss Rachel?"

"That's right," Rachel said.

"Now," Lula said with a huff. "Guess I better let that husband o' yours in before he works hisself into a lather. He probably done wore a path in the ground outside where he been pacin'." She laughed as she moved toward the door. "I'll come back later and see if you need anything," she said.

When White Feather came in, Trace accompanied him. Rachel stood away from the bed and watched with a bemused smile when Hummingbird handed her son up to her husband.

White Feather turned toward Trace and there was much pride in his voice when he spoke.

"See cousin . . . a son. Together, we will teach him the old ways, the language and the pride of our people."

Trace nodded solemnly as he gazed at the child.

Rachel watched him carefully, studying every expression on his handsome face. She was hardly able to look away from him when he reached forward and touched the baby's hand with one finger. His large hand dwarfed the tiny child's and yet Trace's touch was soft and gentle, his entire attitude one of awe and reverence.

Just then, Trace looked up from the baby and across the room straight into Rachel's eyes. Her heart seemed to stop when she met his eyes and saw his look.

There was such sadness there, such regret that for a moment she thought he'd seen something wrong with the child that they hadn't yet seen. But then, with a jolt that shook her and made her tremble, she understood all that was expressed in his tender look.

He was experiencing the same sadness that she had been feeling earlier. The same regret that they would never have children together. She knew it as surely as if he had spoken the words aloud.

Rachel managed to pull her gaze away from his. Then, with a quiet murmur of apology, she turned and left the room.

Twenty-eight

For the next few days, there was an unspoken truce between Trace and Rachel. With the birth of Hummingbird's child, Rachel seemed to return somewhat to her old self. She blossomed beneath the summer sun, helping Dimity and the others as they busily gathered food from the garden and preserved it for winter.

Trace would sometimes see her in the garden, gathering baskets of strawberries. Other times, her arms would be filled with fragrant flower bouquets. He was amazed and pleased that, despite all she'd been through, her face held a quiet contentment and pleasure.

She loved being outdoors and, though Lula often chided her for burning her delicate ivory skin, Rachel couldn't seem to resist.

"Let her go," Trace told Lula one day as they watched Rachel hurry toward the garden. "She's happy there."

Lula clamped her lips together and cast her eyes toward Dimity with a wry smile. Both of them watched Trace as his gaze followed his beautiful young wife.

Over the past few weeks it had become a habit for Rachel to spend her afternoons with Hummingbird. The baby would sleep peacefully in a cradle between them on the porch while their hands were busy with sewing.

Rachel taught Hummingbird the intricate embroidery stitches that she had learned as a little girl. And, in return,

Hummingbird taught Rachel how to weave beads and feathers into soft leather garments and winter boots.

Every day before dinner, after the day's work was done, White Feather and Trace would stop by the porch. And in those moments there was no awkwardness and even moments of laughter.

They would sip lemonade and talk about the crops or cotton prices. Much like Hummingbird and Rachel, the two men were learning together. There was a happiness about Trace that was tempered only by the rift that existed between him and Rachel.

They were sitting there one afternoon when a heavy, stylish carriage drove around the house and toward the stables. The man inside did not look toward the small renovated house. Rachel stood up, laying her sewing aside as she shaded her eyes to gaze after the carriage.

"My father's home," she said. Her glance moved to Trace, who had become very still and quiet. She stepped off the porch and hurried toward the stables.

There was silence among the three left sitting on the porch before Hummingbird turned to Trace.

"Are you actually going to let her go with her father when he returns to Washington?"

"I have no choice."

"Nonsense," she said. "A man always has a choice—especially when the woman in question looks at him the way our Rachel looks at you." Hummingbird's dark gaze turned toward the house and stables. "She is a very special woman. Even with her beauty and all this wealth, she is the sweetest, kindest person I've ever known."

Trace clenched his teeth. Sometimes he wished Rachel weren't so sweet, or so kind. Perhaps it would soothe his conscience, or make it easier for him to let her go.

"I can't blame her for hating me," he said.

"She doesn't hate you," Hummingbird said with an amused little smile.

"Even if she didn't, it would never work," he replied. "We're

too different. Deep down inside she would always resent who
I am and what I've done."

"You're wrong," Hummingbird said. She glanced at her husband as if she wanted him to confirm what she said.

White Feather nodded toward Trace.

"Listen to her, cousin. Women know these things."

"You have hurt Rachel, it's true," Hummingbird continued.
"But there is no hatred in her and there is no difference in
her heart toward our kind. She gives her friendship freely to
us, and is no different with me than she is with her friends
Hallie and Amelia. You know that. You've seen it these past
few days."

"It isn't the same," Trace said, shaking his head.

Hummingbird sighed and put aside her sewing. She gathered
the baby out of his cradle and walked inside the house.

Rachel had informed Trace earlier that dinner that evening
would be more formal. Her father always liked formal dress
when he was home, even when there were no guests. "Our
one attempt at civility out here in the country," he would say.

When Trace walked into the dining room wearing his black
suit and ebony studs, he wondered what Rachel had told her
father.

The Senator was just coming in the front door. He shifted
a smoking cigar to his left hand and reached out to shake
hands with Trace.

"Well, son," he said. "The place has never looked better. I
must say your stewardship agrees with Windridge." The Senator looked up the stairs then and his eyes lit with pride. "Ah,
there's my beautiful daughter. You look lovely, Rachel."

Trace frowned slightly and turned to watch his wife glide
down the stairs. He'd never seen the dress she was wearing.
The shimmering copper color was almost the same as her hair.
It made her skin look golden and as rich as honey.

From the Senator's cordial greeting, Trace knew that Rachel
hadn't yet told her father anything. But, from the look of dread

in Rachel's eyes, he knew that his reprieve wasn't going to last long.

She waited until after dinner, then she stood up and walked to the wide entryway and pulled the huge sliding doors together.

"Father, there's something I need to tell you."

At first, the Senator smiled, as if he expected the news to be happy. But then, seeing the looks between Rachel and Trace, he frowned.

"Why . . . what is it? You're not angry with me because I couldn't be here when Cleo—"

"No," Rachel said. "Of course not. You couldn't possibly have come. I didn't expect it."

"It's the house," Senator Townsend said. "I sensed in your letter, when you questioned my acquisition of Windridge, that you were upset."

"Yes," Rachel answered. "In a way, it all has to do with Wind . . ." Her eyes met Trace's and she faltered. ". . . with the plantation."

Rachel pulled out her velvety skirts and sat down, facing her father. Her voice, as she related the story, was strong and steady. She didn't look at Trace and tended to keep her eyes on the tablecloth or on the wall past her father's shoulders.

Finally, when the gist of what she was saying sunk in, Senator Townsend turned and stared at Trace. His face was flushed, his eyes sparking with anger.

"What in God's name are you talking about? The name of the family living here was . . . Monroe . . . yes, I'm sure of it. It was in the papers I received. It's in the deed I gave you before your wedding."

"Hambleton was my mother's name," Trace said, his voice cold and empty. He had been watching the Senator all the while Rachel talked. He had been patient, letting her tell the story. But he felt his resentment and anger building in him. His black eyes glittered with all the old emotions.

The Senator's heavy jowls actually puffed out and his eyes

had become red with fury and disbelief. Without warning, he pushed himself up and away from the table, sending his chair crashing to the floor behind him.

"You deceitful son of a bitch."

"Father . . ." Rachel stood up and reached a hand toward her father. Her eyes cautioned Trace.

But it was too late for caution.

"You . . . you did this deliberately?" the Senator sputtered. "You came here, deceived my daughter . . . tricked her into thinking you really cared about her, even consummated the marriage? All for the purpose of regaining this land and righting some wrong you think was done to you?" The horror of what Trace had done was reflected in the Senator's eyes. He practically trembled with anger and revulsion.

"I married Trace of my own free will," Rachel said, trying to calm the situation. But her resentful gaze warned Trace not to be fooled. "I loved him." Her words were a bare whisper in the quiet of the room.

"That was before you knew who he was. What he was!"

Trace stood very straight and stiff, his hands clenched at his side.

"I was twelve when the soldiers came to this house," Trace said, his voice quiet and deadly. "Were you with them? Had you even then staked your claim on this place, Senator Townsend? Did you watch my father die? And did you conveniently turn away as my mother and I were dragged from the house and imprisoned before being sent to a cold, ruthless land that wasn't our home?" He was flushed with anger when he finished and his eyes were as black as midnight.

"I . . . I . . ."

Rachel saw the look on her father's face as he tried to speak, tried to think of some excuse. Her eyes widened with hurt and disbelief.

"Father . . ." she whispered. "Tell him it isn't true."

"I had no idea what was about to transpire here . . . But I swear . . . I swear to you Rachel, on your mother's grave, I was not here when it happened. And I had nothing to do with that man's death."

"That man, as you call him . . . was my Father."

Rachel's face was very pale, and even though she had fully recovered from all that had happened recently, Trace felt a jolt of concern for her well being. He took a step, as if intending to steady her, or comfort her.

"No," she said, staring at him with dark, angry resentment and pain. "Don't . . ." she said. "Just . . . don't . . ." Her lips were trembling as she turned back to face her father.

"You knew," she whispered, her voice filled with horror. "You're saying you actually knew that those soldiers were coming here to take this place and to send Trace and his family away?"

She turned away from her father's stricken eyes, as if the sight of him sickened her.

"My God," she murmured. "My God . . . my own father. I can't believe it. I can't believe you made a home for Mother and me in a house bought with someone's blood."

She whirled around to accuse her father. Trace could see the outline of tears streaming down her face.

Senator Townsend stood very still, his jaw clenched, eyes glaring toward Trace.

"Damn you for what you've done, Trace Hambleton, or whatever your name is," the Senator said. "This is your fault. I place the blame for this squarely on your shoulders."

"No, Senator," Trace said, his voice steady. "My only fault was in having Cherokee blood."

"You'll never regain Windridge," the Senator swore. "I'm telling you that right now. This farce of a marriage will never stand in a court of law."

"Rosewood," Trace corrected coldly. "The name is Rosewood, not Windridge. Or have you forgotten the name of the place you stole?"

The Senator cursed and slammed his hand down on the table, causing the dishes to rattle with a loud jangle.

"I want you out of this house." He marched to the door and slid them open with a bang. Then he turned to Trace and pointed toward the door. "Right now! And if you ever set foot on this property . . . if you ever so much as look at my daughter again . . ."

Rachel was afraid her father might actually collapse, he was so angry.

Oddly, Trace smiled and he made no effort to move.

"Well, Senator," he drawled. "As you said earlier, I've done more than just look at your daughter." He ignored the Senator's quiet curse and Rachel's gasp of indignation. "And the truth is, I'm the one who should be ordering you to leave." Trace reached into his jacket and withdrew a piece of paper. "You see, Rosewood is already mine, free and clear. Here . . . see for yourself."

The papers trembled in Senator Townsend's hand as he read the words. He made a choked noise and reached his hand out toward a chair. Rachel hurried to him and helped him to sit down.

"You . . . you've deeded the place to him," he gasped, looking up at his daughter. "My God . . ."

Rachel glanced at Trace, who stood rigidly on the other side of the table. The dangerous, dark look of triumph in his eyes made her want to cry.

"It's his home, Father." Rachel fell onto her knees beside her father's chair. Her dress spread around her like spilled honey. "I've loved this place for as long as I can remember. But I don't want it . . . I couldn't hold onto it knowing what you did to get it." She held her father's arm, leaning toward him and pleading with him to understand her position.

"His father was killed in front of his eyes. And his mother . . . a good, decent civilized woman, like my own mother, was made to live like an animal. She died in a place she hated, always longing in her heart to return here to her home. They were people, father . . . real people, like you and me and Mother. And just because you chose not to be here and see the ugliness of what happened . . . because you chose the easy way, that doesn't mean they weren't real, or that they didn't suffer because of your greed. It was wrong . . . you knew it was wrong and for the first time in my life, I'm ashamed that you're my father!"

All the life seemed to drain from William Townsend. His shoulders slumped and his head was bent as he stared at the papers in his hands.

Then he reached out to touch Rachel's cheek.

"I understand."

With a deep breath he finally looked up to meet Trace's eyes.

"What do you want me to do?" he asked, his voice weary..

"Nothing," Trace said with cold dispassion. "I won't turn you out the way you did my mother. Stay until you're rested and are ready to return to Washington—however long that should be."

"And what about my daughter?" the Senator asked. He seemed completely defeated now and accepting. "It would be best if this is kept between us . . . the disgrace if everyone knew . . ."

"That's up to Rachel," Trace said. For the first time since the evening began, his voice changed. The look in his eyes softened as he turned toward her. "This is her home for as long as she chooses to stay. I would continue to treat her with respect if she wishes to remain here. It wouldn't be the first marriage that's based on a business proposition."

"Business?" Rachel asked, her voice steely.

"Rachel . . ." Trace said, more softly. "You know how I feel."

The Senator watched the two of them with a frown and a sense of curiosity.

"No, Trace," she said, looking him squarely in the eye. "I know how you feel about Rosewood. I know how you feel about White Feather and his family. In fact, I know how you feel about a lot of things. But I don't know . . . how you feel about me."

Trace gritted his teeth. This was hardly the place for such a discussion. He wasn't so sure he was ready for it even it if had been.

"You're my wife," he said stiffly. "And you're welcome to stay here."

Rachel's eyes turned cold and dead. He couldn't say it. She should have known he couldn't bring himself to speak words of love or encouragement to her. With a quiet shudder of resignation, she glanced at her father.

"I'll go back to Washington with you Father, if that's all right."

"Yes," he said, coming to his feet. He looked at his daughter, but he didn't touch her. He knew how disappointed she was in what he had done. He could barely look her in the eye.

"Yes, of course it's all right. Congress will convene again in a few weeks. If staying here that long will be awkward for you darling, then we'll take a room in town . . ." He glanced resentfully at Trace.

"No." Rachel's glance toward Trace was defiant and filled with a quiet grace. "No, Father, it won't be awkward for me at all."

She lifted her skirts and with hardly a sound, she moved out of the room, leaving only the rose scent of her perfume to linger between the two men.

Twenty-nine

The next morning when Rachel woke, the room seemed un-usually dark. She went to the windows, noting the swirling black clouds that blotted out any hint of morning sun. The huge trees around the house swayed first one way and then another. And yet, despite the wind, the house seemed very hot and still.

Rachel frowned and dressed hurriedly, going downstairs to find that Trace had already eaten and left the house. She could see by the look in Dimity's eyes that the weather frightened her.

"Dimity, when Father comes down for breakfast, please in-form him that I've gone out to the field to check the tobacco crop. Looks like it's going to storm."

Rachel's concern for the fragile plants was instinctive, even though she knew Trace would not approve. But she had been tending crops since she was a girl. And if he weren't so stub-born, he'd admit that it was something he was still learning how to do.

Outside, the hot wind wrapped her skirts around her legs and threatened to toss her bonnet into the air. She tied the gossamer streamers beneath her chin and lowered her head as she made her way to the stables.

Jared was there for the first time since his illness and, though Rachel had seen him often, it surprised her.

"Jared, honey," she said, touching his thin shoulders. "It's so good to see you here. Are you sure you're feeling well enough to do this?"

"Oh yes'm," he said. He had adjusted as well as could be expected to his brother Jim's death, but still there was something different about him. He was not as ebullient and his dark eyes did not sparkle the same as before. "Lula has been fussin' about it, but I tol her if'n I don't do somethin' soon I might jes go crazy."

"Well," Rachel said, smiling. "We certainly wouldn't want that."

"Where you goin'?" he asked. "You be needin' yo mare, or you want me to hitch up the little buggy?"

"The mare. Here, I'll help. I need to hurry, before the storm hits."

"If'n you thinkin' about goin' to the fields, Mr. Trace and the Indian, they done gone."

"Well, there's no reason why I can't go, too, is there?" she said, giving him a pointed look.

"No ma'am," he said, grinning.

Within minutes, she was riding hard across the fields. She could hardly see for the wind stinging her eyes. But when she grew nearer and slowed the mare, she could see the field hands working frantically to strip the bottom leaves of the tobacco before it rained. She tied her horse to a nearby tree and hurried to help, shouting instructions above the wind.

She didn't even notice Trace until he was standing beside her.

"What in hell are you doing out here?" he shouted. "Go back to the house. It's going to storm."

She glanced at him briefly, but continued to work.

"Do you think I can't see that for myself?"

She sensed White Feather and some of the Negroes watching them as they worked. Some of them were smiling, and others, like Trace's cousin, looked skeptical.

"Rachel . . ." Trace warned, grasping her arm.

She pulled away from him and for the first time she faced him.

"I'm not going," she said. "In a few weeks, you won't have to worry about me or what I'm doing. But for now, just let me do this, Trace. I like doing it, and I've been helping here since I was a little girl. You can't deny me the right to this one last thing."

Trace's jaw clenched and his dark eyes bored into hers.

"Dammit, Rachel, you are the most pig headed, stubborn female I've ever met. I don't know any well bred lady in the world who would actually admit she enjoys working in the sun and wind and rain the way you do."

His assessment was not a compliment, but Rachel took it as one anyway.

"Thank you," she said with a toss of her head.

Trace sighed and shook his head. Then he walked away, glaring at any man who seemed to glance his way.

"What are you looking at, dammit? Keep working," he growled. "We don't have much time left."

By the time they were almost finished, thunder had begun to rumble continuously in the southwest. The storm was coming closer with every passing minute.

Finally, Trace sent the men to their houses and when he looked back toward the field to make sure everyone was gone, he saw Rachel alone at the farthest end. He called to her and saw her lift her head and look toward him, then go back to what she was doing.

Trace cursed beneath his breath, calling over his shoulder to White Feather. "You go on. I'm going to get Rachel."

On his way across the field, he glanced at the sky. Passing Rachel's mare, he jerked the reins loose to free the animal and kept walking.

For a brief moment, the air around them seemed completely still and lifeless. Then with a sudden, fierce violence, the wind returned, stronger than ever. It roared through the trees, tearing limbs and scattering leaves. It whipped along the ground, stirring clouds of dust into the air. Lightning was close now and almost constant.

It was the lightning that finally captured Rachel's attention. When she looked up, she saw Trace coming . . . striding fiercely through the leafy plants with purpose.

She heard a roar somewhere in the distance, and when she looked up, she could see black clouds swirling in a vicious spiral. Debris was in the cloud, being tossed and pulled higher and higher.

Rachel's heart almost stopped, and when she began running toward Trace, she knew he saw it, too.

"Hurry!" she called, pointing toward the barn in the distance. "It's coming!"

She had gone only a few steps when Trace was upon her, grabbing her around the waist and lifting her off the ground as he moved her away from the outbuildings.

"The barn!" she cried, her voice almost carried away by the roaring wind. "We have to get to the tobacco barn."

"There's no time."

Rachel stumbled and Trace picked her up in his arms, jarring her teeth as he ran across the uneven field toward a deep ditch that was used for irrigation in summer.

By the time he reached the ditch, the air was filled with debris, some of it heavy. Trace grunted as a piece of wood struck him above one eye. Just before he stumbled into the ditch and covered Rachel's body with his, he saw the black cloud dip toward the trees beyond the field, then the forest and earth exploded with a roar.

There had been no time to think, or to consider, any other possibilities besides the ditch. He pushed Rachel against the side of the trench, his body protecting hers as he covered his head with his hands.

Rachel was trembling and the roaring around them filled her ears until she wanted to scream. When debris began to rain down on them, she wrapped her arms tightly around his waist and held on, burying her head against his chest.

It was over in a matter of seconds.

Trace's body was still over hers and the weight of him seemed heavy and lifeless. Rachel couldn't see his face and for a moment she was afraid he was dead.

"Trace," she whispered. "Trace!" she cried louder, trying to squirm her body free.

"It's all right," he said, moving only the slightest bit. He looked down at her face, touching her hair, then her cheek.

There was a small trickle of blood above his eye and bits of dirt and leaves in his hair.

"It's gone over. We're alive," he said. His hand was still cupping her cheek and his face was very close.

"Are you all right?" he asked, running his hands over her arms, then down her body to see if she was whole.

"I . . . I think so." She reached up tentatively, touching his face and examining the cut just at the edge of his brow. "You're bleeding."

Trace touched his fingers to the cut.

"It's nothing," he said. He moved away from her, his body reluctant, as if it had a will of its own. Kneeling in the ditch, he brushed at the twigs and debris that covered them.

All around the ditch, he could see the storm's devastation. Rachel saw the look of disbelief in Trace's eyes and she came up beside him, holding onto his arm to steady herself.

"Dear . . . God," she whispered when she saw.

Trace put his arm around her and helped her stand. She could actually feel her legs shaking beneath her. She briefly thought that she felt Trace's body shaking, too.

They could see the path of the storm, almost directly across them and toward the tobacco barn. But where the building had stood only moments before, there was nothing now except crumpled tin and pieces of scattered timbers. Even the huge trees that had surrounded the barn lay in grotesque, twisted piles.

All the air seemed to leave Trace's lungs. He stared at the

scene of devastation, then put his hands to his head in a gesture of futility and disbelief.

Both of them looked toward the house at the same time.

"It's all right," Rachel said. "Rosewood is all right."

Her words were soft and reassuring. Trace couldn't be certain if she were consoling him or herself. Then he turned to look into her eyes. The concern, the gentleness he saw there, made him groan softly.

"Rachel . . ." he whispered. He reached out, putting his hands at her waist as he pulled her toward him. With a whispered sigh, she came eagerly into his arms.

When he heard a voice calling him, he wanted to ignore it. He wanted there to be no one else in the world but the two of them. With this sweet moment of being together never to end.

"Trace . . . hurry . . . over here. Someone's trapped beneath the barn."

He could see White Feather in the distance, waving his arms above his head and motioning for Trace to come.

He and Rachel began to run, although he soon outdistanced her.

"Go ahead," she said, panting. "I'm coming." But she hardly knew how either of them could force their legs to work after what they'd just been through.

She reached what was left of the barn just as Trace and White Feather and some of the other men were pulling someone from the debris. The young Negro was bleeding from a gash on his leg, but once freed of the heavy timbers, he was able to stand on his own.

Rachel could hardly believe it.

"Is . . . is there anyone else?" she asked.

"They was three of us in the barn," the man said. He pointed to two other young men. "But they ain't hurt."

"We're lucky," she whispered. "Very lucky." Her eyes took in the path of devastation and saw that the tornado had struck ground, then moved up into the air again, taking the tops of some trees with it as it roared across the stables and away to the north.

"I'm going to the house to see if everyone there is all right. Father and Lula will be frantic with worry."

Trace nodded. In his eyes was the memory of holding her against him while the storm raged across. He kept thinking of the sweet look of tenderness in her eyes when she touched his face and when she'd told him that Rosewood was left standing.

Rosewood. She had actually called it Rosewood. And there had been a soft surrender in her voice when she'd said it.

Had it been the danger that had changed her? The possibility that both of them could have died so suddenly on this stormy summer day?

"Trace," he heard someone call.

He shook his head as he watched her go, her hair blowing in the wind, her skirts wet and dragging against the muddy ground. He wanted to go with her, talk to her and hold her until his heart realized that she was truly all right.

What if she had been killed today? What if he never were able to hold her and touch her again? When Rachel had learned who he was and when he thought she hated him, he had told himself that just having her here, where he could see her every day, would be enough. If he could only convince her to stay, he would endure the pretense, even her hatred, if he could just see her.

But after today, after holding her and feeling her arms around him, he knew that it would never be enough for him. He wanted all of her—body and soul. And he had discovered, most of all, that he wanted her to love him again.

"Trace!" White Feather shook his arm. "You coming? We need to get wagons and saws and start cleaning up here."

"Yeah," Trace said, shaking away his dazed thoughts. "I'm coming."

Thirty

The next few days were spent cleaning up after the storm and rebuilding the tobacco barn. They'd need it soon for hanging the tobacco stalks when curing time came.

Everyone worked, including the Senator and Rachel.

Trace would watch her, noting the smudge of dirt on her face, her cheeks glowing from the physical exertion of carrying brush and debris to a burn pile. She actually seemed to thrive in the heat and hard work.

He knew better than to try to persuade her to go to the house to rest. He was finally beginning to realize that she loved the work and the excitement of living on a plantation as much as he did. Being a woman didn't change that.

He even began to admire that in her and told himself more than once that any man would consider himself lucky to be married to such a woman. But in the evening, she would be so exhausted she would not come down for dinner. On those nights, the Senator would refuse to eat with the man who had betrayed his daughter. And Trace would find himself alone in the elegant dining room, the long lace covered mahogany table stretching out before him.

As for Trace, he welcomed the hard work and the exhaustion. It helped him to sleep—and to forget the look of heartache he always saw in Rachel's eyes.

With the storm, summer seemed to have come to Rosewood with a vengeance. The weather was hot and sultry and some days, as they worked beneath the sun, there was little breeze to cool their skin.

It was on such a day that Trace noticed something different about Rachel. She seemed very tired, slower in what she did. And several times within an hour he saw her stop work and go to the water bucket. She seemed pale and when she raised her hand to her head, he walked over to her.

"Rachel?" he asked. "Are you feeling all right?"

She looked at him and her eyes seemed glazed and uncertain.

"You're not all right," he said. "It's much too hot for you to be working out here. Why don't you go back to the house? You can come back this evening when it's cooler."

"I . . . I feel so odd," she said.

He reached out for her just as she collapsed into his arms.

"My God," he muttered, scooping her up against him. He looked over his shoulder and saw White Feather coming toward them. "It's the heat," Trace said. "I'll take her to the house."

White Feather pulled a handkerchief from his pocket and poured a dipper of water over it, placing it on Rachel's brow as he walked alongside Trace and back toward the house.

"I'll get Hummingbird," White Feather said. "She'll know what to do."

Everyone in the household seemed to congregate at the back door as Trace carried Rachel into the house. They fluttered about her like worried hens.

"Lordy, Mr. Trace," Lula exclaimed. "What's happened to our little girl?"

"I don't know, Lula," he said, shifting Rachel's body in his arms. "It's probably the heat."

"I told her," Lula said. "I done told her about workin' out in the sun on days like this. She's such a little thing anyway . . ."

"Dimity," Trace shouted. "Bring some cool water and cloths. Lula, find something cold for her to drink, something with plenty of sugar."

"Yessir, I get it right away," Lula said, hurrying back toward the kitchen.

By the time Trace reached the landing at the top of the stairs, Rachel's eyes were open and she stirred in his arms.

"What . . . what are you doing?" she asked.

"Shh, you're all right, I've got you," he said. "You fainted. How do you feel? Does your head hurt?"

"No," she whispered, touching her head. She still seemed a bit dazed and confused. "No, I feel fine, just a little weak maybe."

He carried her into her room and laid her on her bed. Without thinking, he began to unbutton her blouse. Her hands went to stop his fingers and she looked up into his eyes with a silent entreaty.

Despite her wishes, he continued to unbutton her blouse, pushing the material away from her hot skin. He couldn't seem to resist letting his fingers trail up against her cheek, or brush her hair away from her face.

When Hummingbird came into the room, Trace stepped reluctantly back away from the bed. But he couldn't pull his eyes away from Rachel.

"White Feather asks if you wish him to send for the doctor," Hummingbird said. She came to the bed and touched Rachel's face, smiling at her as she pulled a chair up to sit beside the bed.

"Yes," Trace said. "I'll . . . I'll go back downstairs." Trace then turned to Rachel. "I didn't see your father when we came in—he'll want to know that you're not feeling well."

"Thank you," Rachel said.

Senator Townsend was just coming up the stairs when Trace met him. Someone had already told him about Rachel, and for the time being, he seemed to forget the animosity between himself and the young man he now faced. Trace quickly told him what had happened and that he was going downstairs to send someone for the doctor.

"Good," the Senator said. "That's good."

Later, after the doctor arrived, the two men found themselves together again on the front porch as they waited for the doctor's diagnosis. Trace walked slowly back and forth across the porch, head bent. Periodically, he would brush his hair back impatiently or chew at his lower lip. He seemed completely lost in thought.

The Senator watched him for a while. Then, slowly, he withdrew two cigars from his pocket and handed one toward Trace.

"Here," he said brusquely in the awkward moment. "The best cigar always seems to make things a little better."

Trace looked up, his gaze going to the cigar that the Senator held in his outstretched hand, then up to the Senator's face. With a quiet murmur of thanks, Trace took the cigar and stuck it in his mouth. He didn't light it, but resumed his pacing with the unlit cigar clamped between his teeth.

They heard the doctor inside the house talking to someone. Trace walked to the open door and looked up to see Hummingbird and the doctor talking quietly on the stair landing.

When Hummingbird went back toward Rachel's room, Trace and the Senator waited in the entry hall for the doctor to come down. The man looked at Trace, then pursed his lips and nodded toward the Senator.

"Senator . . . may I speak to you privately?"

Trace took the cigar from between his teeth and watched with a look of disbelief as the doctor and the Senator went out onto the porch. The doctor put his hand on Senator Townsend's shoulder and leaned close, as if telling him of some dark secret.

Trace's heart shuddered, then began to beat again, faster than normal. He hesitated only a moment before going onto the front porch to confront them.

"I think I have a right to know what's wrong with my wife," he said, his voice quietly demanding.

The doctor turned to look at him, then sheepishly he glanced at the Senator.

"Mr. Hambleton," he said. "Your wife is fine."

"What's wrong with her?"

"I, uh . . . all I can tell you at the moment is that she is fine. She's in excellent health and there's absolutely nothing for you to worry about. I'll leave the rest of the details to Rachel."

Trace gritted his teeth together. He still had the Senator's expensive cigar in his hand. He clamped it between his teeth and turned to go inside, bounding up the stairs. He had to restrain himself from barging into Rachel's room. Instead, he made himself open the door slowly and step in.

She was awake now, sitting up in bed and sipping lemonade. She did seem well, happy even. But there were tears sparkling in her eyes and Trace couldn't understand why that would be, if she were as fine and as healthy as the doctor declared.

"I want to know what's going on," he said. "And I want to know now."

"Trace . . ." Hummingbird stood up and reached toward him, as if to quiet him.

"Leave us alone, Hummingbird," he said.

With a lift of her brows, she looked toward the bed. Rachel smiled at her and reached out to take her hand.

"I'll be fine," she said. "You go ahead."

"I'll come to see you later," Hummingbird said. "We'll talk . . ." Her dark eyes turned to Trace and her words faded away. Then with a quiet smile, she left the room.

Rachel placed her glass on a table and looked up to face him. His face was dark, his eyes stormy, as he stood above her like some ancient king—demanding and imperious.

There was so much she wanted to tell him, so many things she longed to say. And yet when he was like this—when he was so cold and authoritative—she found him daunting. When that happened, it only brought out all her stubbornness.

"You seem to think there's a conspiracy against you at every turn, Trace. I assure you, there is not."

Trace noted the sparkle in her eyes. The way she lifted

her chin and faced him with that smug, stubborn little look on her face.

"The doctor walked right past me downstairs and took your father out to the front porch where they stood whispering like two schoolboys. So don't tell me about what I think."

She knew that was her fault. She had pleaded with the doctor not to tell Trace she was pregnant, to let her be the one to tell her husband.

She should tell him the truth. He had every right to know that she was to have his child. Yet, she couldn't. Try as she might to visualize how he would respond, she simply had no idea how he would feel when she told him. She needed a little time to think, to be alone with this wonderful, yet complicating news.

She couldn't bear to have him spoil this joy and happiness. Not yet.

"It's just that it's a delicate female matter, that's all," she lied, drawing her eyes away from his. "I'm sure the doctor felt a little . . . awkward. I'll be fine." She looked at him, trying to force a smile. "You were right," she declared breathlessly. "I was just trying to do too much. From now on, I intend taking your advice and spending more of my time inside the house."

Trace was very still. His eyes narrowed and he turned his head slightly to one side as if he heard a noise that he couldn't quite identify. As he stared at her, she glanced down, fiddling with the lace on the sheets.

"I don't believe that for a minute," he said softly. "And I certainly don't believe that you're planning on taking my advice . . . whether it's working in the fields or riding your horse like a wild little hoyden."

The forced smile left Rachel's face. She clamped her lips together and gave a small huff.

"I'm sorry if you don't believe me," she said. "But after all, it's my body and my health. You'll just have to be satisfied with what I've told you because I don't intend sharing such intimate details with you or anyone else. Now, if you'll excuse me, I'd like to take a nap."

Trace's hands were at his hips, his eyes studied her. He reached up and pulled at his lip.

"Well?" she asked, her voice impatient.

Would he never leave? Would he simply stand there all day until she weakened and blurted out the entire thing to him?

"I'm going," he said. He walked over to the bed and bent toward her, taking her chin in his hand and forcing her to look up at him. "But this is not over, Rachel. Whatever it is you're hiding from me, I'll find out—one way or another."

She watched him walk out and quietly close the door. Then she slid down between the sheets and pulled them up to her chin.

A baby. She was going to have a baby to hold and to love. When she was in Washington missing Trace and thinking of all they might have shared, she would at least have this child.

"Oh Trace," she whispered, her eyes filling again with tears. "Why couldn't it have been different? Why couldn't we be just two normal people who loved one another and wanted to have a family together without all these complications?" Her chin was trembling as she closed her eyes.

She had been so lonely as a child. And she thought of Trace's sad, lonely past. He would never allow her to take his child away from Rosewood—of that one thing she was certain.

And how could she expect it? Wouldn't he be as thrilled as she at having a child to love . . . a little girl or boy to lavish with gifts and attention?

If there was one thing she knew, it was that she and Trace shared this much in common. Neither of them would let a child be alone or lonely. It would be loved and cared for more than any child in the world.

"I want to tell you, Trace," she whispered. "I swear I do. I just don't know how."

Thirty-one

Rachel didn't go back to the fields after that day. And although she found it hard to avoid Trace, she managed to do it for a while. So many conflicting thoughts swirled in her head.

How would he take the news that they were to have a child together? On one hand, she thought he would make a wonderful father. Yet, on the other, this child would be white. Rachel could never allow it to live in any other world. That world was the one Trace professed to hate with all his being.

She spent long hours alone in her room while Trace was away from the house. And when it was time for him to return, she would slip away outside and wander among the wildflowers in the fields, or in the dark cool forests that surrounded the estate.

She had visited the cemetery a couple of times. Somehow it comforted her being there with Cleo and her mother. At least there she could talk about all that was in her heart.

Trace grew more and more impatient with her. He knew something was wrong. Hummingbird told Rachel only that morning that Trace demanded she tell him what was wrong with Rachel.

To avoid Trace at dinner that evening, Rachel walked to the cemetery. She walked silently from one grave to the other, placing flowers here and there. Then she came to Trace's father's grave.

It was now marked by a handsome marble stone with both

his parents' names engraved. Seeing their names, Rachel thought how sad it was that they could not be here to see their first grandchild.

Trace had seen Rachel leave the house. He knew she was avoiding him, just as she'd been doing for the past two days. He was hot and dirty from working, but he couldn't take time to do anything about it now. Once Rachel disappeared into the stand of trees at the cemetery, Trace hurried from the house and headed across the lawn.

When he grew close enough, he heard a voice and he stopped. When he realized it was Rachel speaking, he moved on, walking softly upon the grass and moss beneath the trees.

"I don't know how to tell him," she said. "I wish you were here. Perhaps you could help me decide what to do . . . what to say. I know he loved you both so much. And he misses you."

Trace frowned and turned his head to catch her words better. She was at his parents' grave, speaking to them. Telling them her secret? He knew Rachel would be furious if she suspected he was eavesdropping, but at the moment, he didn't care.

"I don't know what he planned to do with me once this was all out in the open," she was saying. "Maybe he didn't ever expect it to come out. Maybe he would have gone on pretending and letting me believe in this charade until the day he died."

Rachel hesitated and sighed, then walked to the fence. She turned, leaning her arms back across the iron railing.

"I hate lies," she said. "But sometimes I almost wish he'd never told me the truth. Then I could have been blissfully ignorant. I could have told him about the baby we're to have and—"

Trace cursed aloud and stepped from behind the tree. His eyes glinted with fury and disbelief.

When Rachel saw him, she gasped and for a moment she backed against the fence. Then she straightened her shoulders and stepped into the open part of the cemetery, waiting for him to come to her.

He stalked into the cemetery and took her by the shoulders, wanting to shake her, wanting to rant at her for keeping such a thing from him.

"How could you do this?" he asked, his eyes filled with fury. "Did you ever plan on telling me I was to be a father? Or were you simply going to go to Washington and keep this a secret from me for the rest of my life?"

Rachel had expected him to be angry. But she was stunned by the level of anger in his eyes . . . and the pain—she hadn't expected the pain.

"I . . . I hadn't decided what I would do yet," she stammered. She pulled away from him and backed away a few steps.

"*You* hadn't decided," he drawled sarcastically. "Did it ever occur to you that I might have a say in this decision?"

"Yes, it did. I know you probably won't believe me, but all I've thought of these past few days is how I was going to tell you."

"And why didn't you?" he demanded.

"Why?" she said, her eyes growing stormy and as intense as his. "You have to ask me why? Perhaps I should remind you that this child will be white. He will be raised as a white child." She was almost breathless, but she forced herself to continue. "I heard what White Feather said to you when his son was born—that you two would teach him the old ways. You can't do that with our baby, Trace—at least not openly. He can never claim his heritage proudly, the way White Feather's child will be able to do. If everyone knew, you might risk losing Rosewood again, regardless of the fact that it was legally deeded to you."

Trace shook his head and frowned. He put his hands on his hips and paced along the grass. When he looked up, his eyes were dark and steady.

"Only I can make those decisions for my child," he said steadily.

"Oh, no," she replied with a haughty lift of her chin. "I am his mother and I will have a say in this, Trace, whether you like it or not. I will leave this place and you'll never find either of us again before I'll allow you to transfer your prejudices onto him."

"What? My prejudices? What in hell are you saying?"

"I'm saying only what I've heard you say since you came here. You hate whites for what they did to you. I'm not saying that you're wrong or that I don't understand. But I will never stand by and allow my child to be mistreated because of—"

"Mistreated?" His voice was louder now, his look incredulous. "Mistreated? You're saying that I would be cruel to my own child because he is white? Hell, my own mother was three quarters white," he shouted, pointing toward her grave.

"I am not willing to raise my child in a house filled with anger and bitterness," Rachel said, her voice quiet and even. She stepped toward him. Her face softened and she reached out as if to touch him.

"Trace," she whispered. "I don't want to do this. I don't want to take your child away from you. But I can't bring him up in this atmosphere. You can't ask me to do that."

Trace looked deep into her eyes and he knew she meant it. He rubbed the back of his neck as his shoulders slumped forward. His agitation and frustration were evident in the way he took long slow breaths of air, in the way he silently shook his head.

"What do you want from me?" he asked, his voice hollow and empty.

Tears glimmered in Rachel's eyes as she watched him. She didn't like seeing him this way, didn't like confronting him or making demands. She wished she could just walk to him and put her arms around him. She might have done just that a few days ago, before she learned that another life was involved in this fiasco they had created of their lives.

But now she had to put her child first.

"I guess you're going to have to choose, Trace . . ." she said softly.

When he lifted his head and gazed across into her eyes, she smiled wistfully.

"You're going to have to choose between your past and that bitterness that you cling to so vehemently . . . and your child."

Trace's lips parted as he stared at her. And when she turned and walked out of the cemetery, he made no move to stop her. Only after she had vanished into the darkness did Trace turn away. He cursed quietly and kicked at the grass with his boot.

He hadn't expected this. Oh, he had known it was a possibility, their having a child. But after he moved out of their bed, he had hoped . . . prayed even that there would be no child to complicate matters even more.

But now that there was, he wasn't sure how he felt.

Stunned would be a good start . . . troubled . . . frustrated. He also was surprised by Rachel's strong assertion that he had to choose. But before he chose to include this child in his life—before he made the decision to bring another innocent person into this mess—he had to make damned sure he could handle the consequences.

First of all, Rachel would have to stay here at Rosewood. Trace would never agree to her raising their child anywhere else, especially not in a place like Washington.

He wanted the child to feel loved and to feel at home here. And he wanted to ensure that it would be secure and never be dragged from its own home in the middle of the night because of the color of its skin.

The bitterness rose in him again, as it always did when he thought of his past. That past and bitterness that, according to Rachel, he would have to put away if he expected to be a part of her child's life.

"This is my child too, dammit," he muttered.

He felt a tiny flicker of determination deep within him. A

very small, distant light of pride and joy for this life he and Rachel had created between them.

Then it was gone.

"Damn." Trace shook his head in bemused wonder.

Was this enough for him to build on? This small, unexplained spark of exultation? He had wondered over the years if there could ever be joy within him again. He had experienced pleasure and moments of genuine happiness with Rachel.

But always he had held back something. He had refused to give in to that happiness, afraid it would all be taken away.

But this time, the joy was real. It had come upon him unexpectedly, pleasing him at the same time.

He looked into the darkness and shook his head again as if he could not quite believe what was happening. Then slowly a quiet, bemused smile curved his lips and he walked out of the cemetery toward the house.

He didn't go immediately to Rachel's room, although that was what he wanted, as every instinct within him urged him to do. Instead, he stood at the door of the back bedroom where he'd been staying and let his gaze wander over the walls and the small bed.

This would be his son's room. Trace could take the larger room across the hall, next to Rachel's.

He was tempted to move his few belongings immediately. Then, glancing back down the hall toward Rachel's closed door, he decided he'd better wait.

She hadn't yet agreed to stay. And Trace was discovering that even without the child, her presence in this house was something he wanted very much.

Thirty-two

Rachel had to admit that she felt a wonderful sense of relief after finally telling Trace about the baby. And, even though she was afraid of going through childbirth, she thought she was even more afraid that Trace's decision would be for her to leave Rosewood.

She wanted to stay, but she wasn't yet ready to forgive what he had done. Still, sometimes at night, when she lay alone in her bed, she actually felt a physical longing for that day to come.

The next morning, she was a bit disappointed that Trace was already gone when she had breakfast. She had hoped . . . dreamed, that he would begin a new habit of having breakfast with her, if for no other reason than as a token that he intended to try and rid himself of the bitterness and resentment he felt.

She felt the old fears and insecurities return. She pushed her plate away—she hadn't been feeling particularly well in the mornings anyway—and with an excuse to her father, she left the table.

"Now daughter," he said, as she walked toward the door. "You need to eat. That's one thing the doctor did say—that you should get plenty of rest and nourishment."

"I will father," she said. Impulsively, she went to him and placed a kiss against his hair.

She had been cool to him the last few days, since learning about what he had done. And although she still could not understand how he had done what he did, she felt guilty for condemning him. He was not a bad man—perhaps only selfish and thoughtless. She wasn't a child anymore, and like it or not, she could see him, not through innocent girlish eyes, but as an adult.

He had not considered the consequences of what he had done, like many men his only focus had been on the goal, on the treasure he wanted for his own. Possession. It was the same thing Trace wanted. To possess Rosewood and her, and now it seemed he expected to possess their child as well.

With a deep breath, she left the dining room and went toward the kitchen. Perhaps she'd have something to eat there. Food always tasted best to her when she took it directly from the cooking pots and skillets in Lula's kitchen.

At the back door she stopped, her eyes moving with curiosity toward the man who stood at the washstand outside the kitchen.

She was surprised to see Trace there shaving. He had an elegant wash basin and shaving stand of his own upstairs. She stepped out onto the small back stoop, letting her eyes take in every inch of him.

He had taken off his shirt and the straps of his suspenders hung down from the waist of his trousers, leaving his muscular chest bare and glistening with sweat in the sultry morning heat. She held her breath as she gazed at the strong arms, the way the muscles flexed as he shaved, the strong curves and angles of his back, tapering down to a lean waist.

Trace saw Rachel's reflection in the mirror and the hand that held the razor stopped, suspended in the air as he studied her. He washed the soap off his face, then dried his skin. He picked up a pair of scissors and turned to face her.

"Good morning," he said.

"Good . . . good morning." Rachel tried to pull her eyes away from his body. But she found her gaze going back again and again, as if she had absolutely no control over herself.

"Why are you—?"

When she saw Trace gather his hair in one hand and lift the

scissors behind his head with another, she stopped, unable to say another word. This was why he was outside. Because he intended cutting off his long hair.

Her lips were parted in a look of disbelief. She heard the snip of the scissors and watched as the dark locks fell away to the ground. Her gaze followed, then moved again back up to Trace's face.

"What are you doing?" She quickly moved forward toward him with a look of consternation. "Stop . . . don't—" She reached out, but it was too late. The rest of his beautiful, shining hair fell to the ground.

She stood in front of him, staring at him as if he had committed some unpardonable sin.

"Why did you do this?" she whispered.

Trace seemed a little puzzled, then amused.

"It's hot," he answered, watching her carefully through narrowed eyes. "And it's in the way."

He looked so different. He was still as breathtakingly handsome as ever, but the loss of his lustrous long hair made him look not quite the wild young savage that he'd looked before. He looked younger . . . sweeter somehow.

Or was it the way he was looking at her that did that?

"But I . . . I liked it," she managed. She stooped to the ground and picked up a few strands of his hair, staring at it in her hands with an odd expression of sadness.

Trace turned his head as if he wasn't sure he could believe her sincerity. And he continued to look at her with that mixture of curiosity and amusement. Slowly, the smile left his face as his look became more serious.

"I thought it more fitting for a man who's about to become a father," he said, his voice quiet. "White men don't wear their hair this way anymore."

It was the first time since Rachel had known him that he seemed a little tentative and uncertain, the first time she saw the need for her approval in those black eyes. Rachel was afraid she might break down in tears.

"I . . . I have to go." She held the long dark strands of his hair against her and ran from the small porch and out toward Hummingbird's house.

Trace watched her go. He had hoped to tell her more and to ask her to stay. But she seemed so unhappy that he couldn't decide what she wanted.

By the time Rachel reached the house, she was sobbing. She leaned against the house's siding, letting the tears come, letting the sobs come from somewhere deep down in her soul. What right did she have to take this heritage from Trace? She stared at the strands of hair in her hand. What right did she had to demand that he choose between his way of life and his child?

But she didn't want him to leave. God, she didn't want him to be captured and taken back to that hell in Oklahoma, where she'd never see him again. He would live a terrible, lonely existence, hating every moment and longing for this compelling Black Delta land . . . for his home and his child. It would kill him, especially after this taste of freedom.

Yet she knew that those were the only choices for an Indian: living on a reservation or denying his heritage and living a lie. She straightened her shoulders and wiped her eyes before going in to see Hummingbird.

White Feather was not there and the two older children were outside playing.

Hummingbird, seeming to sense Rachel's distress, came forward and put her hands beneath the other woman's elbows, guiding her toward a chair near the baby's cradle.

"Little one," she said. "What is it? Why have you been crying? And what is that you have in your hand?"

In halting sentences, Rachel managed to tell Hummingbird everything. From the scene with Trace last night in the cemetery, to what had just happened outside the summer kitchen.

"Sun Killer has cut his hair?" Hummingbird asked, her eyes wide with disbelief.

"Yes," Rachel said, bending over with a moan. "It wasn't

what I wanted. I can't bear this, Hummingbird. I just can't bear it. It's as if I've forced him to strip himself of his identity, and his people's ancient past. He's doing this for me and for the baby."

Hummingbird waited until Rachel's sobs subsided. Her look was tender and full of sympathy.

"But isn't this what you wanted?" she asked quietly. "For him to choose? All of us know that, for him to stay, it must be done. The authorities might allow him to stay, but they would never allow him to own property, or to participate in local government the way he wants to do."

"It *is* what I wanted," Rachel admitted with a slight nod. "But . . ."

"But you had not thought it would be so painful? This changing from one life to another. Could you imagine yourself denying your life here and coming to live with our people?"

Rachel's eyes were troubled as she looked up and into her friend's eyes. It was the first time she'd ever seen that spark of resentment in those gentle eyes, a hard look of disapproval that Rachel never expected.

"Hummingbird . . ." she whispered. Rachel's eyes were bleak as she took a deep breath.

"Perhaps I *should* go to Washington," she said. "Just leave everything the way it is here and go."

"No," Hummingbird said. The small hands that clasped Rachel's were strong. "Running away will not fix it."

"But I'm only making him miserable by being here. By making these demands . . ."

Hummingbird's smile was gentle.

"Sun Killer is miserable for the same reason you are miserable, Rachel," she said. "You are here together . . . but you are apart." With a knowing lift of her brows, she nodded.

"If he is anything like my husband," she continued. "He has cut his hair and he has made this decision because it is what *he* wants . . . not because you have demanded it."

Rachel leaned back in the chair with a sigh.

"This is all so complicated," she said.

"Yes," Hummingbird agreed with a smile. "Love is a very complicated thing." She grinned and nodded toward the hair that Rachel still held. "Well . . . are you going to hold onto that for the rest of your life, or would you like me to show you how to weave it into a keepsake?"

By the time Rachel left hours later, she was smiling, and feeling much better. Hummingbird was right. Love was complicated and it would take more than one day to work out the problems that existed between her and this enigmatic man she had married.

That evening, dinner was still awkward between Rachel and her father and the man who was her husband.

She couldn't seem to take her eyes off him. With his dark hair cropped short, she thought he looked even more handsome and masculine than before. Somehow, it emphasized his deep set eyes and the darkness of his face and neck.

The Senator noted that his daughter seemed fascinated with her husband's new looks. At first, he was appalled by the blatant look of hunger on her face. Then he was a bit amused.

It was much the same way his wife had once looked at him. Yet when he'd done something that she had not thought "civilized," when he'd made some comment that she considered crude and ungentlemanly, her eyes could change in an instant. Were things so different after all between his beautiful daughter and this mysterious man she had chosen to love?

Perhaps not. The only thing different was something he himself had caused. And he felt a great deal of guilt for what he'd done. Perhaps, for Rachel's sake, he should give this stubborn young man a chance to prove himself.

After dinner, Trace stood up and looked at Rachel.

"Could I talk to you alone?" he asked.

"Yes," Rachel said quickly. She glanced at her father, who nodded. She placed her napkin on the table and followed Trace out toward the front porch.

It was a beautiful, sultry Alabama night, one filled with

the scent of sun warmed roses and the quiet murmur of wind in the trees. Rachel took a deep breath of the sweet familiar scent and sat in a chair at the end of the porch. The same place she had sat that night when Trace admitted that he was an imposter.

She turned to look at him, but in the shadows, she couldn't see his eyes or the expression on his face. She caught the scent of some masculine spicy shaving balm and she had to close her eyes against the intense longing it brought.

Trace lit a lamp that sat on a nearby table, throwing a dim wavering light over the place where Rachel sat. He pulled a chair within the circle of light.

She thought he might take her hand. Instead, he stretched out his legs and put his hands into his pockets, as if to deliberately keep himself from reaching toward her. His eyes, however, couldn't hide the emotion he was feeling. She thought his gaze was like a caress—soft and entreating.

"Rachel . . ." he said. "There are so many things I need to say to you."

Rachel held her breath, thinking she'd never heard such poignancy in his voice.

"I need to tell you I'm sorry." His voice was very low and he didn't look at her. "When I thought up this crazy idea of marrying you to regain Rosewood, I never meant to hurt you."

Rachel clamped her lips together to keep them from trembling. It still hurt to hear him admit that he had not married her for love.

He looked at her then, his eyes searching hers in the dim light.

"I didn't know you well, then," he said. "Except that you were a sweet, beautiful young woman."

Trace was restless. He pulled his legs back, and bent over, his forearms resting against his muscular thighs. He gazed down at his hands, then back at her.

"I used you, because of my own selfish need for revenge," he whispered. "And I'm sorry."

Rachel felt the tears in her eyes. This was not what she expected. Somehow, she had hoped that he wanted to talk about other things. He knew that she loved him. She had not been able to hide that fact very well. And she still couldn't.

"What do you want me to say?" she asked, her voice unsteady. "Do you want me to say I've forgiven you?"

"I don't expect that," he said. "Maybe some day . . ."

"Then what do you want, Trace? Please tell me. Because, I swear, I have no idea."

"I want you to stay," he said, his voice deep and barely audible. "I want you to stay here at Rosewood . . . with me."

"Why?" She didn't mean to be hard, or stubborn. But she had to know. The time was past for playing games.

Trace frowned and his mouth worked. Then with a shrug of his shoulders he answered.

"Because of the baby," he said. "I want my child to be born here at Rosewood, the way I was. And I want him to have both a father and a mother."

Rachel could feel her hopes dying. His words, as sweet and honest as they were, moved over her with a coldness that reached to her very bones.

"I see," she whispered. "And what about us? Are we to be friends? Acquaintances?"

"We will be . . . whatever you want us to be, Rachel."

She sighed and shook her head. Why couldn't he understand that they could never be anything—not until he loved her as much as she did him.

Trace unbuttoned his shirt and reached his hand inside, pulling out a leather cord around his neck on which a gold coin glittered in the lamplight.

"Do you know that this is?"

Rachel frowned and leaned toward him, gazing at the necklace he wore around his neck. The gold coin, flanked by colored beads, was thin and misshapen, but it possessed a raw beauty.

"I . . . is it a Cherokee symbol of some kind?"

Trace nodded. "My father gave several of these coins to me when I was a very small boy. When I left this house I wore this one every day. I never took it off until the day I set foot on Rosewood property again. The day I came back I buried another up there . . ." he nodded. ". . . on the hill, in Monroe soil."

Hearing his deep voice, being so close to him, Rachel felt her skin tingle. She glanced into his eyes, waiting for his further explanation.

"His grandfather wore one and his father before him. It is a symbol of our family's position. My family were peacemakers, spokesmen for our people. I am the first to wear it who did not seek peace with the white men."

"But you could still do that," Rachel said. "It isn't too late." She listened to his words, and to the deep tone of regret in his voice. "You are a wonderful lawyer. And I think you would be an even better statesman."

Trace laughed, the sound harsh in the gentle night air. He stood up, turning to stare down at her.

"Have I behaved like a peacemaker? Do I look like a statesman?"

Rachel let her eyes move over his dark suit, up to his strong handsome face and hawk-like eyes. Whether he knew it or not, he had an authority about him that made people listen. She'd seen it with her own people at Rosewood, even with her own father.

"Yes," she said, smiling slightly. "As a matter of fact, you do."

Trace seemed surprised. He frowned and shook his head in denial. He went to stand with his hand on one of the white columns as he gazed out into the darkness.

"I want this child, Rachel." He turned then, coming back to kneel in front of her and take her hands in his.

His touch stirred something in her. That same irresistible something that always happened when he was near.

She wanted him still. Dear God, but she thought she would never stop wanting him. Or loving him.

"I know you do," she answered.

"Then say you'll stay," he said, his look intense.

Rachel bit her lip.

"You have such pride . . . such fierce pride," she whispered, touching his hair. "But you made love to a white woman, not because you cared for her, but for some dark revenge that even now I don't understand. As a result, you're going to have a child with this white woman . . . this enemy."

"Not an enemy," he murmured. "Never have I considered you my enemy, Rachel."

"Then where do I fit into your high Cherokee sense of moral justice and the outrage you feel toward my father?"

He frowned at her. Had he been so hard . . . so embittered that she thought he regretted their lovemaking for one moment?

"I can't explain it," he said. "But you asked me to choose . . . and I've chosen. Is there no forgiveness in you for what I've done? Has everything changed so badly that we can never go back?"

His breath whispered against her skin. He was so close . . . so tempting.

"And where is it we would go back to?" she asked. "To your using me as if I were your white captive?"

Trace gritted his teeth together and took a deep breath.

"I probably deserve that remark," he said. "What I want to know is, can we live here together . . . as man and wife?"

She wanted to say yes. Dear God, but she wanted that with all her heart and soul. But something deep down inside kept her from falling into his arms—the same something that made her stand up and move away from him.

"I'm not sure I'm ready for that . . . not yet." Her eyes glittered with unshed tears. *Not until I know you love me,* she wanted to add.

"But I will stay," she said. "And our child will be born here at Rosewood . . . as you wish."

Trace felt a deep, aching pain in his chest as she turned away from him and walked slowly back into the house.

Thirty-three

Despite the way they had parted that night, Rachel found herself almost deliriously happy during the next few days. She didn't know why, exactly, unless it was the euphoria that most women told her accompanied pregnancy.

Except for some nausea in the mornings, she felt well, better than she had in months. There was a new glow to her skin and a fullness to her figure that made her feel feminine and beautiful.

Trace treated her delicately, always making sure she was getting enough rest and that she was eating well. Rachel could almost convince herself at times that he was doing it because he cared about her.

One day, Mr. Copeland and Marshall drove up to the house with the large cherry armoire strapped in the back of the wagon. Trace had seen them coming from the barn where he was working and he followed them around the house to the front porch. Rachel met them at the door, her eyes sparkling with pleasure.

But as soon as they had the piece of furniture in the entryway, her shoulders slumped. She looked up the stairs and back at Trace.

"This will never fit in your small bedroom," she whispered to Trace.

He took her arm and pulled her toward the stairs, glancing back at the others.

"We'll be right back," he said.

His and Rachel's problems were private, although everyone in the house certainly knew something about them. The fact that they did not share a bedroom was not unusual. But he sensed that Rachel didn't want everyone to know. She glanced at him curiously as he motioned her along the upstairs hallway and opened the door to his room.

"I've been thinking . . ." he said. "This room would be perfect for a nursery. The room across the hall is larger; the armoire would fit and the baby's room would be close to both of us."

How strange, thought Rachel, to be discussing this so impersonally, after all they had shared. She watched his face as he spoke. Did he experience none of the loneliness she felt every night when she lay in her bed alone?

"Well?" he asked.

Rachel had been lost in thought and now she shook her head and smiled.

"Yes," she said, her voice more breathless than she intended. "This would be perfect." She glanced into his eyes only briefly before turning and going back toward the stairs. "I'll have them bring the piece to this room."

Trace watched her go, aware of nothing else except the lingering scent of her perfume. Standing here with her, he'd wanted to touch her, to kiss her soft parted lips until she was gasping for more. Until—

"Dammit," he muttered beneath his breath. He took a deep breath of air and tried to compose himself before the others came. He ran his fingers through his newly cropped hair and went into the bedroom that he would now make his own.

The room was larger even than the one Rachel had. He stood for a moment, trying to make his heated body relax as he gazed around the room. There was a door in the wall between this room and Rachel's. He stared at it.

He had forgotten it was there and that these two rooms were connected. Or had he known somewhere deep in his mind that it was there when he chose this room?

Not that it would do any good, he told himself. He forced himself to turn away from the door that brought even more forbidden thoughts. By the time the two men arrived with the piece of furniture, Trace felt strangely irritable and anxious to be out of the room and away from the house.

"Put it over there," he said, motioning across the room.

Rachel frowned at him and put her hands at her waist.

"But Trace . . . it would completely cover the windows there." She stared at him.

"I have to go," he said, pushing past her. "Put it wherever you want it."

Rachel shook her head. Only a few minutes ago, he had been so sweet as he talked about the nursery. And now he had changed completely, reverting back to the cold, mysterious man who trusted no one.

Would she ever really know him?

Rachel worked in the room all day, replacing some of the furnishings with more masculine items from the attic, changing the bed's counterpane to something darker and more tailored.

She picked roses from the gardens and arranged them herself in vases of dark green and gold that her father had imported from Austria.

When Trace came back late that afternoon, he hardly recognized the room. His dark eyes took in the roses—the scent of them making him close his eyes and grit his teeth. The scent was so much like Rachel's.

Must he be reminded now with every moment he spent here of her sweet provocative scent? And the fact that she lay sleeping just on the other side of the wall?

Trace had been irritable all day and, as he paced the room, his irritability grew even stronger. He could think of nothing except Rachel. His traitorous body wanted her even now and he couldn't seem to convince his mind or his heart that she was forbidden.

He might manage to keep her here through the child. And, as an honorable woman, she would remain married to him and live a life of pretense before others. But she was young and beautiful and Trace wondered how long it would be before she would turn to another man. To someone kind and loving— someone like Edmund who would give everything he owned to possess a woman like Rachel.

Trace was so lost in the fantasy that he wasn't aware of anything in the room. Suddenly his hand lashed out blindly, striking one of the vases of roses and sending it crashing across the room where it shattered with an earshaking crash.

"Goddamit!" He was breathing as heavily as if he'd just fought a battle. And he couldn't seem to make his heart stop pounding. The anger that he felt just seemed to rise up from somewhere unknown, until it consumed him.

"Trace . . . what . . ."

He turned and saw Rachel at the door, her eyes troubled as she gazed from him to the scattered roses and the water that seeped across the floor and onto the expensive rug.

"You . . . you hate the room . . ." she said.

"No," he groaned. "It isn't that."

Rachel hurried over to the roses and began to pick them up, gathering them into her arms as if they were abandoned kittens.

"Don't," Trace said, going to kneel beside her. "You don't have to do this. I'm the one . . ." He reached for the roses and heard Rachel's gasp as one of the thorns dug into her finger.

"Dammit to hell," he muttered. He took the roses from her and tossed them onto the floor. Then he took her hand and pulled it up before his face to search for the thorn.

Rachel stared at him, unable to understand why he was so angry, or why that terrible, tortured look was in his eyes.

"Trace . . ."

He was concentrating on the thorn that pierced her skin. The touch of his warm fingers caused such sweet, unexpected pleasures that she could hardly breathe. When the thorn was removed, he pulled her finger to his mouth and kissed it, as if he had forgotten all the anger and anguish that lay between them.

"I'm sorry," he murmured. The look in his beautiful black eyes stunned her. "I'm so sorry."

Rachel wasn't sure if it was her condition that made her feel such strange feelings toward him. She wanted to console him, to comfort and nurture him like a lost little boy. It was those feelings, so strong she could not deny them, that made her reach forward. She pulled her hands free and slid them around his neck and shoulders. Her fingers gently rubbed the corded, tensed muscles there.

"Shh," she whispered. "It's all right. I'm not hurt."

Trace raised his head to look into her eyes. Then his troubled eyes slid closed as he made a quiet choked noise in his throat.

He pulled her against him, making Rachel cry out with stunned pleasure as he buried his face against her neck. His mouth, hot and devouring, moved from her neck to her ear, sending shivers of pleasure down Rachel's back.

His hands moved over her with searching eagerness, as they came up to their knees on the hard floor.

Rachel clung to him, yielding to his every move. Her senses, so alive, reeled in the wonder of the moment that she'd feared would never come. Her hands tangled in the hair that she had longed to touch since she saw him cut it.

She was drowning in him, in the heat and pleasure of the way he held her so tightly, with such need and desire. She loved the way his strong hands moved over her.

"Oh Trace," she whispered. "My own love . . ."

With a strangled sound, Trace pulled away from her. He was breathing heavily, and his eyes stared with tortured wonder into hers.

"I'm sorry . . . I didn't mean to do this . . ."

"I want you to," she whispered, her hands going up to his face. "We're man and wife, Trace," she said, her eyes searching. "There's no reason—"

"I've never felt this way about anyone in my life," he said. He seemed troubled by that fact, as if he couldn't quite understand how it happened. "You have to believe that."

Rachel's mouth opened and her eyes grew brighter.

"But you have to understand . . ." he continued, his voice finally becoming more controlled. "I've never known what it was to worry about anyone except myself . . . and staying alive from day to day." He pulled himself away from her and stood up.

Rachel sat on the floor, uncertain if she would be able to move if she stood up. She watched him pacing, saw the genuine anguish and indecision on his face.

He came to her and stood for a second, then reached down to pull her back into his arms.

"I hurt you so badly before," he said, touching her face. "How can I be sure I won't disappoint you again?"

"Oh Trace," she sighed. "You won't. I'm not afraid of that."

"But I'm afraid *for* you," he said, grinding out the words between his teeth. "No one has ever been as kind to me . . . as loving as you've been, Rachel. You're the last person on this earth I would ever want to hurt. I would rather die . . . go back to Oklahoma, even, than do that."

"Don't . . ." she whispered. She placed her small hand against his mouth, as her eyes searched his. "Don't ever say such a thing again."

She had no idea what had caused this revelation from Trace. But it was such a fragile, tentative thing that it frightened her, too. More than she was willing to admit.

"Close the door," she said. "Make love to me here . . . now. We'll start all over again and—"

Trace pulled away from her and turned away. With a heavy sigh, he rubbed his hand wearily over his eyes and down his face. When he turned back to face her, there might as well have been miles between them instead of mere feet.

"I want to be sure," he said. "I have to know for certain that I will be content to deny who I really am for the rest of my life. That I won't just give up on the life I'll have to live here and leave in the middle of some night." His eyes met hers. "Because of you, Rachel . . . I need to be sure. Do you understand what I'm saying?"

Rachel bit her lip and gave a small nod.

"I think so."

She knew he was telling her that he cared. But it was something neither of them was willing to put into words yet.

Rachel felt such disappointment that she actually ached from it. She should have felt hope and elation. This was the closest he'd ever come to saying that he loved her. But instead she felt empty and afraid.

Her body ached for him—longed for him with a white hot passion that she'd never experienced before. And she wondered if she would ever know his love again. She turned and walked slowly to the door, not bothering to look at him when she spoke.

"I'll send Dimity up to clean up the roses. Have her take the rest of them downstairs, if they bother you."

Trace's shoulders slumped and he cursed again beneath his breath. Hadn't she understood a damned thing he was trying to tell her?

But it wasn't her fault. It was his. But this time, the paralyzing fear that kept him from committing himself to her was not for his own safety. It was for Rachel.

That night, long after the house was quiet, Trace lay awake in the new room. His bed was against the same wall as Rachel's and a few times when he was about to drift off to sleep he actually thought he could hear her soft breathing.

He would grit his teeth and sit up in bed, vowing that tomorrow he could have the bed moved to the other side of the room.

Frustrated and irritable from lack of sleep, he walked to the door between the two bedrooms. Slowly, he turned the knob and pushed the door open.

Rachel's windows were open and a cool night breeze stirred the curtains. A small lamp flickered near the bed.

Trace stood for a moment, staring down at her, at the woman

who had changed his life forever. Her skin had never looked so beautiful and her hair had a new brilliance these days.

This was the woman who had taken him to her bed, despite all her misgivings and without him ever having told her that he loved her. And when she'd learned his true identity and what he'd done, she had returned love for betrayal by giving him the house he coveted.

And now he coveted her.

She was pure goodness, while he was angry and bitter and often filled with what he thought must be pure evil.

Yet she loved him. Despite everything, this good, sweet woman loved him.

And she was joyful that she was to have his child.

There was an aching lump in his throat and chest and it seemed to grow bigger with every passing moment. It consumed his entire being, filling Trace with such anguish that he almost cried aloud.

"What have I done to you angel?" he whispered. "God, what have I done?"

Thirty-four

After that, Trace came to Rachel's room every night after she was asleep. He would stand beside her bed, watching her as his mind went over every moment, every event of their life together.

He wanted her just as desperately as before. But his wants and needs became secondary as he examined himself and his motives—what he wanted and needed in his new life at Rosewood. Oddly, he found a peace and contentment in those clandestine ventures to her room. He was experiencing more and more peace anytime he was with Rachel.

On Sunday they went to church together. When Rachel and her father walked out onto the front porch, they found Trace waiting there. He'd been talking to Justus who stood brushing the horse in the drive. When Trace heard her, he straightened and turned, giving her a soft smile that made Rachel's eyes grow wide, then warm and glowing.

Her father grunted and handed his daughter toward Trace.

"Guess you'll have to bring a horse for me," he said to Justus, "since my son-in-law only saw fit to order the one seat buggy this morning."

With a grin, Justus walked to the corner of the house, coming back with the Senator's favorite horse.

"We done thought of that," he said with a wink toward Trace.

After church, they stood outside talking to neighbors and

friends. Hallie and Roland stood among them, and Rachel thought it was as good a time as any to tell her about the baby.

Hallie squealed and jumped, catching everyone's attention. Even if Rachel had considered waiting to tell the others, she knew it was too late.

She and Trace stood awkwardly for a moment, hardly knowing how they should act, and each of them extremely conscious of the other. By the time the third or fourth person had come to congratulate them, Trace's arm had gone around Rachel's waist, and he was grinning like any proud, expectant father.

Rachel could hardly believe the change in him. And she could hardly believe the look in his eyes when she glanced up at him. Even the fact that Edmund watched them from a side angle couldn't change the happiness she felt.

When the crowd began to disperse, she and Trace walked toward their buggy. It was then that Edmund came to them. Rachel hoped that he meant to add his congratulations to the others.

"Rachel . . . Trace . . . I need to speak to you."

Trace's jaw tightened and his nostrils flared as he stood staring at Edmund. He meant to be civil, if only for Rachel, but he wanted whatever the man had to say to be done in a hurry.

"You both seem . . . very happy," Edmund said tentatively.

Rachel glanced at Trace.

"We are," she murmured. Rachel was almost afraid to say the words out loud. She placed her hand in the crook of Trace's arm, noting the tenseness in his muscles. She patted his arm softly and glanced up at him from beneath her lashes.

Trace didn't miss that little gesture, or the soft look of pleading in her beautiful blue eyes.

"Yes . . . we are," he said, his lips curving slightly into a smile.

Edmund took a deep breath of air and let it out slowly. His eyes darted about him, as if he might bolt and run.

"You wanted to add your congratulations?" Rachel asked, thinking to ease Edmund through the awkward moment.

"Something bothering you?" Trace asked him.

"God, Rachel, please forgive me. I wouldn't blame you, Trace if you knocked my head off. But I've done something . . . I had no idea . . . I thought you had only used her and I—"

"What?" Trace demanded, his face growing fierce again. "What have you done?"

Edmund's face was pale and a thin layer of perspiration had popped out on his brow.

"I . . . I told Major Nelson that you were . . . an impostor." Edmund's look flew to Rachel's face. "I couldn't stand to see you hurt, Rachel. I thought he might even be cruel to you or—"

"He's not cruel," she said, her eyes flashing. "He would never be cruel to me."

"What did you tell him?" Trace asked, his voice cool.

"I . . . I didn't tell him who you really are, because I don't know. But he was asking around town about some Indian that had lived here. He'd escaped from a reservation in Oklahoma and they thought . . ."

Rachel gave a quiet, choked little sound and Edmund stopped, his eyes moving from her to Trace.

Trace clenched his teeth and looked off into the distance.

"My God . . . you aren't him? You aren't really this—"

"What else did you tell him?" Trace asked.

"Nothing. It's all I knew. God, Rachel . . . Trace, I'm sorry. I only meant to do something that would make you leave so I—"

"So you could have my wife to yourself?" Trace's gaze was hard as he stared at Edmund with frighteningly intensity.

"God, I'm sorry. If I had known about the baby . . . that you two were trying to work things out, I'd never . . . I wouldn't blame you if you bashed my head in."

"Believe me," Trace growled. "I'd like nothing better."

"Oh, Trace," Rachel said. "What will we do?"

"I don't know." There were lines between his brows and he seemed lost in thought.

"More than likely nothing will ever come of it," Edmund said, his voice quick and strident. "You know how the Major is—he has easy duty here. He's not going to bother with some trouble way out in Oklahoma territory."

Trace turned and placed his hand on Rachel's waist, helping her up into the seat and ignoring Edmund, who walked over to the buggy and looked up at Rachel with pleading eyes.

"I'll see what I can find out," he said. "I'll tell the Major that it was a mistake. Perhaps that will put an end to it. Rachel, I'm so sorry."

"Just leave it, Edmund. Please. You might only make things worse." Rachel was more frightened than angry. She nodded curtly at Edmund as Trace flicked the reins and they pulled away.

Trace glanced over at Rachel. She held her hands tightly together in her lap and she was trembling. He reached across, taking both her hands in his.

"I don't want you to worry," he said. "Unless they send someone here to identify me, there's no way they can know for sure. I'll think of something."

There was no more talk until they reached Rosewood. When Trace turned to Rachel, he frowned with concern and reached out to take her hands in his. They were icy cold.

"Rachel," he murmured, touching her hair and her face. "You're trembling. I didn't know that Edmund's words had upset you so much."

"I . . . it isn't that," she said, her words catching softly as she spoke. "I . . . I think I have a fever. I felt ill all during church, but I thought it was only the usual sickness. But now . . ." She reached up to touch her forehead and her eyes when they met Trace's were filled with a quiet desperation.

"Oh, Trace . . . I couldn't stand for something to happen to the baby. Not now."

The dazed look in her eyes stunned Trace, and he pulled her quickly into his arms, holding her and feeling the heat emanating from her small body. She was burning up—he should have been able to see it before now. But he'd been lost in thought about Edmund's revelation and concentrating on what he was going to do to keep from losing everything.

"Shh," he said. "It's probably just a cold. You'll be fine." He stepped over her and jumped down from the buggy, then lifted his arms for her. "Let me take you upstairs. Lula and Hummingbird will know exactly what to do."

Rachel put her arms around his neck and hid her face against his shoulder. He could feel her shaking and hear her muffled breathing.

"It's my fault," she said. "If I hadn't been so stubborn about working . . . if I haven't taken all that laudanum when Cleo died . . ."

"Stop it," Trace muttered, carrying her up the stairs and into the house. "It's not your fault. None of this is your fault."

"I wouldn't have done any of it if I'd known I was pregnant, Trace," she said, her voice rising almost hysterically. "You have to believe me . . . I would never have done anything to endanger our child."

"God, Rachel," he muttered. "Don't you think I know that? You'd never harm a fly, let alone your own child."

Trace frowned down at her as he laid her down on the bed. The look in her eyes was fevered and wild, and he realized that she was just at the edge of delirium.

That thought struck fear in the deepest, darkest part of his heart.

"Rachel . . . angel. God, you're burning up." Trace felt his heart thudding against his ribs as he pulled a quilt up over her. "I'm going to get Lula . . . don't move or try to get up, do you hear?"

She nodded and reached out her hand toward him. He took it, feeling the heat from her skin and small delicate fingers. She pulled him back toward the bed and as he gazed down into her eyes, he could feel a muscle twitching in his jaw.

Unshed tears swam in her eyes.

"I'm afraid," she whispered. "I don't want to leave you."

Trace could feel his heart hammering in his chest. Heat rushed over him, then a sheet of cold sweat.

"Don't say such a thing," he said fiercely. He knelt by her bed, holding her hand so tightly that he was afraid he might break her delicate bones. "Do you hear me? Don't say it, or even think it. I won't let anything happen to you."

"Promise me," she whispered. "Promise you won't let me go."

"I promise, angel. I swear, I will not let you go."

She closed her eyes and tears slid silently down each cheek. Then she nodded and released his hand.

Trace hurried from the room, taking the stairs in a run. By the time his feet hit the landing, he was calling for help.

"Dimity!" he shouted.

The young Negro woman appeared almost immediately, her eyes large with fright.

"Bring Hummingbird and Lula upstairs. Tell them Miss Rachel has taken ill."

"It ain't the baby . . ." Dimity cried.

"No . . . I don't know," Trace said. "Just hurry. And send someone for the doctor." He turned and raced back up the stairs, almost afraid of what he would find when he went back into Rachel's room.

Thirty-five

Rachel's eyes opened when Trace came back into the room. He was shocked, however, at how quickly her condition had worsened. He went to her and took her hand, but she seemed too weak to speak.

Her teeth chattered and Trace piled more covers over her, even though it was a hot, summer day. He wished he could crawl into the bed with her, hold her shaking body tightly against his and make her well.

But he couldn't. He could do nothing except watch and wait for the doctor.

Hummingbird and Lula were just as puzzled as he by Rachel's sudden illness. And though both of them offered remedies, nothing seemed to work.

The doctor's arrival gave Trace some relief. But when he pulled Trace with him out into the hallway, he shook his head.

"I'll be honest with you son," he said. "Sometimes there just doesn't seem to be any explanation or anything a doctor can do."

"But you must know what's wrong with her," Trace replied.

"Well, it could be anything. There's an outbreak of typhoid over in Swan's Creek. Or it could be influenza. It's not unusual to see a fever get so high in either of those cases. But it's serious," he said nodding sadly. "Especially with the baby coming and all. If we don't get the fever down . . ." The doctor shrugged his shoulders as if he had no other words to offer.

Trace raked his hand across his face, feeling the ache in his shoulders from sitting so long. Feeling a heavy sense of frustration that no one seemed to be able to do anything for Rachel.

Through the afternoon, Rachel lay lifeless, waking occasionally to gaze about the room. She couldn't eat and her body shook miserably. Only when her eyes found Trace would she smile and close her eyes again.

She'd reach her hand out to him, and he would take it. Hummingbird and Lula had left, telling Trace to call them if there was any change. Hummingbird had left a small offering of sage burning in a nearby tray and the scent filled the room until Trace finally took the burning embers and set them in the hallway.

He kept cold wet compresses on Rachel's forehead, changing them often. He didn't leave her bed, even though there were times when his eyes burned and every muscle in his body ached.

It was late when the Senator returned from visiting friends. When he was told about Rachel, he hurried upstairs. He could see the fatigue in Trace's eyes.

"Son," he said. "Why don't you go downstairs and eat something? I'll sit here with her for awhile."

"No," Trace said, shaking his head. He hardly took his eyes away from Rachel's face. "I promised I'd be here. I don't want her to wake up and find me gone."

The Senator sighed. He sat on the other side of the bed for a while and then silently left the room. He doubted that Trace even noticed.

It was dark, but still early evening when Trace drifted off to sleep in his chair. He woke with a start and found Rachel sitting up in bed, her eyes wild and searching.

"Trace," she cried.

He bent toward her in an instant, taking her hand until she turned to see him. Her eyes seemed confused as she stared at him.

"I'm here angel," he whispered. "I'm here."

"Where's my wrap?" she asked. "I'm cold and I don't want to go out on the porch without my wrap."

Trace shook his head and his mouth worked soundlessly.

"Sweetheart . . . lie down. You're very sick. You don't know what you're saying."

Rachel smiled and reached out to touch his face.

"Of course I know what I'm saying," she said.

He could feel her hand trembling against his skin. She felt even hotter than before.

"Rachel . . . please . . ."

"Sun Killer," she murmured. "My beautiful Indian warrior."

"Sun Killer is gone," Trace whispered. "He no longer exists."

"No," she said. "You're wrong. He's the man I fell in love with. He's still here . . . I know he is." She touched his chest weakly. "I'm so tired. I feel so awful."

"I know you do, baby. I know. Why don't you lie down again? Are you hungry? Thirsty?"

Rachel lay back down lifelessly, her eyes so blank that it frightened Trace. He held her hand as if he might hold her back from the dark cloud that threatened to claim her.

"Can the baby live?" she asked weakly. "Even if I die?"

"God!" Trace stood up and stalked away from the bed, shaking his head. He didn't know what to do, or what to say to her. He wished Cleo were here to help him.

"Don't . . ." he whispered. "Don't do this."

But she didn't hear him—she was sleeping again.

He stayed with her all night, holding her hand and bathing away her fever. Sometimes he slept sitting up, with his upper body bent over the bed, his head resting against her stomach.

"I won't let you go," he whispered fiercely. "Do you hear me? I won't let you go."

Sometime near morning she roused again. He felt her hand on his hair and looked up to find her watching him, her eyes still glazed and feverish.

"Would you take me outside?" she asked weakly.

"What? Honey, you're—"

"Take me out on the porch, Trace," she pleaded. "Where I can see the sun shining on the treetops. I want to see how the roses are doing."

Trace's heart ached. He wanted to scream and curse. He wanted to kill someone for letting this happen. And yet, his voice, when he spoke, was gentle and held no hint of what he was feeling inside.

He bundled her in one of the quilts and picked her up. She seemed to weigh almost nothing when he carried her down the stairs.

He was surprised to find Hummingbird sitting at the foot of the stairs. She was burning some other incense in a nearby dish. When she saw him, she came to her feet, the fear of death in her eyes.

"She isn't . . . ?"

"No," Trace said. "But she wants to see the sunrise . . ." he said, his voice choking. "And the roses." He closed his eyes and his knees almost gave way before he caught himself. "I don't know what to do, Hummingbird," he whispered. "I don't know what to do."

Hummingbird gathered up a nearby leather pouch, motioning him out to the front porch. When Trace sat in one of the big rockers, the earth was still dark. But the birds had started to sing in the trees. Sunrise was not far away.

He held Rachel close to him as he dispassionately watched Hummingbird pull items from her bag.

Silently, she waved an eagle's wing over Rachel's body.

"Spirit of death," she chanted. "Leave this place and our Rachel."

Then she took a small gourd and shook it, sending a soft rattling sound into the cool morning air. As Hummingbird began another quiet chant, Trace gathered Rachel even closer to him, holding her tightly.

When Hummingbird was finished, she gathered her things and rose to go.

"I've done everything I can do," she said, "as the white doctor did all he could do. If she lives, it will be because the great spirit does not yet want her. You must ask him to spare her, Sun Killer," she added. "The prayers of a warrior are heard above all others."

After Hummingbird had left, Trace held Rachel's heated, limp body against him and buried his face in the quilts that covered her.

"I'm not a warrior," he murmured. "I'm just a man. A man who loves his wife and child."

He didn't know how to pray. The prayers he'd offered for his mother had never been heard—neither had the ones he'd prayed for his own freedom. He had finally decided that his salvation would have to come from himself, from his own plans and thoughts and his own intelligence. That was what had delivered him from the reservation, not prayers.

He moved his hand to the pulse at Rachel's throat. Her skin seemed cooler, but perhaps that was only his wishful imagination. He could feel her heart beating rapidly. He traced his fingers down her face, along the delicate bones of her shoulders.

"You are so beautiful," he whispered. "Have I ever told you how beautiful you are? No," he added with a choked sigh. "I suppose I haven't. Or how proud I am of you because of your kindness and your goodness?" He picked up her small hand and drew it softly to his mouth. He kissed the palm of her hand and each finger before bringing it to lie against his chest, his large hand covering it.

Trace began to rock her as he talked, softly murmuring all the feelings he had never been able to express out loud.

"You are the woman I dreamed of when I was alone. The vision I imagined when I was most afraid," he said. "When I came here and saw you, I could hardly believe that you were real. Yet when you loved me and reached out to me, I pushed you away. I hurt you probably more than I've ever hurt anyone. And you are the one person on earth I should not have hurt."

Trace felt hot tears on his face, something so foreign to him that he could hardly explain it. But he couldn't stop them, or the choked sobs that swelled up from his chest and finally engulfed him.

"God," he cried, bending against her. His tears wet her skin and hair. "Please . . . please don't take her from me. She doesn't deserve this. She's good and kind and loving . . . all the things that are best in a person. Punish me . . . not her," he cried until there were no more tears left inside. Then, completely exhausted, he leaned his head back against the chair and fell asleep.

The sun was just coming up when Rachel stirred and opened her eyes. For a moment, she didn't know where she was. Calmly, she turned her head and saw Trace. She smiled as she studied his handsome, unshaven face, then reached out to touch his lips.

Trace's eyes came open and he blinked.

For a few seconds, he seemed speechless and unable to react.

"My God . . . Rachel!" He sat up straighter and reached to touch her as if to make sure she was real.

"You're awake . . . you're better," he exclaimed.

Rachel wanted to laugh aloud. She thought she'd never seen him the way he was that morning. And she couldn't figure out what they were doing out here on the front porch with her wrapped in a quilt in his arms.

Whatever the reason, she wasn't about to complain.

Trace ran his hands down her arms, wrapping his fingers around her delicate wrist.

"You're alive," he murmured. "Thank God . . . thank you."

Rachel turned her head and looked at him oddly, then she touched his face tenderly.

"I thought I'd lost you," he said. "I'm so thankful . . . I can't believe it. How do you feel? Is there anything you want?"

When Rachel laughed, her voice sounded weak and hoarse.

"Am I dreaming? Is this really Trace Hambleton's voice I'm hearing?"

"This is real," he said, hugging her again him. "I'm real. Here, touch me . . . feel my heart beating." He felt like shouting. Even as exhausted as he was, he felt like grabbing her up in his arms and dancing across the floor with her.

"Lord, Rachel, I love you," he whispered. "God, if I hadn't been so blindly stubborn and selfish, I'd have told you long before this just how much you mean to me."

Rachel's mouth opened and she stared at him. Tears welled up in her eyes.

"You . . . you love me."

"I love you," he repeated, kissing her hands, then her cheeks. "I adore you. With all my heart. From the very first moment I saw you, I knew I could never let you go." He looked into her eyes. "Can you forgive me for being so stubborn . . . for taking so long—"

"Yes," she whispered. "I forgive you. I told you before, all you have to do is ask."

Thirty-six

Rachel thought those next few days were the most glorious of her life. She hadn't been able to believe it at first, that Trace really loved her. In her heart she'd been afraid that once she was well, he would come to his senses and realize it wasn't true.

But it was. Delightfully, wonderfully true. She could see it in his dark eyes, hear it in his voice. Everything he did was for her and was filled with the deepest, most passionate meaning.

She was still very weak, but continued to grow stronger every day. Her only concern was for the baby, and the doctor couldn't say if her illness had caused any damage to the child or not.

"We'll just have to wait and see," he said solemnly on the last day he was at Rosewood. He still couldn't explain what had caused her sudden, dangerous illness, any more than he could explain her miraculous recovery.

"You're very lucky," he said, as he was leaving.

"We know," Trace said, looking at Rachel. "Very."

When she finally was able to leave her bed, Trace would take her on long, quiet carriage rides. He took her back out to the springs where they'd once made love.

Things were so different then and yet Rachel thought this was where it all had started. All of Trace's soul searching had begun that day when he realized that his feelings for her ran deeper than he thought.

There was a new kind of joy between them, and a sweet forgiving acceptance of their life together. And yet Trace treated her like a fragile flower and had made no effort to make love to her.

As they stood at the springs, Rachel shivered, remembering that other day that seemed so long ago.

"You're cold," Trace said. "I should get you back to the house."

"No," she answered. "I'm not cold." She turned to him, sliding her hands around his trim waist.

When she lifted her mouth toward him, Trace groaned and kissed her soft parted lips. Gently, tenderly, he kissed her mouth and her face.

"Sometimes I can hardly believe this has happened and that you love me," she whispered.

"I do," he said. "Always and with all my heart."

She kissed the corner of his mouth, then with nipping little bites along his bottom lip. She could feel him against her, his body needing her as much as she did him.

Trace moaned and pulled away, his breath hard and fast. Her sweet kisses were driving him crazy. The scent of her was in his nostrils, and he couldn't seem to pull his eyes away from where her breasts rose above her soft muslin dress.

"We'd better . . . stop this . . ." he said, his voice deep and husky. "We can't make love here the way we did before. The ground is cold and damp and I—"

"You worry too much," she whispered against his mouth.

He drew in his breath as her mouth and small teeth continued to tease and bite. And when she reached her hand inside his shirt, he gasped and grabbed her hand, laughing with her.

It had been so long. He'd wanted her so badly now, and with a few teasing kisses, she'd made him completely aroused. He smiled, thinking how unworthy an opponent he was against this small, sweet-smelling foe.

"We're going back to the house," he said. He scooped her

up in his arms and carried her to the carriage. And when he heard her laughter, he laughed, too.

For the first time in years, he felt free. He couldn't be sure how long it would last before the authorities came, but today, for whatever time they had left, he was free. And happier than he'd ever been in his life.

A long while later they lay in each other's arms in her bed, both completely exhausted. Trace felt as if he'd come home, as if the fighting was over for good. He had mistakenly made Rachel his adversary. But she was one no longer. She was his love and the mother of his children to be, the woman he wanted to spend the rest of his life with.

Rachel thought that day was the beginning of their new life together. One they had sealed with their love as surely as they had bonded their heated bodies. It was a never to be forgotten day when they were able to share physically the fact that they loved one another.

They lay all night, cozy and safe in each other's arms—making love, talking, sharing thoughts and feelings they had never shared before. Just as Trace was going to sleep, he heard Rachel gasp, then laugh.

"What?" he asked, reaching out to touch her. "What's wrong?"

"Nothing's wrong," she said, still laughing. "Everything's perfectly wonderful." She pulled his hand toward her and lay it against her rounded stomach. "I felt the baby move. Here . . . can you feel it?"

"Yes," he said with a sense of awe.

"It's going to be all right," she whispered. "Everything's going to be all right."

That next morning, Major Nelson and his soldiers came riding into the yard at Rosewood. They were armed and there was another officer with them—one that Trace recognized immediately.

"You . . . you know him," Rachel said. She'd seen the recognition in his eyes. She also saw a surrender there and she wanted to scream out her protest to the world.

"Yes," he said, looking into her eyes. "His name is McDermott. He was at the Fort in Oklahoma."

"Oh, no," she said quietly. "Trace . . . don't go out there. I can't let them take you away. I can't!"

"It's too late, angel." His voice was filled with resignation as he touched her face gently. "We haven't talked about it because we didn't want it to spoil what we'd found. But in the back of our minds, I think we both knew this was coming."

"You can leave," she said, her voice desperate. She clung to his shirt and stared up into his eyes. "They haven't seen you yet and they don't know for sure you're here. You can go out the back and ride away from here."

Trace took her hands and kissed the tips of her fingers.

"I'm through running," he said. "And I don't intend to spend the rest of my life looking back over my shoulder. I'm going to tell them the truth. Who knows . . . perhaps McDermott will ride on back to Oklahoma and pretend he never saw me."

The Senator came out of his study. He'd heard enough to realize what was going on. Now he gazed through the curtains out toward the soldiers in front of the house.

"Perhaps she's right, son. I have money here in the study. Maybe you can make your way up to Canada and later, after the baby is born, Rachel can join you."

"No," Trace said, shaking his head. He turned to look at Rachel, hoping she would understand.

"Trace . . . please. We've only just found one another. I can't bear it if you go . . ."

"I have to talk to him," Trace said. "Just let me go and do this. I would never feel right if I ran—don't you see that? This is my home and I won't leave it again. This is where I'll have to make my stand, no matter what happens."

A glint of determination sparkled in his eyes. How could

she fight him and how could she deny him his right to do this thing that he considered honorable?

"Then I'll go out on the porch with you," Rachel said, straightening her shoulders and wiping her eyes.

"So will I," the Senator said. He put his hand on Trace's shoulder and together they walked outside.

Trace's eyes met Colonel McDermott's eyes right away and he saw sadness and disappointment in their depths. For some reason, the Colonel had been the one officer who was kind to him as a boy—kinder probably than he'd deserved in those wild, rebellious days. He knew McDermott was a fair and honest man.

But would he listen? Would he turn his back on his duty and let Trace remain here in Alabama?

"Is this the man, sir?" Major Nelson asked, nodding toward Trace.

McDermott frowned and swung his leg over his horse.

"I can't be sure. Might we go into the house gentlemen . . . Mrs. Hambleton? I'll explain why we've come. Major Nelson, you and your men wait here."

Inside the house, they went into the front parlor. Rachel stood beside Trace, holding onto his arm as if she could protect him somewhat from what was about to happen.

The officer removed his hat, revealing thinning gray hair. Rachel thought he must be about the same age as her father.

"You've changed, Sun Killer," he said with a wistful smile.

Rachel practically gasped aloud and Trace squeezed her hand where it lay on his arm. She had hoped, by the officer's seemingly calm disinterest, that he didn't remember Trace.

Colonel McDermott glanced around the elegantly appointed room.

"So . . . this was your home as a boy."

"This is still his home," Rachel corrected.

"Yes ma'am. I didn't mean it that way." The officer's look was apologetic and infinitely kind. That, more than anything, made Rachel relax a bit.

"I only meant that it was a shame . . . what happened here. Sun Killer . . . I'm sorry, I hardly know what to call you now. I never called you by your English name when you were on the reservation."

"Trace."

The man seemed as unnerved by what was happening as the rest of them. He took a deep breath and wiped his hand across his forehead.

"It's hot," he said. He looked toward the settee and its surrounding chairs.

"Here . . . Colonel, why don't we sit." Senator Townsend waved his hand toward the settee and then stepped to a nearby table to open a wooden box. "Cigar, sir? We have the best Havana tobacco there is."

"This is Senator William Allen Townsend, my . . . father-in-law," Trace said.

McDermott, with a grateful look, seated himself on the settee and reached for the Senator's cigar. Rachel and her father also sat down, but Trace continued to stand near the fireplace, with his arm propped on the mantel.

"Colonel," the Senator began. "I don't know if you're aware, but I am as responsible as anyone for what happened to Trace's family and to this house."

McDermott frowned and his gaze moved with curiosity between Trace and Rachel.

"Oh? And how's that?"

The Senator explained quickly about the land grant and how he had always coveted Rosewood.

"I'm ashamed to say that I, like many people in this country, did not see Trace or his family as important people. But he is and always should have been, the owner of Rosewood. When he fell in love with my daughter, she placed the deeds back into his name."

Rachel smiled when she heard her father's slight stretching of the truth.

"I must tell you that the President and I are more than just casual acquaintances, and I believe if I propose to him that he pardon Trace and allow him to keep his home, then he will do just that for me."

"Well," said Colonel McDermott. "You must be a very influential man."

Senator Townsend cleared his throat and continued.

"The point is, this man has done nothing to deserve what happened to him. Do you realize that his mother was three quarters Irish and a woman of quality? She died in that forsaken land with no representation whatsoever?"

"Sir," the Colonel said with a solemn nod. "Believe me, no one regrets that fact more than I do." There was an odd note of remorse in his voice.

"Trace is a good man. Intelligent and hard working. His only sin was—"

"Senator . . ." the Colonel snuffed out his cigar and came to his feet. "You don't have to tell me any of this. I already know what kind of man Trace Hambleton is. And as an officer, I am ashamed of my apathy in the entire matter."

Trace frowned and pushed himself away from the fireplace. McDermott turned now to Trace.

"Son, I came here to tell you that I'm sorry for all of this."

Rachel held her breath. One moment she thought that the Colonel intended to help them and the next she thought he might take Trace away, regretful as he was about what happened.

"I guess I came here today to see for myself how you were doing. I see this house . . . your home. And your beautiful wife who obviously loves you very much and needs you here with her. I understand you're expecting a child . . . congratulations ma'am."

Rachel nodded and clasped her hands together to keep them from shaking.

"I've been thinking during the entire trip about what I could do to help—or if I could help at all. And if you'll listen to my proposition, I think I've come up with something."

"I recall you always wore a necklace . . . something with a small coin on it?"

Trace's eyes narrowed, but he reached inside his shirt and pulled out the leather cord.

"Yes, that's it. Now the way I see it, the government or the army doesn't really care about one Indian . . . if you'll pardon my saying so. All they really want is something to put in their records. You know what I mean?" he said, speaking directly to the Senator.

"I sure do," the Senator said with a laugh.

"I figure if I take this necklace back with me, tell them you were killed in some saloon fight, they'll be satisfied. As an officer of thirty years, with a reputation of integrity, I think I will be believed."

"Why would you do that for me?" Trace asked, his eyes glittering and filled with suspicion.

"Well, it's a long story," the Colonel said. He seemed nervous and defensive, unwilling to explain anything else.

"How do I know that I can trust you to do that?" Trace asked.

The Colonel frowned and looked skeptically from Trace to the Senator and Rachel.

"I hadn't intended on telling you this," he said. Slowly, he reached into his watch pocket, pulling out a watch and turning it over. When he opened the lid, a small coin fell out into his hand. He handed it to Trace.

Trace frowned and turned his head, staring at the coin.

"Do you recognize it?" McDermott asked.

"It's one of my Father's coins, but—"

"It was your mother's," the colonel said, his voice suddenly growing soft. When he glanced up, his eyes were troubled and dark.

Trace made a small noise. His eyes narrowed as he stared from the coin up into the older man's saddened eyes.

"I loved your mother, son," he said. "No one on this earth knows that fact except me. And I will regret to my dying day that I didn't turn my back on the army and take her away from the place she hated so much. If I'd had your courage . . . or your wife's, your mother might still be alive."

Trace's mouth was open, his look one of disbelief.

"I don't know what to say." He looked at Rachel and saw the hope in her eyes. Even the Senator seemed a little shaken by the colonel's revelation.

"You don't have to say anything," he said. "I'll take care of the matter. And on your mother's name, I swear you can trust me to do what I say I will do." McDermott offered the coin to Trace.

Trace shook his head and looked into the man's eyes.

"She gave it to you, sir," he said. "She would want you to keep it." Slowly he reached behind his neck and unfastened the necklace, with its coin so similar to the one the Colonel held.

He placed it in the man's hand.

"I'll write to you," McDermott said, "and let you know when all the details are taken care of. But as far as the army is concerned, the man named Sun Killer is dead. His records are closed."

Traced reached forward and shook Colonel McDermott's hand.

"I don't know how to thank you."

"You just have a healthy baby and a happy life," McDermott said. "I think your mama would be pleased on this day."

"Yes sir, I think she would."

The man had hardly left the room before Rachel threw herself against Trace with a small squeal of delight. The Senator cleared his throat and discreetly excused himself, smiling as he closed the door behind him.

Trace picked her up off the floor and whirled her around, sitting her down with a quick, laughing apology.

"Trace . . ." Rachel whispered, looking up into his black eyes. "Can you believe it? Can you believe something has finally gone right in our lives?"

"I think that happened the moment I met you," he said, still smiling.

"Oh God, I love you," she whispered. "I'm so happy I could just . . . explode . . ."

Trace laughed and kissed her. "Don't do that," he teased.

"But I have to know . . . do you have any regrets . . . any at all?" she asked, her face becoming solemn.

"Regrets? About what?"

"That you've had to say goodbye to the boy named Sun Killer . . . that your Indian heritage is gone, or must remain a secret at best . . ."

"Sweetheart, the entire Cherokee way of life is gone. It can never be the same." Trace took her in his arms and kissed her parted lips. "And as much as I regret that, I can't change it and neither can you. But don't ever think I regret what I've found here with you. Your love and our child . . . this house, is all I ever wanted. It's all I will ever need. The past is gone, just as Sun Killer is . . . buried and forgotten."

"You mean it?"

"I mean it," he said, looking into her eyes.

He smiled mischievously and pulled her tighter against him.

"Will you stop talking now, woman?" he asked. "We have a lifetime to talk. And there are a few things that have been sadly neglected during these past few weeks . . ."

She was smiling as she reached up to meet his kiss.

ROMANCE FROM FERN MICHAELS

DEAR EMILY   (0-8217-4952-8, $5.99)

WISH LIST   (0-8217-5228-6, $6.99)

AND IN HARDCOVER:

VEGAS RICH   (1-57566-057-1, $25.00)

DANGEROUS GAMES   (0-7860-0270-0, $4.99)
by Amanda Scott

When Nicholas Barrington, eldest son of the Earl of Ul-
combe, first met Melissa Seacort, the desperation he
sensed beneath her well-bred beauty haunted him. He
didn't realize how desperate Melissa really was . . . until
he found her again at a Newmarket gambling club—being auctioned off by her father to the highest bidder. So,
Nick bought himself a wife. With a villain hot on their
heels, and a fortune and their lives at stake, they would
gamble everything on the most dangerous game of all:
love.

A TOUCH OF PARADISE   (0-7860-0271-9, $4.99)
by Alexa Smart

As a confidence man and scam runner in 1880s America,
Malcolm Northrup has amassed a fortune. Now, posing
as the eminent Sir John Abbot—scholar, and possible
discoverer of the lost continent of Atlantis—he's taking
his act on the road with a lecture tour, seeking funds for
a scientific experiment he has no intention of making.
But scholar Halia Davenport is determined to accompany
Malcolm on his "expedition" . . . even if she must kidnap
him!